Sly, Slick & Wicked

A KENDRA CLAYTON MYSTERY

Angela Henry

PRAISE FOR THE KENDRA CLAYTON SERIES

The Company You Keep
"A tightly woven mystery..."
—Ebony Magazine

"This debut mystery features an exciting new African-American heroine... Highly recommended."
—Library Journal

Tangled Roots
"Smart, witty, and fast-paced, this second Kendra Clayton novel is as likeable as the first."
—CrimeSpree Magazine

"…appealing characters…witty dialogue…an enjoyable read." 4 Stars
—Romantic Times Magazine

Diva's Last Curtain Call
"It's the perfect script for a great summer read."
—Broward Times

"…this series is made of inventive storytelling, crackling wit and that rarity of rarities in American publishing: an authentic, down-to-earth slice of Black life."
—Insight News

PROLOGUE
July 1982

Lila Duncan's feet were killing her. But she was much too angry to take notice of the throbbing pain. She was busy peering through the lobby's glass double doors waiting to see the faint glow of headlights in the distance that would indicate her husband, Leonard, had pulled into the McPherson building's large empty parking lot to pick her up. She'd been waiting for nearly an hour and still no Leonard. He was late. And Lila was pissed.

"Where the hell are you, Leonard?" she whispered through gritted teeth. Her lips were tight and bloodless with anger. Her forehead was pressed against the door causing her breath to fog up the glass.

"You better not be where I think you are!" Lila said aloud, her voice echoing in the empty lobby as she turned to look yet again at the large clock mounted on the wall above the receptionist station. It was 11:47, two minutes later than the last time she looked. She'd gotten off work at 11 o'clock. She'd been cleaning the McPherson office building five nights a week from 5:30

to 11 for the past eight years. She always got off at 11 o'clock on the dot. Her supervisor at Masterson's Cleaning Service had a strict no overtime policy. Lila didn't arrive for work a minute before she had to or stay a minute longer than she was required. Leonard knew better than to be late picking her up. But here she was, still waiting.

It was hot and airless in the lobby and her cotton work smock stuck uncomfortably to the sweat on her broad back. It was Friday and maintenance always turned the air-conditioning off for the weekend every Friday night to save money, which Lila thought was stupid since she knew they probably had to crank the air up full blast to cool off the sweltering building on Monday morning. Unable to stand the heat any longer, Lila pushed through the lobby doors and walked outside into the much cooler night air. She heard a soft click as the doors locked behind her and it made her even more furious. Lila bent down and loosened the laces on her tight tennis shoes giving her swollen feet some much needed relief. She didn't dare take them off for fear she wouldn't be able to get them back on and the pebble strewn parking lot was no place she wanted to be barefoot.

For the next ten minutes Lila paced, angrily swinging the cheap canvas purse she carried to work, with its frayed shoulder strap, like a warrior ready for battle. In the murderous mood she was in, when Leonard's sorry ass finally did show up, he was going to get her purse upside his head. Only her purse must have sensed her plans because the strap broke sending it flying out of her hand and halfway across the lot. With the sight of her purse laying broken and forlorn on the ground, Lila felt her anger dissolve into tears of weary frustration and she limped over and bent down to retrieve it.

She'd barely touched the purse when she was suddenly bathed in the bright lights of on oncoming car. Lila looked up, and through eyes blurred with tears, saw the rapidly approaching car. She froze, her hand still outstretched. The car wasn't going to stop. Lila saw who was behind the wheel and after a fleeting moment of disbelief, stood and feebly threw up her arms to shield herself as the car slammed into her with such force that she was knocked out of one of her shoes and sent flying, much like her purse only moments before, into the brick wall thirty feet behind her.

The driver of the car slammed on the breaks hard enough to send the car skidding almost sideways, and watched in horrified fascination as Lila smashed into the wall with a sickening crunch. Her broken body sagged into a heap on the ground leaving a smear of bright red blood behind on the weathered brick. The driver got out of the car, walked slowly over to the body, and pressed trembling fingers to the side of Lila's still warm neck, trying hard to avoid looking into her empty, staring eyes, or at the thin ribbons of blood trickling out of her nose, ears, and the corner of her slack mouth. Not surprisingly, no life pulsed under the driver's fingers, which were quickly snatched away.

The driver took a step back from the blood pooling under the dead woman's head and looked around wildly to make sure no one was watching. But there was no one around and the only sound, besides that of crickets chirping furiously, came from the idling car. Feeling a little braver, the driver looked down at the stunned almost comical expression frozen on Lila's face without a trace of pity or remorse, then quickly got back into the car and sped out of the lot.

ONE
Fifteen years later

"Leonard, honey, would you like some more pie?" asked my grandmother, Estelle Mays, of the elderly gentleman sitting to her left at the dining room table. It was Sunday and I, along with my Uncle Alex, and his girlfriend of nearly a decade, Gwen Robins, ate dinner almost every Sunday at my grandmother's house.

Usually Sunday dinner at Mama's house was the highlight of my week. She put her heart and soul into the food she cooked and it showed in every single piece chicken she fried, every potato she mashed, and every pie and cake she baked. Mama's cooking made me happy. It was better than Prozac, and a whole lot cheaper.

However, for the past month we'd had an extra guest for Sunday dinner in the form of Mama's new boyfriend, Leonard Duncan. Mama met Leonard while playing bid whist at the Willow Senior Center. Leonard was seventy-five, and like Mama, widowed. Unlike my late grandfather, who'd been tall and thin, Leonard wasn't much taller than Mama, and was thick around the middle. He sported a neatly trimmed graying goatee and kept his thinning hair cut short with a small part on the side. He seemed like a nice enough man, and was polite, and well dressed. And he made my grandmother laugh and smile in a way I hadn't seen since before my grandfather died. But there was something about him that rubbed me the wrong way.

I couldn't put a finger on just what it was. But Leonard Duncan was just a little too good to be true. Or maybe I was just suspicious of men in general because my own man, Carl Brumfield, had unceremoniously dumped me and moved to Atlanta after a huge misunderstanding. And of course there was also the little matter of me being unable to give Carl an answer to his marriage proposal.

But if pressed to give an immediate reason as to why I didn't like Leonard Duncan, I'd say it was because Mama had just slid the last piece of pecan pie onto Leonard's plate. It was his third piece. Everyone knew not to stand between the last piece of pie and me. Mama usually wrapped it up for me to take home. Since Leonard arrived on the scene, I was crap out of luck on the pie front. No man and no pie, my life couldn't get much worse.

"Stella, baby, you have outdone yourself, again," Leonard said, taking a big bite of pie, and grinning at Mama.

That was another thing that I couldn't stand about the man, his stupid nicknames for people. He couldn't be bothered to call any of us by our God given names. No, that was too boring he declared during his first Sunday dinner appearance. From then on Mama was dubbed Stella usually followed by baby, Gwen was simply called G, Alex was Lex Luther or LL for short, after the bald arch nemesis of Superman, and I was Ken because I wore my hair short and natural like a boy.

Mama, who got tickled every time he called her Stella, beamed back at Leonard over the compliment to her cooking. Gwen and my uncle Alex also smiled. Though they both hated their nicknames as much as I did, unlike me, who thought he was a pie hogging pain in the ass; Alex and Gwen thought Leonard Duncan was the best thing to happen to Mama since Polygrip came out in cherry flavor. I rolled my eyes as he finished off the pie. Gwen saw me and cleared her throat and frowned.

Usually, Gwen isn't anyone I'd want mad at me. At five ten and almost two hundred pounds, Gwen had a way of inspiring obedience with her sheer presence alone. However, I was finding it hard to feel intimidated by her today because she was wearing a white blonde Afro wig that looked like dandelion fluff. I had to resist the urge to blow on her head. For Gwen, wigs were a form of self-expression. I had no idea what she was trying to express today other than a total lack of self-consciousness.

"Kendra and I will do the dishes, Mama," Gwen said, tossing me a venomous smile. "So, you and Leonard can just kick back and enjoy yourselves."

"Come on, Stella, baby. You're too pretty to be sittin' around. I bet we can catch the last little bit of Lawrence Welk." Leonard pulled Mama to her feet and twirled her around.

"I know that's right," replied Mama, laughing, as they danced their way into the TV room.

I watched them go, repressing the urge to upchuck

into the gravy bowl, and turned to meet the disapproving gazes of Gwen and Alex.

"What is your problem?" whispered Gwen so the lovebirds in the TV room wouldn't hear her. But judging from the sounds of the laughter coming from the next room, our conversation was the last thing on their minds.

"Yeah, why don't you like Leonard? Seems like a pretty harmless old dude to me," added Alex before I could even answer.

As I've already admitted, irritating as I thought he was, I couldn't put a finger on any serious reason why he bothered me. He treated Mama like a queen. But there was something in his eyes, lurking just underneath the surface, that I didn't like. I knew they wouldn't understand. So instead of answering, I proceeded to pile up the dirty dinner dishes.

"I don't know what you two are talking about," I said.

"Liar," replied Gwen. I stuck my tongue out at her when she turned her back earning me a snort of laughter from Alex who made no move at all to pitch in.

"Either you can get off your bony ass and help us LL, or you can go in the TV room and get some pointers from Leonard on how to treat a lady. Take your pick," said Gwen irritably.

Alex shrugged nonchalantly, refusing to let Gwen's moodiness bother him, stretched his long legs, then left the room to go join Mama and Leonard, who's continued laughter indicated they were having a lot more fun than we were. Gwen and I continued to clear the table in silence.

I followed Gwen into the kitchen with my arms

loaded down with dirty dishes. I set the dishes next to the sink, which was already half full of hot soapy water. Gwen had put on a pair rubber gloves to protect her fresh manicure and was purposefully ignoring me.

"Fine. If that's the way you want it," I mumbled under my breath, as I got busy rinsing and drying the dishes she'd started to wash. After ten minutes of the only sound in the kitchen coming from the silverware clinking together at the bottom of the sink, I finally spoke up.

"So, you don't think there's something a little off about Leonard?" I whispered and turned to make sure the swinging door to the kitchen was closed.

"Like what?" she asked not looking at me.

"I don't know. He's just too...too... I just have a weird feeling about him that's all," I concluded.

"Are you for real?" Gwen asked, finally turning to give me an incredulous look. "He's a nice man and he makes your grandma happy. Would it kill you to be happy for her? She's been alone a long time, Kendra."
Gwen didn't need to remind me how long Mama had been alone. She hadn't been romantically involved with anyone since my grandfather's death ten years ago. She and grandpa Mays had been high school sweethearts and inseparable the entire forty-nine years of their marriage. Contrary to what Gwen seemed to think, I did want Mama to find love again. Truly, I did. But Leonard Duncan felt wrong. I just wished I could figure out why.

"All I'm saying is —" I began before Gwen cut me off.

"Look, you don't have to like the man, Kendra. You aren't the one dating him. But it sure would be nice if you'd stop being so selfish. I'm sorry you're so miserable over Carl, girlfriend, really I am. But it's not Mama's fault your man dropped you like a hot potato and skipped town. Just because your relationship didn't work out, doesn't mean no one else has the right to be happy."

My mouth fell open. No she didn't just go there. Gwen and I glared at each other for a few seconds before I shrugged and went back to drying dishes. Clearly, I had no ally in my uncle's girlfriend when it came to the subject of Mama's new man. But, was Gwen right? Was I taking my disappointment over my break-up with Carl out on Mama and Leonard? Could I actually be jealous of my own grandmother?

I balled up my dishrag and threw it on the counter, and then headed back into the dining room to get the remaining dinner dishes. I looked through the dining room door through the TV room and saw Mama and Leonard standing by the front door deep in conversation. Then Mama reached into the pocket of her skirt and pulled out what looked from where I was standing to be a large wad of cash. Leonard held up his hands in mock protest until Mama pressed the cash into his hand and gave him a big kiss on the cheek that made him grin. I watched with a sinking sensation in my stomach as he stuffed the money into his pocket. I looked over at Alex, who was sitting on the couch, to see if he'd witnessed what I had. No such luck. Alex was glued to the TV screen and had missed the whole thing.

I went back into the kitchen feeling somewhat vindicated. Surely what I'd just witnessed was proof that that geriatric gigolo was up to no good. My grandmother wasn't a wealthy woman. Her only source of income was from my grandfather's Social Security pension. She'd always been thrifty for as long as I could remember, and lived on a very tight budget. She leapt at any freebie in her path to save herself some cash and was the queen of coupon clipping. She just wasn't the type to freely give money away, and I ought to know. On the rare occasions I'd asked to borrow money from her, you'd have thought I'd asked her for a kidney...and a lung. So why then was she giving a grown ass man a big wad of cash? There were only a few reasons that sprang to mind and none of them good. If Leonard Duncan thought he was going to use my grandmother as a meal ticket, he'd have to go through me first.

After helping Gwen finish the dishes, I made my excuses and headed out the door. But not before Alex reminded me that I had agreed to help serve the food at Joy Owens' art show at the Ramey Gallery the next night. Estelle's, Alex's restaurant, named after my grandmother, was catering the event for free as a graduation gift to Joy because she worked at Estelle's part-time as a hostess, along with me and Gwen, and had recently graduated with an art degree from Kingford College.

Joy Owens is not my favorite person. While there's no denying her talent as an artist, she was so obnoxious and abrasive she made sandpaper look like Kleenex. She had the whole angry, young artist routine down to an art form. Needless to say, I wasn't real enthusiastic at the prospect of spending my evening serving economy class champagne, bacon wrapped shrimp, and Thai chicken skewers to snotty art lovers and tacky folks, who don't give a crap about art, but who'll show up because of the free grub and booze, while Joy barked orders at me like a drill sergeant. I'd only agreed to do it because Alex was paying me double. Joy's less than sparkling personality had ensured that one else was willing to work the event. Plus, it meant I wouldn't have to spend another evening home alone thinking about Carl and all the southern beauties that were probably throwing themselves at him in Atlanta.

I was stopped at a red light two blocks away from my duplex on Dorset when I noticed the same brown Chevy that had been behind me since I left Mama's house was still behind me. I looked in my rearview window but couldn't see who was behind the wheel because the windows were tinted. Was this person following me? When the light finally turned green, I made a left turn. The brown Chevy made a left turn, too. Next, I made a right turn. The brown Chevy made a right turn, too. Okay, now I was getting freaked out. And I had damned good reason to be.

Several months ago a murderer named Stephanie Preston tried burn my best friend, Lynette, and me alive in a cabin in John Bryan State Park. The fact that I'm still alive to tell this tale means she failed. Actually, Stephanie herself was the one seriously burned over thirty percent of her body. Up until a month ago, she was languishing in isolation at the Ohio Reformatory for Women's medical ward awaiting trial on two counts each of first degree murder, attempted murder, kidnapping, and arson. The trial was scheduled for this fall.

Angela Henry

Lynette and I were all set to testify against her when the unthinkable happened. With the help of Dr. Walter Dillon, the prison doctor treating her, who turned out to be a former john from her hooker past, Stephanie Preston escaped custody while being transported to a nearby hospital after developing a burn related infection. No one knew where she and Dr. Dillon were, unless, of course, they were in the brown Chevy currently behind me. I sped up leaving the Chevy behind at a stop sign.

I pulled into my usual parking space in front of my apartment and reached into my purse for the can of pepper spray I keep at all times. Yeah, I know pepper spray can't stop bullets. But since I refuse to buy a gun—because I'm too klutzy to operate one without shooting off my foot—pepper spray was all I had. My hand closed around the cool aerosol can and I felt instantly reassured as I peered through my rearview window to see if the brown Chevy had followed me home. I could see the headlights of an oncoming car. It was the brown Chevy. I was now convinced that the Chevy was bringing my inevitable demise. Stephanie Preston had made it quite clear in the numerous interviews she'd given since her arrest that I was the cause of all of her current legal problems. Her coming after me to keep me from testifying against her seemed only logical to my overworked imagination.

But as I cowered in the driver's seat trembling and awaiting certain death and dismemberment at the hands of a murderous, burnt up, lunatic and her lovesick accomplice, the brown Chevy sped past so fast I couldn't even make out the license plate number. I sat in my car, with the pepper spray can still clutched tightly in my right hand, until I could no longer see the car's taillights. I barely had time to let out a sigh of relief when a sudden tap on my passenger's side window almost made me crap my pants and caused my index finger, which was firmly poised on the can's discharge button, to press down releasing a mushroom cloud of pepper spray inside my car.

The shock and burning pain was almost enough to make me faint. I practically fell out of the car gagging, coughing, and half blind with tears in my attempt to get away from the noxious fumes. I was rolling around in the street unable to even scream as I clawed at my eyes and a river of snot streamed out of my nose. I could hear the concerned voices of several people including that of Mrs. Carson, my 72 year-old landlady, as she repeatedly asked me what was wrong.

"Kendra, good Lord what's the matter?" Only I couldn't answer her because I was still coughing. She roughly turned me onto my stomach and started pounding me on the back. She thought I was choking and my face bounced off the concrete with each blow of her palm.

"No! Burns! It burns!" was all I could manage to get out. "Water! Water!" I croaked in a raspy voice I didn't recognize.

And water is just what I got. Lots of it. Seconds later, I was not only doused with a couple of large buckets of cold water, but felt a steady, narrow stream of water hit me in the forehead indicating that someone must be spraying me with their garden hose. In less than a minute I'd gone from burning to almost drowning. And the water just kept coming until I finally waved my arms and yelled, "Stop! Stop!"

I was soaking wet, and sputtering on the water that had run into my nose and mouth, but I was finally able to open my eyes to see myself surrounded by Mrs. Carson and about half a dozen other neighbors all holding either buckets, or large plastic tumblers. What I thought had been a garden hose was actually a jumbo sized super soaker water gun that Mrs. Carson was clutching like an assault rifle. It probably belonged to one of her great grandkids. It was also apparent, after I was helped to my feet, that water wasn't the only thing I got doused with. My white shirt and tan crop pants had stains from what looked and smelled like cherry Kool Aid, iced tea, and Mountain Dew.

"Better?" Mrs. Carson asked, fingering the super soaker's trigger like she'd be happy to oblige me with more water if I needed it.

"Loads," I replied sarcastically as I stood there dripping. Even my shoes were soaked through and squelched water as I walked up onto the sidewalk.

I explained what happened. And my dignity and I were quite thankful that Mrs. Carson and the neighbors at least let me get inside my apartment before laughing like hyenas. The words *idiot*, *dumb ass*, and *airhead* managed to reach me through my front window, which was open a crack. I didn't care. I was just happy to be alive and that the burning had subsided into a dull throb. I stripped off my sopping clothes and shoes just inside my door and walked naked to the bathroom making a brief stop at the mirror. Not a good idea. I flinched when I saw myself. My eyes were bloodshot and swollen almost to slits, and the skin around my eyes and cheeks was also swollen and sore to the touch, my nose was bright red and still running, and my lower lip was puffy from Mrs. Carson flipping me on my stomach and slamming my face into the ground. I looked and felt like I'd been beaten with a club.

After scrubbing away every trace of the pepper spray, washing my hair, and letting cold water from the shower run over my sore face for what seemed like forever, I put on a night shirt, avoided all mirrors and reflective surfaces, and got ready to do what I'd been doing every night since Carl left. Eat. I was settling in front of my TV with a pint of chocolate Hagen Daz and a tin of homemade double chocolate chunk cookies, when there was a tap at my door. It was Mrs. Carson, again.

"All those theatrics of yours made me forget what it was I needed to give you, missy," she said, handing me a letter. She was staring at my swollen face trying not to wince.

"That new mailman delivered it to my place yesterday by mistake. Would have brought it by sooner but I been out. You want some cocoa butter?" she asked. She reached out to touch my face but stopped when I flinched. In Mrs. Carson's opinion, there wasn't much that a little cocoa butter couldn't cure.

I mumbled a thank you and watched her go. I stared at the letter for a long time. It was a letter I'd written to Carl apologizing for the way things had ended and wishing him well on his new job. I didn't have a home address for Carl in Atlanta, or an email address, or phone number, not that he'd have spoken to me if I'd called. I'd resorted to sending the letter to his new law firm. The words *return to sender* had been scribbled across the front of the letter in Carl's sloppy, slanted handwriting. He hadn't even opened it. He could have just pitched it and I'd have been none the wiser. Instead, he'd sent it back to me because he wanted me to know he wasn't interested in what I had to say. I torn up the letter and tossed it in the trash.

I flopped down on my couch, turned on the TV, and avoided every love and romance related offering finally settling on the movie Gremlins on the Sci Fi channel, which is exactly how I looked and felt. I devoured the cookies and ice cream, trying hard to fill the emptiness inside me, as a flood of silent tears cascaded down my sore cheeks.

TWO

I felt like crap the next morning and barely made it to the bathroom before heaving my guts up. I discovered, after pulling my head out of the toilet, that I looked a lot better. My eyes were still bloodshot, and had thick yellow crust in the corners, but were no longer swollen. I'd bet money that all the crying I'd done had probably washed away the remainder of the pepper spray. My nose was caked with dried snot, and my cheeks weren't red any more. But they were still sore and tender to the touch. My bottom lip was still a little puffy but a couple of thick coats of lipstick could easily hide it. It was my stomach of all things that felt the worst and it was no wonder. I walked into the kitchen after showering and saw the empty Hagen Daz container in the trash. The almost empty cookie tin was on the counter. There had been two-dozen cookies in the tin last night. Now, there were only four left. No wonder I threw up. I was in sugar shock. I skipped breakfast and headed to work.

My workday flew by. Normally, I was happy when

were busy because it meant enrollment was up at the literacy center that I've taught English at for the past six years. But the end of this particular day meant the arrival of Joy Owens' art show and running around all night being the only server. Alex had told me he'd help out but I knew I'd get little help from him since he thought his only contribution should be the preparing and bringing of the food. He'd be mixing and mingling along with everyone else while I worked my ass off. The actual showing started at seven o'clock. But, I had to get there early to set everything up and stay when the showing finished up at nine to clean up and help Alex load up his van. It could be after eleven before I got home. My lack of enthusiasm caused me to be twenty minutes late getting to the gallery. Alex wasn't happy, and neither was Joy. Both of them were waiting for me at the gallery's back door.

I'd only been to the Ramey Gallery once before with Carl for an exhibit of abstract sculpture by a college buddy of his. I'd enjoyed the exhibit, but not the snobby, elitist attitude of Justin Ramey, the owner of the gallery. Ramey had been very friendly to Carl, who was a lawyer, and thus deemed worthy of his attention because he thought Carl might buy something, which he did. He'd been very nice to me, too. Until, he discovered that I was a mere broke and lowly, adult education teacher, and a part-time one at that. His attitude towards me turned on a dime. This was my first time back to the gallery since that night and I planned to steer well clear of Justin Ramey.

"Sorry, I'm late," I mumbled to Alex and Joy, avoiding eye contact with either of them, and grabbing the serving trays from the back of Alex's van. In true

Joy fashion, she didn't miss a trick.

"Damn! You been smokin' blunts or what?" Joy asked, referring to my still bloodshot eyes. "I don't know if I want you servin' lookin' like that. People might think you're a crack head or somethin'." Good old Joy.

"It's allergies," I said flatly, moving past her to go into the gallery.

"Yeah," she said, laughing in her horse smoker's voice. "I guess once they get a good look at that double chin you're gettin', they'll know you can't be smokin' crack."

I glared at her. Alex just looked at me, chuckled, and shook his head without speaking. He was one of the few people who actually thought Joy was funny.

If I looked like crap, then Joy was looking better than I'd ever seen her. Gone was her usual uniform of jeans, baseball cap, and T-shirt. Tonight she was dressed in a tailored black men's wear style pants suit with a vest and a crisp white shirt with tiny ruffles at the cuffs and down the front. She had on black patent leather flats with tuxedo bows on the toes. Her hair was still tinted auburn and pulled into the usual knot at the back of her head. But her bangs had been trimmed and she had let some longer tendrils hang down in front to frame her face making her look softer. She even looked like she had on a little make-up. For once she looked like an adult instead of a juvenile delinquent. I couldn't stop staring at her. She actually looked pretty.

"Don't hate me 'cause I'm beautiful," she said, looking both pleased and self-conscious over my shocked expression. "Just get your ass in gear. I ain't lettin' no one mess up my big night. Are you feelin' me?"

The outside may have gotten an upgrade but the attitude was still the same. I rolled my eyes and ignored her and helped Alex unload the rest of the van.

An hour later, the Ramey Gallery was hopping. Joy's show, which featured twelve of her strangest and most colorful paintings, was called *Dark Revelation*, and featured such oddities as flies with human faces and angel wings, and teddy bears that looked like they had leprosy. I found the paintings the same way I found all of Joy's work, extremely depressing and very weird. Apparently, I was the only one who felt this way because everyone else was raving over them.

"I love they way they jar their minimalist surrounding, don't you?" sniffed one well dressed, and overly tanned, middle-aged redhead whose diamond toe ring alone looked like it cost more than everything I owned.

"The sheer surrealism quite takes my breath away," replied the redhead's companion, a short, ruddy faced, bald man wearing a beret and a goatee.

I had to agree with both of them, though. Joy's paintings could definitely take ones breath away and they were as colorful as they were weird, which really livened up the Ramey Gallery's stark white walls and shiny blond hardwood floors. Each painting was mounted on the wall and positioned under a bright white spotlight. But the rest of the gallery was in almost complete darkness making it hard for me to navigate, especially loaded down with two trays at a time. Thankfully, Alex was manning the drinks table so I didn't have to worry about tripping and spilling liquids on the gallery floor.

Joy was holding court in a corner being interviewed by poufy haired channel four news reporter Tracy Ripkey and acting surprisingly joyless for someone in the limelight. She looked very nervous and was looking at her feet while Ripkey grilled her about everything from her art influences to what kind of paint she used. I almost felt sorry for her. Almost. The more I watched, the more I realized it was Ripkey I should feel sorry for.

"So, Roman Beardman was a huge influence for you growing up?" Ripkey said brightly. Joy glared at her.

"It's Romare Bearden," Joy said, correcting her. "And, yeah, his stuff is the shit. I've been diggin' him since I was a kid."

All the color drain from Ripkey's face. I truly hoped this wasn't a live interview.

"How would you describe your work?" Ripkey asked, quickly regaining her composure if not her spark.

"I'd describe it as a straight-up mind fuck, an acid trip without the acid. Look at all these people, man. They're trippin'. They don't know what in the hell just hit 'em," Joy replied proudly, gesturing around the room without a trace of embarrassment.

Ripkey blinked rapidly several times before turning back to the camera.

"And there you have it. Tracy Ripkey reporting live from the Ramey Gallery in Willow. Back to you Dave," she said with a tight smile.

I could barely contain my laughter as a furious Ripkey stormed out of the gallery mumbling angrily about not realizing she'd need a time delay to interview a small town nobody, while being trailed by her hysterically laughing cameraman. I was so caught up in the drama that I didn't see the person standing directly behind me. I whirled around and almost dumped an entire tray of crab and Gruyere stuffed mushrooms down the front of Justin Ramey himself. Uh oh!

He took an instinctive step backwards and then gave me the most disdainful look I'd ever had the displeasure of being on the receiving end of. And it was really a shame he was such an ass. He was kind of fine for a guy kicking sixty in the butt. Not that he looked it. He certainly knew how to dress, I couldn't help noticing as he inspected his tan Italian suit for the tiniest stain. He was of average height, caramel-skinned, and clean-shaven with keen features and thick, curly, dark hair streaked with silver strands. His eyes were light brown and currently narrowed to slits. He smelled like Burberry cologne.

"I realize that this kind of an event might be a bit beyond the scope of your social experience. But while you're standing around with your mouth hanging open, the food is getting cold, and my patrons aren't being taken care of," he said in a frosty voice.

If he recognized me as being the girlfriend of the guy who'd spent a crap load of money in his gallery last year, he sure didn't act like it. But that was hardly a surprise. Something happened once you put on a serving uniform. You became somehow less than human. People will say and do all kinds of things in front of you because as far as they're concerned, you're only one step above the furniture. Even though Alex had supplied the food and drink for free, I didn't want him to lose out on a potential future customer. Word had it that Justin Ramey was loaded and threw lots of fancy parties at his big house out in the country. So, I as much I wanted to see his arrogant ass wearing the tray of mushrooms, I did my best bowing and scrapping routine.

"So sorry, sir, it won't happen again," I said, quickly moving away from him.

"See that it doesn't," I heard him hiss at my retreating back. Asshole.

There was only forty-five minutes to go before the showing ended and I was counting the minutes. My feet hurt and my arms and back ached from lugging the heavy trays around. I'd just come from the galley's small kitchenette with a tray of white and dark chocolate dipped strawberries, when I saw a couple just arriving and being greeted warmly by Justin Ramey. It was Reverend Morris Rollins and his new girlfriend, my arch nemesis, Detective Trish Harmon. The bottom dropped out of my stomach and the tray would have dropped out of my hands had Joy not caught it.

"See, I knew your ass was high," she said, then following my gaze started smirking. I tried to get past her but she blocked my path.

"You got *no* luck when it comes to men, Clayton. That lawyer of yours dumped your ass, and now even the man who tried his best to hook up with you when you *had* a man has moved on." Ignoring her, I walked away.

I'd met Morris Rollins, the attractive and charismatic minister of Holy Cross Church, last year when one of my students was accused of murdering one of his loved ones. And even though technically he was old enough to be my father, there was an undeniable attraction between us that had resulted in a couple of very steamy and very illicit kisses, illicit because I was still dating Carl at the time. The last time I'd spoken to Rollins had been the week before Carl had dumped me, when he'd told me that he was moving on because he knew I loved Carl. Talk about bad timing.

Only I had no idea who he was moving on to. Detective Trish Harmon, of the Willow Police Department, and I hated each other with a passion because of all of the murder investigations of hers that I'd gotten myself mixed up in. Harmon saw everything in black and white, while I could see all the shades of grey that she chose to ignore. I should have known there was a new man in her life because she'd recently gone through an amazing transformation by coloring her grey hair and buying a whole new, up-to-date wardrobe. I had no idea Rollins had been behind her change from caterpillar to butterfly. Love has a way of doing that to women.

Rollins had just spotted me and was coming my way. I pushed past Joy and headed in the opposite direction. The last time we'd talked, he had told me we'd always be friends. Yet, I hadn't heard a peep out of him in weeks, even after the news of Stephanie Preston's escape had hit the news and I could have really used a friend. I didn't want to see him now.

"You can run but you can't hide," came Rollins seductively deep voice in my ear after he finally cornered me next to Joy's painting called *Nightcrawlers* depicting, of all things, babies with scorpion stingers sticking out of their diapers crawling across a moonlit desert.

"Isn't your girlfriend going to miss you?" I said nonchalantly trying hard to ignore how good he smelled and looked in his jeans and tweed sport coat.

I had to look up to meet his eyes because he was well over six feet tall. He'd recently cut the full beard he'd been sporting and was wearing the neatly trimmed goatee he'd had when we first meet. Good God he was hot!

"So, is this the way it's going to be, Kendra?" he said, sighing heavily.

"Look, I'm working, Rollins. That uppity Justin Ramey already chewed me out once. I don't want that man jumping on my case again because you've suddenly remembered I exist and want to chat." I knew I was rude, but I was also tired, and miserable, and just didn't care.

"I haven't been a very good friend to you lately, have I?" he asked, looking appropriately contrite. "Have there been any sightings of Stephanie Preston?"

"Don't you have a direct pipeline to the police department? You probably know more than I do."

He looked at me sheepishly for moment without speaking then said, "I'm sorry about you and Carl."

I didn't even realize he knew about our split but nodded and started to walk away when his voice stopped me. "I have the right to be happy, too, Kendra. You never wanted to be more than friends, remember?"

I whirled back around almost flinging the chocolate strawberries against the *Nightcrawlers*.

"But, with her?" I hissed through clenched teeth. "Why her? Of all the women you could have hooked up with, you had to pick the one who goes out of her way to treat me like a paranoid idiot. The woman who arrested my sister for a murder she didn't commit, and tried to arrest me! And then you didn't even tell me you were seeing her. I had to find out on my own," I said, thinking back to the night I'd gone to his place needing to talk only to see him and Harmon through the window locked in a passionate embrace.

"I don't need your permission on who I can date, Kendra. And Trish was just doing her job. You're being unreasonable. I didn't do this to spite you. People can't pick who they fall for. It just happens," he said, putting his hand on my shoulder.

"Sure, whatever you say." I shook off his hand. For some reason the warm touch of his hand on my shoulder made me want to cry.

"Kendra, please don't be like this. I never meant to —" But he didn't get to finish whatever it was he'd been about to say. Loud voices were coming from the front of the gallery.

We turned to see Justin Ramey arguing loudly with a woman waving a piece of paper in his face. Looking for any excuse to get away from Rollins, I went to see what the problem was.

The young woman's arms gestured wildly as her voice rose higher and higher. She was cinnamon skinned, very pretty, and looked to be in her early twenties. She had curly, shoulder length hair, and big brown eyes. Her jeans, leather thong sandals, and embroidered black tunic were casual but expensive looking. I wondered who she was, Ramey's girlfriend? She looked way too young for him but I guess that wasn't impossible given my own recent attraction to an older man. Rich men often had young wives and girlfriends.

"You can't do this! It's not just me you'll be hurting. There are a lot of talented kids who'll be back on the streets with nothing to do if the art center closes!" she wailed.

I could see the tears in her eyes from where I was standing and the pleading in her voice made me embarrassed for her. But Justin Ramey was unmoved and stared coldly at her.

"You did this to yourself. I warned you what would happen if you disobeyed me. I'm not responsible for a bunch of ignorant, young thugs, and future welfare mamas with no ambition, and going nowhere lives, and neither are you. If you need a job, you can help me out here at the gallery," replied Justin Ramey haughtily.

She shook her head in astonishment as the tears flowed freely down her cheeks. She wiped her eyes with the back of her hand and headed towards the galley's front door. But before she opened it, she turned to face Justin Ramey, her face flaming.

"You are one soulless bastard, you know that? If it weren't for an art center like the one you're closing, where would your ass be today?"

I looked over at Ramey. His face was as hard as stone. The small crowd that had gathered were watching and whispering. I could only imagine what they must be thinking witnessing fancy pants Justin Ramey's personal drama.

"I'll tell you where you'd be," the young woman continued. "You'd be broke and broke down just like the poor people you despise so much."

"I don't despise them because they're poor," Justin said, shrugging matter-of-factly. "I despise them because they're weak and stupid. And if you want to roll around in the mud with those people, you go right ahead. But, you won't be doing it with my money anymore. Now get out of here and go home before I cut you off and you get to be one of those poor people you love so much." He turned and walked away.

The young woman grabbed a brass penholder from the counter by the door and hurled it at Justin Ramey's head. It missed him but hit the wall next him making a big, ugly dent. He kept right on walking—like a parent walking away from a child having a tantrum in public—and didn't look back, which infuriated her even more. She shrieked at his retreating form.

"I hope you die you sad, empty monster! I hope someone cuts your heart out just like you did mine and everyone else who's made the mistake of loving you!" She slumped against the door crying so hard her shoulders were heaving.

Surprisingly, Joy rushed over and grabbed the girl's hand and tried to comfort her, but she angrily shook her off and rushed out the door into the night. You could have cut the tension she left behind with a knife. Thankfully, by this time many people had already left. There were only about a dozen people in the gallery now. A few more people left immediately after the drama ended, no doubt having had their delicate sensibilities ruffled.

I was more than ready to go home myself and hoped people wouldn't linger so I could clean up. But forty minutes later, as the clock struck nine, I was unhappy to see Joy still surrounded by well-wishers, including Rollins, Trish Harmon, and Alex. Justin Ramey must have been more upset than he'd appeared. He'd yet to resurface from wherever he'd gone since the mystery woman's departure. I was so sure he'd be the type to rush around smiling and apologizing for the unfortunate display of bad manners, but, apparently not.

I noticed Joy wasn't paying much attention to her admirers. She kept glancing over at the gallery's front door like she was expecting someone, while Rollins kept sneaking peaks in my direction as I was picking up empty cups and plates. Trish Harmon, looking disgustingly fab in a sleeveless cranberry colored wrap dress and killer heels, noticed her man looking at me and purposefully snuggled up next to him and gave him a slow lingering kiss on the cheek. He smiled down at her and kissed her affectionately as he rubbed her back. There was softness in his eyes as he looked down at her. This was not a summer fling. He actually had feelings for her. I felt like I'd been punched.

That was it for me. I headed off to the bathroom and spent the next ten minutes bawling like a baby. And I didn't know why. I wasn't in love with Rollins, was I? There was a time when I definitely wanted to jump his bones. Cut could I actually have been in love with two men at the same time, both of who now no longer wanted me? No! I refused to believe I was feeling anything but sorry for myself. I quickly pulled myself together enough to leave the bathroom and ran into Alex on his way to the kitchenette.

"You okay?" he asked, looking at me funny.

"Of course," I said, avoiding his probing gaze. He squeezed my shoulder.

"We can pack up in a few minutes," he said, walking past me into the kitchenette.

I started to head back out into the gallery when I saw Rollins headed in my direction. I couldn't take one more minute of him tonight. I backtracked and headed down a long narrow hallway just off the gallery's back entrance. I heard Rollins softly calling my name and ducked into the nearest unlocked door closing it a crack, and peering out into the semi dark hallway until I was sure he was gone. Once the coast was clear, I shut the door and leaned wearily against it. Suddenly, my foot slid out from under me and I landed hard on my ass. I tried to get up but kept slipping.

"What the hell?" I said aloud trying to get up and slipping again.

The room was pitch black. There was something wet and sticky all over the floor and I couldn't see what is was. I finally managed to grab the doorknob and pull myself to my feet. I felt around on the wall for a light switch. Once I got the lights on, I froze. I was in what appeared to be an office. At first I thought the red pattern on the walls was wallpaper. I quickly realized I was wrong, very wrong. It was blood. Blood as far the eye could see. There was blood all over the floor, blood on the walls, and blood on the ceiling. There was blood all over me, the coppery tang of it—and another scent I couldn't immediately place—filled my nostrils. My clothes and hands were covered in blood. But that wasn't the worst of it. Lying across his desk, dripping blood and gore all over the floor, was Justin Ramey. The only reason I knew it was him was because of his eyes. His face was unrecognizable but his light brown eyes were open and staring at me. I couldn't pull my horrified gaze away from his dead one.

It was only after I finally realized that the smell I couldn't place was Ramey's Burberry cologne that I snapped out of my trance and frantically tried to get out of the office. My blood and sweat slicked hands kept slipping on the doorknob. I had to get out. If I didn't get out I'd lose my mind. I got the door open and lurched into the hallway leaving bloody smudges behind on the wall as I felt my way down the hallway. My stomach was roiling. My head was spinning. I almost fell in my haste to get away from the horror behind me. I stumbled out into the front of the gallery where Joy was, thankfully, still talking to Rollins and Harmon. They all turned to stare at me. Rollins' mouth fell open in shock. And feeling like *Carrie* after she'd been drenched in pig blood at the prom, I screamed and then fainted.

THREE

When I came to I was outside on a stretcher with an oxygen mask over my face being tended by a female paramedic taking my blood pressure. I tried to sit up but was gently pushed back down.

"Not so fast, Kendra. You've had one hell of a shock," said Rollins deep voice. He was standing next to the stretcher holding my hand.

I could see that the front of the Ramey Gallery had been cordoned off with barriers and crime scene tape and was swarming with police. Flashing lights from police cars and the emergency vehicles lit up the night sky. People were gathered across the street watching the drama unfold. Harmon was in full detective mode and had put on some latex gloves and plastic booties over her high heels. She was talking to some uniformed officers. Alex, and Joy were talking to Harmon's partner, the terminally rumpled, overweight, and ever friendly, Charles Mercer, probably giving him statements.

"It was Justin Ramey, wasn't it?" I asked, pushing

the mask away from my face.

"Yes, unfortunately, it was. Now, stop talking and let this nice lady take care of you," Rollins said, putting the mask back over my face.

I gave his hand a grateful squeeze and closed my eyes only to have the grisly image of Justin Ramey's battered and bloody body force them open again. I'd certainly seen my share of dead bodies, though never the blood bath I'd walked in on tonight. The blood was bad enough. But, it's the victim's eyes and their forever frozen stares that always got to me.

By now my clothes were stiff with dried blood and I wanted nothing more than to get out of them and stand under a hot shower until the water turned cold. The urge to go home and get clean was so strong it had me sitting up and taking the oxygen mask off my face against the wishes of the paramedic and Rollins.

"I'm fine, really," I insisted. I swung my legs over the side of the stretcher. I still felt a little wobbly but I'd live.

"Glad to hear it," said Trish Harmon. I hadn't even noticed her approach. Probably something she learned in the academy. "We'll need those clothes and shoes you're wearing," she said, handing me a large brown paper bag.

"Gladly, I never want to see them again." I shuddered.

"Anybody have any idea who could have done this, Trish?" Rollins asked.

"No, and it doesn't help matters that the scene has been completely contaminated," she said, giving me a hard, accusatory look.

"I'm sorry but I didn't realize there was a dead

body in that room when I walked into it. It was dark in there and I slipped in the blood. It's not like I rolled around in it on purpose." Man, this woman had a way of getting under my skin. How could Rollins stand her?

"What am I supposed to think, Miss Clayton? You're attracted to dead bodies the way flies are to shit."

"Being attracted to dead bodies is called necrophilia, Detective. I'm just always in the wrong place at the wrong time," I snapped, though technically I should be grateful she hadn't arrested me for Ramey's murder. That was Harmon's usual method of operation. I couldn't help noticing that getting laid on a regular basis was doing wonders for her temperament. That is until she opened her mouth again.

"And just why were you in Justin Ramey's office in the first place?"

I wasn't about to tell her I'd been ducking her man and went into the office to hide from him. Harmon wasn't the understanding type. As much as I hated the thought of them being together, I wasn't looking to make trouble for Rollins. Not much anyway. I sighed heavily while my mind raced trying to figure out a good excuse for being someplace I shouldn't have been. Fortunately, someone arrived at the scene that could take the heat off of me. It was the mysterious young woman who'd argued with Ramey. I'd forgotten all about her. She was now arguing with one of the officers and trying to push past the barrier.

"Why are you grilling me? She's the one you need to talk to." I pointed to the young woman. "Didn't you hear her telling Ramey she hoped he died and that someone would cut his heart out?" They both turned to look.

The young woman had changed from jeans and tunic into a yellow halter dress and her long hair was pulled into a ponytail that hung down her back. Joy rushed over and said something to the officer who finally let the woman through. We watched as Joy gently took her hands and told her what happened after which the young woman started screaming and trying to break away from Joy to get back into the gallery.

"Daddy!" she shrieked. "No! No! Daddy!"

Seeing the trouble petite little Joy was having keeping the young woman from rushing back into the gallery, Mercer and two officers ran over to help restrain her. She struggled wildly for a minute before falling to the ground screaming and sobbing. Joy pulled her into a tight embrace and she went limp in her arms.

Daddy? She was Justin Ramey's daughter? Two more people, who I deduced were also family members of Ramey's, arrived at the scene. A tall, slender, striking white woman in her early thirties with short, black hair, a sun-kissed tan, elegantly dressed in a green off-the-shoulder mini dress and gold stiletto heels; and a young black man in his mid twenties who vaguely resembled Ramey but was shorter and stockier and dressed casually in black chino's and a grey button down shirt. We watched as Harmon's partner, Charles Mercer, gave them the bad news.

The young man looked stunned and leaned against a police car for support. The woman's hands flew to her mouth in shock. And though they were both clearly upset, neither of them was as distraught as the young woman who was still sobbing in Joy's arms and wailing, "I'm sorry, daddy. I'm so sorry. I didn't mean it." I felt like an intruder. I didn't want or need to be witnessing this family's darkest hour. No one did.

"Can I please go home?" I asked Harmon before she headed off to go talk to the family.

"I'll have an officer run you home. But make sure you come by to see me tomorrow to give a statement and don't forget to give one of my officer's your clothes," she said curtly. Any other time she'd have made me wait around in bloody clothes until they were ready to get my statement. I could tell she wanted me gone.

"I can run her home, Trish, it's not a problem," said Rollins. Trish wasn't having it.

"I really need you to stay here with me, Morris. I was hoping you could offer support to the Ramey family," she said, referring to the fact that Rollins was a minister and used to dealing with grieving families. However, Harmon's eyes met mine and I knew it was all just a bunch of bullshit. She didn't want us to be alone together. I didn't have time for this.

"Actually," I said, jumping down off the stretcher and grabbing the paper bag. "My car is here and the clothes I wore to work are in the trunk. I can change out of these bloody things in the back of Alex's van and be on my way."

This seemed to appease Harmon, who headed back to the gallery with Rollins in tow, without a backwards glance. Rollins winked at me to let me know he knew his girlfriend was being insecure. I just rolled my eyes.

Ten minutes later, I left, too.

GALLERY OWNER BRUTALLY SLAIN screamed at me from the front page of the Willow News-Gazette the next morning after I stumbled bleary eyed out of bed from a night of blood soaked nightmares. The account of Justin Ramey's murder didn't yield any new information other than the names of his family, whose photographs caught in various expressions of grief at the scene, were under the headline next to a picture of Justin Ramey looking rich, handsome, and smug.

The young woman he'd argued with before his death was identified as his daughter, Pia Ramey, a twenty-two year-old who ran Graffiti, a non-profit art center for underprivileged kids. This must have been the art center they'd been arguing about. The one Justin Ramey had apparently been about to pull his funding from. The young man was identified as twenty-seven year-old Link Ramey, an aspiring filmmaker— translation—he was unemployed. The white woman in the green dress was Justin Ramey's wife, thirty-two year-old Lauren Ramey, a former model.

I read the rest of the article while I scarfed down a lemon poppy seed muffin and got dressed for my date with Harmon at the police station. The one new thing that I did learn was that the weapon used to kill Ramey was thought to be a mahogany pineapple sculpture that sat on his desk and was now missing It was hard to believe that while I was serving finger food, someone had been battered to death with a piece of wooden fruit a mere forty feet away. The killer must have knocked Ramey out first while his back was turned because I couldn't imagine him not defending himself or screaming for help. It was awfully ballsy to kill someone in a gallery full of people.

I headed out and was opening the door of my car when I spotted something that made me stop dead in my tracks. It was the brown Chevy. It was parked across the street two houses down from my apartment. I couldn't tell if anyone was in it because of the tint on the windows. It could have been a neighbor's car but I doubted it. The only time I'd ever seen the car was when it was following me home from Mama's. Here it was again. I pulled a notepad from my purse and was crossing the street to get the license number, when the car suddenly roared to life and pulled out from the curb coming to a dead stop ten feet in front of me as I stood in the middle of the street. I was frozen to the spot like a deer caught in headlights with my hand gripping the pen so hard it almost snapped in two. Was this it? Was I about to be run down like a chipmunk in the road? And if so, did I have on decent underwear?

The car sat idling for what seemed like forever but was probably less than a minute, then switched into reverse, backing all the way down the street and around the corner without hitting any parked cars like some stunt driver in a movie. If I weren't about to wet my pants, I'd have almost been impressed. Was this person playing with me? Surely, if it had been Stephanie Preston or Walter Dillon behind the wheel they'd have just run me down and been done with it. Unless, of course, the plan was to torment and scare me half to death before killing me, something that would appeal to a sick twisted mind like Stephanie Preston's. The loud horn blast from a car behind me sent me scurrying back to my white Toyota.

I had already called and told them I'd be late to work, so when I spotted Leonard Duncan walking his dog Queenie near the Kingford College campus, I parked and got out. I knew Harmon was probably as unenthusiastic about talking to me this morning as I was. I still had plenty of time to get to the bottom of a more pressing mystery before going to give my statement. When I finally caught up to Leonard, Queenie, a Beagle mix, was frantically barking at something that was hiding under a bush, while Leonard sat on bench nearby smoking a cigar. He looked surprised to see me when he finally looked up.

"Ken, what a surprise," he said with a smile that didn't quite reach his eyes. "Queenie, look here. We've got company," he said to the dog. Queenie was too busy racing around chasing squirrels and barking like mad to pay any attention to her master.

"Hi, Leonard. I was on my way to work and saw you. Thought I'd stop for a little chat." I sat down on the bench next to him.

He took a puff of the cigar and then hooked a thumb behind one of his suspenders, eying me speculatively. I'd never been alone with Leonard and had never really had any kind of in depth conversation with him. I was surprised at how nervous I felt.

"Uh Oh, Queenie. I must be in big trouble. Ken's never wanted to chat before. Usually, she treats me like dog doo on her shoe," he said sarcastically to the dog. Queenie was now panting tiredly in the grass at his feet. He'd made exaggerated quotation marks in the air with his fingers at the word *chat*.

This wasn't going to be fun. But given his already less than thrilled attitude, there was no reason to beat around the bush.

"It's just that I couldn't help noticing my grandmother giving you money the other day," I began. "She lives on a very tight budget. She's not a wealthy woman, Leonard, and I don't want to see her getting hurt because you have some kind of ulterior motive."

Leonard's eyes got big. Then he started laughing so hard he choked on his cigar smoke.

"You hear that, Queenie? Ken here thinks I got an ulterior motive. Ain't that somethin'? She must think her grandma doesn't have sense enough to make her own decisions," he said, reaching down to pet the dog. Queenie immediately rolled onto her back to offer him her pink and brown spotted belly.

"I'm not playing, Leonard." I glared at him all pretenses at friendliness gone.

"Oh, neither am I, Ken. Neither am I. And the last thing I would ever do is to hurt Stella." He gave me an indignant, misunderstood look.

"Then why was she giving you money? Aren't you a little old for an allowance?"

His eyes suddenly turned as hard as marbles and the smile evaporated off of his round face. "You know what, Queenie?" he said, bending over to connect the dog's leash to her collar and sitting back up. "I think Ken here needs to stay out of grown folks business and get to wherever it is she was going, don't you?" Queenie barked her agreement.

"Excuse me? My grandmother *is* my business. I don't want to see her taken advantage of." I stood up to go but stopped when it looked like Leonard was about to say something.

"What is it that funny Martin Lawrence is always sayin', Queenie? Oh, yes," Leonard said, looking up at me. "Get…ta…steppin'."

"Gladly. But don't think I won't be watching you, Lenny, baby," I said and was happy to see him wince.

Apparently, he didn't appreciate being given a nickname of his own.

"Okay, Miss Clayton. You last saw Justin Ramey alive when he was arguing with his daughter, Pia, at approximately 8:15 pm, after which he went to his office and you didn't see him again until you discovered his body almost an hour later?" Harmon looked like she'd had no sleep. I wondered how long she'd been tied up at the Ramey Gallery last night.

"That's right, except I don't know where he went after he argued with his daughter. He left the front of the gallery. I have no idea if he went straight to his office. He could have gone to the bathroom for all I know."

Harmon peered at me over the top of the statement she was typing and gave me an annoyed expression, like I was purposefully making life hard for her. She sighed heavily and then whited out the part about Ramey going to his office after the confrontation with his daughter.

"Wouldn't it be easier to use a computer?" I asked. Harmon snorted in amusement.

"It would be easier if you'd quit adding and subtracting things from your statement. We've been at this for over an hour, Miss Clayton."

"I just want to make sure you have all the facts down right," I replied sweetly.

"Of course you do because you're always only too happy to help us out and provide us with accurate information, isn't that right? Never mind the fact that you've been nothing but obstructive in the past," she said sarcastically.

She was right. I've never been anything but a burr in Trish Harmon's behind. But that was because the cases involved either me, or people I was close to, people I loved and cared about. This time was different because I had no personal stake in Justin Ramey's murder. I hadn't liked or been close to him or his family. So, Harmon could have all the details she wanted. She'd have my full cooperation.

"I'm sorry you're having such a bad day, Detective. But you're the one who told me to come down here this morning. We could have taken care of this last night. Maybe I should talk to your partner, instead. He's always happy to see me," I said, looking around for Charles Mercer and expecting to see him rounding the nearest corner with a big box of Dunkin Donuts in one hand and a coffee in the other.

All the color left Harmon's face and she leaned back in her chair. "Mercer had a heart attack, Miss Clayton. I got the call at about three this morning from his wife."

"He isn't ..." I said as my voice trailed off.

"Dead? Oh, no. He's not dead. He had emergency bypass surgery this morning. His prognosis is good. He'll be fine. Now, let's finish up this statement. As you can imagine, this turn of events increases my workload and I have a murderer to catch," she concluded sourly.

I stared at her incredulously. Her longtime partner suffered a heart attack and all she could think of was the extra work? Underneath all of her woman-in-love glow, the real Trish Harmon was alive and well. I noticed a picture of her and Rollins smiling, and mocking me with their happiness, sitting on one corner of her desk in the same spot a picture of her late husband had resided. Clearly, she was moving on, and moving on in a hurry given the fact that she and Rollins had been dating less than two months.

"Speaking of murderers," I said, leaning forward in my seat. "Someone in a brown Chevy with tinted windows has been following me for the past two days."

"Did the person in this car harm or threaten you in any way?"

"No."

"Well, did you happen to get the plate number of this mystery car?" inquired Harmon disinterestedly.

"No."

"Then I fail to see how I can help you."

"You fail to see?" I sputtered before she cut me off.

"I know exactly what you're thinking, Miss Clayton. But there've been no new sightings of Stephanie Preston in weeks. If we thought for a minute that you were in any danger, we would have you under round the clock police protection. Stephanie Preston would be crazy to come back to Willow."

"But she *is* crazy. That's the problem. If she weren't crazy she wouldn't have killed two people and tried to turn my friend Lynette and me into human torches. And since when do crazy people act rationally?"

"Okay," she said, sighing and rubbing her temples. "If it is Stephanie Preston, then why hasn't she tried to kill you? What is she waiting for? If getting rid of you is her reason for being here, then why not be done with it and be on her way? Why risk hanging around here and getting caught?"

"I don't know. Maybe she wants to drive me insane

first."

Harmon gave me a thin, snakelike smile that told me that if that were the case, it would only be poetic justice for all the times I'd driven others—namely her—insane with my antics.

"What about your friend, Lynette? Has this brown Chevy been following her around, too?"

"Lynette's out of town," I replied.

In fact, Lynette, her husband Greg, two kids, mother, and the dog had made like the Griswolds and were on a cross-country trip to Disneyland in a rented RV. Call me crazy, but I think I'd rather be home being stalked.

"Want to know what I think?" she asked, pulling my statement out of the typewriter.

"No. But, you'll tell me anyway, right?

"I think you're hyper paranoid and imagining danger where there is none. Not that I can blame you given what you went through. However, that doesn't change the fact that you have absolutely no proof that someone is following you. Here," she said, handing me the typed statement. "Sign this and you can be on your way."

I snatched the piece of paper from her and was scrawling my name on it when her phone rang. Within seconds of answering it, her whole demeanor changed. Her voice softened and she started smiling and playing with a strand of her hair. It was Rollins. Had to be. Only a man can account for a change that drastic. She shot me a dismissive look when I tossed the signed statement onto her desk and swiveled around in her chair giving me a prime view of the back of her head. I left and tried not to cringe at the sound of her low seductive laughter.

I could hear my phone ringing as I hurried up the steps to my apartment after work. I hadn't seen the brown Chevy again but took the long way home just to be on the safe side. My landlady, Mrs. Carson, was in her usual spot on the front porch when I arrived.

"I'm glad you're home, missy. That phone of yours has been ringin' off the hook for about an hour now. Someone's sure hot to get a hold of you. Maybe it's that nice Carl callin'," she said hopefully. Mrs. Carson didn't like many people. She'd liked Carl, though. Everyone liked Carl.

"I doubt it, Mrs. Carson. He's long gone," I said firmly as I rushed up the remaining steps.

Once through the door, I grabbed my cordless off the coffee table and breathlessly answered it. It wasn't Carl. It was Mama. And she was pissed.

"Kendra Janelle Clayton if I had a switch I'd light up your behind so good you wouldn't be able to sit down for a month! What in the world did you say to Leonard?"

Crap! I'd been so preoccupied obsessing over the brown Chevy all day, I'd forgotten all about my little chat with Leonard. I couldn't believe that old blabbermouth had run back and tattled on me.

"Answer me, girl! What did you say to him that has him so upset? He said you threatened him!"

"Threatened him? I did not threaten him! All I did was let him know that I saw you giving him money and pointed out that you're on a fixed income. I don't want him taking advantage of you. I was just looking out for you," I protested.

"Kendra, my money is my business, and if I want to burn my money on a bonfire, and dance the jitterbug around it in my underpants, I can because it's *my* money! You had no right to be so disrespectful to Leonard. You weren't raised like that. He is so upset."

"I was just looking out for you!" I said again feebly.

I couldn't remember the last time Mama had been so mad at me. It felt like the time I was in the second grade and had broken her good lead crystal flower vase, the one Grandpa Mays had given her as an anniversary present, the one I wasn't supposed to touch.

"I'm a grown woman. I've looked out for myself since I was seventeen and I don't need you, the girl who can barely take care of herself, and who ran off her nice lawyer boyfriend, looking out for me. Now, get over here and apologize to Leonard this instant!"

She almost had me until she threw Carl up in my face. I hadn't told anyone but her just how devastated I was over Carl. I hadn't even told Lynette how truly upset I was, and she'd been my best friend since grade school. I'd poured my heart out to Mama alone. Hers was the shoulder I'd sobbed on. She was the one who'd told me it wasn't my fault he'd left and had encouraged me to write the letter. If she was mad over what I'd said to Leonard, fine. But to have her bring up Carl in this way, after I'd confided in her, was like having salt poured in an open wound.

"No." I said simply.

"What did you say?" I could hear the incredulity in her voice.

"I said no. I'm not apologizing to Leonard."

"You're not going to apologize?"

"Didn't I just say I wasn't?"

There was silence on the other end for what seemed like an eternity before she finally spoke again.

"Then until you can apologize and show my friend some respect, I don't want you over here, Kendra," she said in a soft, slightly trembling voice.

"What!" I was stunned. I thought she'd be mad. I thought she'd pitch a fit. Telling me that she didn't want me around wasn't in the equation. She couldn't be serious, could she?

"You're putting a man you've known for all of five minutes before me, your own granddaughter? You're picking him over me?"

"It's not a matter of choosing him over you. It's a matter of respect. Until you can show Leonard and me some respect, I don't want you around." I could tell it took a lot of effort on her part to say this but that didn't make it hurt any less.

I refused to cry. And I refused to apologize. I started to tell her that if that's the way she wanted it, then that was just fine by me. But, she'd already hung up.

Hours later, I'd fallen asleep on my couch when loud pounding on my door startled me awake. Bleary eyed, I looked at the clock on my VCR. It was almost midnight. Who in the world would be pounding on my door this late? Was it the driver of the mysterious brown Chevy? I wasn't taking any chances. I stood up, legs trembling, and crept over to the door grabbing my baseball bat along the way. I looked through the peephole in the door and the pounding started again. I jumped away from the door before I could see who it was.

"Who is it?" I said with the bat poised over my shoulder. I'd tried to sound forceful and menacing but only succeeded in sounding like I had asthma. Instead of an answer, I got more pounding.

"Go away! I'm calling the police!" The pounding got even louder.

"I've got a gun. Go away and leave me alone!"

The pounding stopped immediately. I waited a full five minutes before opening the door. I cautiously stepped out onto my landing, bat held high. There was no one there. At least I thought there was no one there. A hard tap on my left shoulder made me whirl around, swinging the bat wildly, and taking out my mailbox with a deafening clang.

"You've got to be the goofiest chick I've ever known in my life," exclaimed Joy Owens, laughing so hard she was doubled over.

"Joy? What are you doing here? Why didn't you answer me when I asked who it was?" I practically yelled, as I rubbed my sore arm irritably. The impact from hitting the mailbox had hurt like hell. I kept staring at my late night visitor like she was a ghost. I didn't realize Joy even knew where I lived.

"Sorry. I was just messin' with you. I couldn't help it. That shit was funny." She straightened up. "Go away. I have a gun," she said, mimicking me in a high-pitched girly voice. It was a good thing I didn't have a gun. I would have gladly shot her.

I hadn't seen her since Justin Ramey's murder and noticed she was back to looking like her old self again in jeans, T-shirt, and baseball cap worn backwards. She smelled of her usual perfume of cigarettes and baby powder. I saw that a couple of the neighbors were peeking out their windows to see what all the racket was and hurried back into my apartment with Joy on my heels.

"It's midnight, Joy. What do you want?"

Joy plopped down on my couch uninvited and I heard a crunch. She pulled an empty Fritos bag out from under her and held it out to me. Her nose wrinkled up when she looked at the floor around the couch and saw that it was littered with empty pop cans, candy bar wrappers, and a Hagan Daz container. Cookie crumbs were all over my coffee table. It had been a stressful evening.

"You need to seriously tighten up your housekeeping skills."

"It's midnight, Joy. What do you want?" I repeated.

"And your hospitality skills," she replied, refusing to be rushed.

"It's *after* midnight, Joy. What do you ...?"

"Okay. Okay. Chill out. Damn! You ain't exactly makin' this easy for me. I ain't used to askin' for help," she said, looking down at the floor.

"You need help? From me?" I laughed and she glared at me.

"Yeah, I need your help," she admitted grudgingly and nudged a Snicker wrapper with the toe of her black Air Jordan.

"With what?"

"I know you're good at all that investigatin' and shit. I know how you helped people out before. I need you to help me prove to the cops that my best friend ain't a murderer."

"Your best friend?" I said in confusion, not realizing Joy had any friends, then remembering how chummy she was with Justin Ramey's daughter the night of the showing. "You mean that Ramey girl?"

"Her name's Pia," Joy said indignantly. "And, yeah, I mean her. They're tryin' to pin her daddy's murder on her all because of that disagreement they had at the gallery."

She couldn't possibly be serious. In all the time I'd known Joy Owens, she'd done her best to insult and aggravate the hell out of me at every opportunity. And had succeeded every time. She was rude, crude, inconsiderate, lazy, foul-mouthed, and had the social grace of someone raised by wolves. The only thing I wanted to help Joy do was leave my apartment by way of my foot to her ass.

"What your friend Pia needs is a good lawyer. There's nothing I can do to help her." I walked over and opened the door for her.

Even if Pia Ramey was innocent—and I could truly care less one way or the other—I had problems of my own. Being dumped by Carl, having Rollins defect to the enemy camp, and being followed by a loony in a brown Chevy was bad enough. Now, my own grandmother had disowned me. I had a cosmic *kick me* sign hanging on my back. Joy sat unmoving on my couch and a sly gleam settled into her eyes.

"You might want to rethink that decision," she said smugly.

"I don't have time for this. It's late and I have work in the morning. Goodbye." I held the door open wider.

"Don't your granny kick it with a cat named Leonard Duncan?" Joy asked. I nodded slowly.

"You know Leonard?"

"He used to live across the street from my aunt. That dude's a trip," she replied with a grimace.

"What are you talking about? What do you know about him?" I could feel my stomach start to knot up, though that could have also been from all the crap I'd eaten.

"If you want to know what I know, then I'd be changing' that fucked up attitude of yours real quick. Unless, you want me to walk right out that door and take what I know with me. And you definitely need to hear what I know about that dude." She grinned like a Cheshire cat.

I slammed the door shut and rushed over to her grabbing her by the front of her T-shirt and pulling her to her feet.

"What do you know about Leonard?" I demanded, shaking her like a rag doll. She pulled free and shoved me away.

"Tit for Tat," Joy said, pissed now. "You help me out and I'll tell you all the dirt on your granny's man. Deal?"

I'd rather climb a barbed wire fence butt naked than be involved in anything to do with Joy Owens. But I had to know what she knew about Leonard. If my gut feeling about him was right, then Mama would need to be warned whether she liked it or not.

"Deal," I said, regretting it almost as soon as the word was out of my mouth.

FOUR

"Alright, Joy, I agreed to help your friend. Now, what do you know about Leonard?"

"You must think I'm stupid. You ain't gettin' nothin' from me until you help Pia first."

"What exactly is it that you think I can do for your friend?" I asked in exasperation. It was now almost twelve thirty and I'd given up hope that Joy would be leaving any time soon.

"You know. Talk to people and shit. Snoop around. Do what you do."

"Has she been arrested?" I asked.

"No," Joy replied defensively.

"Then why does she need my help?" I asked on my way into the kitchen. I got a trash bag and started picking up the wrappers from the floor.

"'Cause those detectives are tripping', that's why. Everyone who was at the gallery last night claims Pia threatened to kill her father. So, now, she's a person of interest."

"Uh, Joy. I was there last night, too. I heard what

she said like everyone else. Not only did she threaten him, she threw a pen holder at him and almost hit him!"

"Almost doesn't count and she didn't threaten him, man," Joy said, throwing up her hands in disgust. "What she said was, she hoped someone else would kill him. Not once did the words *I'm gonna kill your ass* come out of her mouth."

Thinking back on what Pia had said, I realized Joy was right. Pia had said she wished someone would cut her father's heart out, someone other than her. Technically, Pia hadn't threatened Justin. But what she did say and do was still pretty damning.

"Why was she so mad at him in the first place?"

"He pulled the funding for her art center. That center, and the kids that hang there, are her heart and soul. She had a couple of small grants from the arts council but the bulk of the funding came from her father. Without it that place doesn't have a chance."

"Why was he pulling it?"

"Some kinda family disagreement. You can ask her yourself tomorrow when I introduce you two."

"You mean today?" I pointedly looked over at the clock hoping she'd get the hint. She didn't. She leaned back against the cushions of my couch like she was settling in for a nice long visit.

"Yeah, whatever," she replied.

"What about her family? Doesn't she have a mother and a brother? Why does she need us to help her?"

"Her real mom lives in Paris. Pia only sees her every couple of years. She don't get along with her brother, Link. He's a straight up hater. He's been jealous of Pia since they were kids. Justin's second

wife, Lauren, is a first class gold digger. She and Pia
barely speak unless it's to say *fuck you*. Both of those
fools would be happy to see Pia get convicted of
murder. That way they'd have one less person to split
all Justin's loot with. Lauren's already been to a lawyer
to freeze Justin's accounts. Pia comes into a trust fund
in three years when she turns twenty-five. But that
don't help her now when she needs a good lawyer. I'm
the only one lookin' out for her," she concluded.

"Okay, she's not close to her family. I get that. But,
she still hasn't been arrested, which means there must
not been any evidence beyond that argument to charge
her with, right?"

"Not exactly," Joy said, looking down at her feet.

"Not exactly? What else have they got?"

"Pia got rid of the clothes she was wearing when
she came to the gallery last night."

I did remember Pia showing up at the scene
wearing different clothes. It only just occurred to me
how bad that looked for her. If I were the police, I'd
think she changed her clothes because they were
covered in her father's blood.

"What do you mean she got rid of them?"

"When she left the gallery she went back to the art
center. The kids left the place a mess as usual. She was
cleanin' up and spilled a whole can of black paint down
the front of her. She figured the clothes were toast, so
she pitched 'em. And she told the cops about her
clothes when she gave her statement. But, she can't
prove it cause the clothes are gone from the art center's
dumpster."

"You mean the trash already got picked up?"

"I mean someone took the clothes from the

dumpster."

"Why would someone take clothes covered in black paint?"

"How the hell should I know? Maybe some homeless motherfucker took 'em. All I know is the clothes are gone and she ain't got no way to prove she didn't kill her father. But they ain't really got any evidence to charge her, yet."

"Sounds like she just needs to prove she wasn't anywhere near the gallery during the time her father was murdered. Was there anyone there with her or anyone near the art center who saw her and could vouch for her whereabouts?"

"No, she was alone at the center," Joy said sullenly.

"No one saw her at all?"

"The art center ain't in the best of neighborhoods and the people who live 'round there didn't exactly welcome Pia with open arms. They think she's some rich bitch who'll leave when she gets bored. Plus, they're real allergic to cops. Suddenly turn deaf, dumb, and blind whenever any come 'round askin' questions. They ain't gonna vouch for Pia, even if they did see her last night."

This was sounding worse by the minute. Not that it mattered. As far as I was concerned, I just had to give the appearance of helping. I just had to go through the motions to appease Joy into giving me the info on Leonard. Despite what I'd agreed to, I had no intention of getting any more involved in this investigation than humanly possible.

"Okay, Joy," I said, stifling a yawn and getting up to hold the door open for her. "I'll meet with your friend tomorrow at Estelle's when I get off work. But I've got to get some sleep first."

Joy reluctantly got up to go and rolled her eyes as she walked past.

"There's one more thing," she said after she stepped out onto my landing, before I could close the door.

"What?" I glanced over at the clock. It was 12:42.

"That sculpture they think was used to kill Justin, Pia made it for him for father's day when she was in junior high. Took her months to sculpt it. He loved that ugly ass pineapple."

I could think of few things sadder than being murdered by a gift given in love, unless, of course, the giver was the murderer.

Pia Ramey may have nobly set up shop in the hood, and been dedicated to the underprivileged kids that came to her art center, but the look of distain she was currently giving me told me she was probably more her father's daughter than she'd ever admit to. When I'd arrived the two of them were already in a booth in the back of the restaurant. Joy was chowing down on baby back ribs, while Pia nibbled on a veggie burger and half-heartedly pushed sweet potato fries around on her plate. Joy had introduced me—around a mouthful of slaw—as the woman who could clear her name. Pia begged to differ.

"I'm sorry," Pia said, giving Joy a confused look. "Who is she and what the hell is she supposed to do for me?" She was dressed in the same expensive boho chic look, of artfully torn jeans and gauzy tunic, she'd sported at the gallery the night her father died. Her hair was hidden under a green silk head wrap. Large silver hoops hung from her ears.

"You need all the help you can get, P," replied Joy as she wiped her sticky fingers with a moist towelette. "Kendra's nosy as fuck. She's real good at turning up shit the cops miss. She's helped out other people the cops tried to jam up."

I could tell Joy meant what she'd just said as a compliment. However, the *nosy as fuck* part, though true, wasn't a compliment no matter how you put it.

"Really?" said Pia, clearly unconvinced.

"Really," I said, giving her a reassuring smile. She just stared at me in much the same way her snobby father had the night before. I started to do a slow burn.

"Yeah, right. I don't think so," she said, dismissively and busied herself by reapplying her frosted plum colored lip-gloss.

"Oh, come on, Pia. She can help," pleaded Joy.

"I'm not talking to her," Pia said flat out when I continued to sit there and stare at her. For the first time, Joy looked like she might have been wrong and maybe this hadn't been such a good idea after all. Finally, something we both agreed on.

"Okay. Well, since you don't seem to mind going to prison, I'll be on my way." I got up then added. "Hey, maybe they'll let you teach painting to the other inmates. I bet there's a lot of talent up in Marysville. Just make sure and stick to finger paint because no telling what they might do with pointy end of those paint brushes." I barely made it to the door before Joy grabbed my arm.

"Hold up. Where the hell are you goin'? We had a deal," she hissed at me. I looked back at the booth. Pia was staring straight ahead stony faced with her jaw clenched.

"I can't help someone who doesn't want to be helped. And she sure has a f'ed up attitude for someone the police consider a person of interest who can't afford a lawyer."

"It's all an act. She's just scared, damn, wouldn't you be? Come back here," Joy said, practically dragging me back to the table.

I slid back into the booth avoiding eye contact with Pia. A waitress came over and put a menu and place setting in front of me. I ordered a tuna melt, fries, and a chocolate shake. When I finally looked at Pia, she was looking more than a little contrite. I also noticed she looked completely exhausted and her eyes were drooping.

"I'm sorry," she said in a small voice. "I haven't had any sleep in two nights. It's like I'm trapped in a waking nightmare," she said wearily.

"I'm sorry, too. This must be so awful for you. Did Joy tell you I'm the one who found your father?" I asked.

"No, she didn't." She gave Joy a surprised and slightly irritated look.

"What difference does it make who found him?" Joy said defensively. "What we got to figure out is how to get you out of this mess, especially after what happened this morning."

"What happened?"

Pia and Joy looked at each other. It was Pia who finally spoke up.

"My father's bitch of a wife told the detectives working his case about another argument my father and I had last month at his house. I didn't even realize she was home. Usually, when I go visit my father she's out spending his money. I had forgotten about the argument and didn't tell the police. So, now it looks like I lied to them when I told them my father and I got along just fine and that was the first argument we'd had in years."

"What was the argument about?" I asked.

"Personal family business," Pia replied a touch frostily.

"You may as well tell her, P. It ain't like it'll be a secret much longer and she needs to know." Joy pushed her plate to the side and pulled a toothpick from her shirt pocket.

"My father has a younger sister named Janette. They had a falling out a long time ago and haven't spoken in years. A couple of months ago, she contacted him and told him she had cervical cancer. She doesn't have health insurance and needed money for treatment. He said no. Wouldn't give her a dime. I couldn't believe it."

"Wow," was all I could say but remembering how cold Justin Ramey could be, I could certainly believe it.

"I couldn't just let her die," Pia said. Her eyes filled with tears.

"You helped her and he found out and got mad?" I asked. She nodded and continued on.

"I have a trust fund that I come into when I turn twenty-five. I get a check for the interest on it every month. My father found out that I've been giving those checks to Janette for her doctor bills. He told me if I didn't stop, he'd pull his financial support for Graffiti, my art center for underprivileged kids. I couldn't just leave her high and dry. The chemo is working. She's getting better. I didn't really think he was serious. Then

I got a letter in the mail the other day from his lawyer saying he was officially pulling his support effective immediately."

"Joy told me about you getting paint on the clothes you wore to the gallery. Isn't there anyone who saw you after you left the gallery that can confirm you were at Graffiti or saw you tossing those clothes in the dumpster?"

"Are you kidding? I was so upset when I left the gallery, I could barely see straight, let alone notice if anyone saw me."

"Well, who do you think killed your father? Did he have enemies?" I asked.

"Yeah, he had two living under his roof. His gold-digging wife and his spineless son," said Joy with a humorless laugh.

"Had he argued with either of them recently," I persisted.

"My father had been trying to put Lauren on an allowance for months. She wasn't having it. Every time he'd complain about her spending, she'd start whining that shopping was all she has to do out here in the sticks and would threaten to go back to New York. He'd shut up real quick. As for my brother, it would have been in his best interest to keep my father alive. He got his trust fund when he turned twenty-five and blew it all in two years on cars, women, and bad investments. The monthly allowance my father gave him was his sole source of income. Now, he's screwed."

"Is there anybody else besides your brother and stepmother who might want to hurt your father?"

"Well," said Pia thoughtfully. "About six months ago, my father left Link in charge of the gallery when he and Lauren went to Italy. Link charged a couple of my father's regular clients double for some paintings they bought and pocketed the extra money. But once my father found out, he was able to smooth it all over by refunding the money and firing Link before his latest scam ruined the gallery's reputation."

"There were no hard feelings? No one wanting revenge?"

"No. They all got their money back and everyone was happy."

"What about your father's will?"

Pia shrugged. "As far as I know, all his money goes to Kingford College's school of Art. He always wanted a building named after him," Pia said sadly.

"Do your brother and stepmother know that?"

"He told us all enough times but I don't think Lauren believed him. I bet she probably thinks she gets it all. And I can't wait to see the look on her face when she finds out all she has is the Mercedes he gave her, and the designer clothes on her bony back." Pia and Joy both chuckled but I didn't see the humor.

My food arrived and Pia got up to go.

"Sorry, but I've got to cut this short. I have an appointment with the funeral home director. Was there anything else you needed to know?" Pia asked unenthusiastically.

I thought for a minute while I took a long sip of my milkshake. It was perfect, thick, but not too thick to suck through my straw, and just the right amount of chocolate syrup. Personally, I thought ice cream and chocolate were the foods of the Gods.

"Yeah," I said, looking up at her. "Why'd you come back to the gallery that night?"

Pia smiled and her face relaxed. "To pick up my best friend here." She reached over and gave Joy's shoulder an affectionate shove. "We were going out to celebrate her showing."

She left and Joy watched her go with a wistful expression and I wondered just how close the two friends were. She turned and noticed the look on my face.

"Don't even think about it," Joy said. "We're just friends. She's the only friend I got. So, you can't fuck this up. Got it?"

"You just make sure you hold up your end of the bargain. I'm going to ask around to see if I can find anybody who saw Pia during the time of the murder, then I want—."

"Hold up," she said, cutting me off. "What you need to do is go talk to Lauren Ramey. If anybody would want Justin's ass dead, it would be Lauren. You heard Pia, didn't you? Justin was tryin' to slow Lauren's roll by puttin' her on an allowance. I bet she killed him so she could get all his dough."

"And didn't you hear when Pia said Justin was planning to leave all his money to Kingford College? And besides, our agreement was for me to prove Pia didn't kill her father, not find out who did. Once I find a witness who saw her at Graffitti last night, I'm out of this, and you better tell me what you know about Leonard. Have *you* got that?"

"Maybe. Depends on what you find out, don't it?" she replied cryptically.

It suddenly dawned on me that Joy could string me along forever while she dangled the information about Leonard in front me like a sardine in front of a cat. The more I thought about it, the more I realized that was exactly what she planned to do. Joy was never one to play fair. I didn't even know if the information she had was any good.

"On second thought. I want to know what you know about Leonard right now, or I'm not going anywhere to talk to anyone."

"Yeah, right. You ain't done one damned thing to help Pia and you think I'm gonna just start spillin' what I know?" She started laughing like I'd told a big joke.

"I'm not a damned puppet. If you want my help, you need to tell me what you know or I'm walking right out of here and Pia can go to jail. It's your choice because I could care less. She's not my friend."

Joy sat and glared at me for a long minute, during which I proceeded to eat and drained half my shake. I wasn't backing down.

"Fine. You wanna know 'bout Leonard? Here it is."

I leaned forward in anticipation.

"Leonard and his wife, Lila, used to live across the street from my aunt right up until Lila got her ass killed."

"Killed? She didn't die from a disease?" For some strange reason, I'd always thought Leonard's wife had gotten sick and died like my grandfather had.

"Do you wanna hear this shit or not?" snapped Joy irritably. I nodded for her to continue.

"Like I was sayin'. Leonard's wife got run over in the parking lot of the office building she used to clean. Whoever hit her just left her there for dead," she said stiffly. Joy had been the victim of a hit and run last year. I could understand her bitterness.

"Everyone just thought some stranger ran her over. Then Leonard starts actin' real shady."

"How?" A chill went down my spine.

"He got rid of his caddy. That man loved that car. I was only seven or eight at the time, but I remember him washin' it practically everyday. You never saw a drop of bird shit on that car. He kept it shinin' like new money. After Lila died, it was gone. Poof. No one ever saw it again. Used the life insurance money to buy a brand new car."

"That's not so strange, Joy. He probably just traded the old car in when he got the new one." Joy sighed in exasperation and rolled her eyes heavenward.

"You ain't listenin', Clayton. I said no one saw the car again after Lila was killed. Meaning when the police came and told him his wife was dead, the car wasn't at his crib. He'd already gotten rid of it, like that night. Why would he have done that unless he used it to kill her?"

"They never asked him what happened to his car?"

"He told them he didn't have a car. Said the caddy we all thought was his was actually his uncle's car. His uncle 'sposedly gave it to him when he went into a nursing home. But his uncle's kids didn't like Leonard and sold the car before he could sign it over to Leonard."

"And that story checked out?"

"I guess if it didn't, his ass would be in jail, wouldn't it?"

There was a lump in my throat.

"Then there was all her stuff," Joy continued.

"Stuff?" I said.

"Yeah, you know, her possessions. Leonard got rid

of all her stuff the day after Lila was killed. I mean everything. Bagged all that shit up and dropped it off at the Goodwill. I heard the only thing of hers he didn't give away was the dress he had her buried in."

I just stared at her big eyed.

"Then there was the big ole' lie he told the police," she said smiling. Now that she could tell she was seriously freaking me out, Joy's mood had improved tenfold.

"Go ahead," I said. I didn't really want to hear any more but since I'd demanded she tell me, I couldn't turn back now.

"Leonard told the cops that the night Lila died, he had a cold and took some cold medicine and went to bed. He said Lila knew she'd have to take a cab home that night because he couldn't drive on account of the cold medicine making him drowsy. He didn't even know she hadn't come home until the police knocked on his door early the next morning. But, my aunt told me she swore she saw Leonard leaving the house earlier that evening and his ass sure didn't look sick to her."

"Was he driving the Cadillac?"

"Yep, and that's why his story about the caddy not being his was so suspect," Joy replied.

"Why?"

"Because according to a friend of my aunt's who knew Leonard's uncle, the caddy that Leonard claimed belonged to his uncle, the one that got sold, was sold a full week before Lila died, which meant that it couldn't have been the same car that everyone in the neighborhood thought was his. Plus, the uncle's caddy was black and Leonard's was dark midnight blue."

"Those would be easy colors for people to mix-up," I said with a sinking heart. Much as I loathed Leonard, I really wanted to be wrong about him.

"Exactly," Joy continued. "But when the cops checked the DMV records, they couldn't find any kind of vehicle registered to Leonard, not a black, blue, or pink one. They dropped it and didn't look any further."

"Is this uncle still alive?" I asked.

"Are you kiddin'? He was sick and older than dirt when all this went down. He kicked not long after Lila did."

"Well, what would Leonard's motive for killing his wife have been? Did they not get along? Was the life insurance payout huge? Was there another woman?"

"How would I know some shit like that? I was just a kid back then."

"Why not? You seem to know about everything else. Are you telling me you never noticed how they got along or if you ever saw him with other women?"

"Hold on. I'm thinkin'," Joy said, staring off into space like she was trying to recall something. "I heard my aunt and her friends talking one day about Leonard getting a lot of money when Lila died. But there couldn't have been too much life insurance 'cause the only thing he bought was a car and he lost that house they lived in a few months later and had to move."

"Anything else?" I persisted.

"Yeah, I remember Lila Duncan being a straight up bitch. If she said jump, Leonard's ass better be askin' how high, or he'd catch ten kinds of hell. She treated the dog better than him. The whole neighborhood could usually hear her yellin' at him. No wonder the man drank. Any man would have to be drunk all the time to be married to her ass."

"He's an alcoholic, too?" Could this get any worse?

"I don't know about now. First time I saw him in years is when I saw him hugged up with your granny at the grocery last week. But back in the day," she said, shaking her head and letting out a low whistle, "he got tore up regularly. Anything else you wanna know?" She asked brightly.

"No. I'm good," I replied, glaring at her.

"Glad to hear it. Now, you need to stop stuffin' your face and get a move on 'cause you owe me big time, Clayton. And if Pia gets arrested over some bullshit 'cause you fucked this up, you'll need more than that baseball bat to keep me off your ass."

She left and I watched her go wrestling with the urge to either laugh, or toss my milkshake glass at her.

"Everything, okay?" asked my waitress. "Want me to top off that milkshake?"

In my opinion, there were few things in life that ice cream and chocolate couldn't help make better, unless, of course, you're lactose intolerant. I eagerly held out my glass for another shot of ice cold comfort.

FIVE

Despite Joy's threat, instead of going to talk to Lauren Ramey, I headed over to Mama's to talk to her about Leonard. However, when I got there Leonard's white Lincoln was parked in front of her garage, and while confronting him about his shady, alcohol soaked past in front of my grandmother had its appeal, I knew it would only make things worse. I needed to talk to her alone. It would just have to wait.

After leaving Mama's, I drove past the Ramey Gallery. It was predictably still closed. There was a shrine to Justin Ramey of flowers, candles, cards, and stuffed animals piled high in front of the Gallery's door. I had no idea stuck-up Justin had been so popular. I drove on for less than half a block until I came upon the edge of the Kingford College green, not far from where I'd had my confrontation with Leonard earlier. The area was dense with trees and had a paved walking path, as well as park benches, strategically placed to take advantage of the shade, where people sat to feed the birds and squirrels.

On a whim, I parked and got out. I headed over to the nearest bench and sat down. I looked up the street towards the Ramey Gallery and saw that I had a prime view of the side of the gallery and the alley next to it. Anyone sitting here the night before could have easily gotten a glimpse of Justin Ramey's murderer leaving the gallery. I went back to my car and pulled a stack of English assignments out of my tote bag, took them back to the bench, and started to grade them in the hopes that someone would come along who may have been sitting there the night of Ramey's murder. If the person had seen someone other than Pia, both she and I were off the hook.

An hour later, after stretching out the grading of the papers for as long as humanly possible, I had gotten up to leave when a man showed up on a bike, parked it under the nearest tree, and sat down on the bench I'd just vacated. He had a paper sack full of crumbs and proceeded to start feeding the birds. With each handful of crumbs he spread, more and more birds, some of them crows that looked big enough to carry off a full-grown person, arrived and started fighting for the crumbs. I'm not usually scared of birds. But I was starting to feel like I was in a Hitchcock movie. The man noticed my discomfort and started laughing.

"Don't worry. They only want the crumbs. They won't hurt you unless you're made of bread."

He was tall, thin, and wiry with a long grey ponytail hanging down his back. He looked to be in his late fifties and was dressed in faded jeans, leather sandals, and a tie dyed T-shirt that looked like he'd had it since the sixties. After the crumbs were gone, he sat down on the bench and I sat back down next to him.

"I haven't seen you here before. You a student?" he asked.

"No. I just needed a quiet spot to grade papers and thought this spot would do. I'm Kendra Clayton," I said, holding out my hand for him to shake, which he shook hardily.

"Randy Farmer, nice to meet you. You a teacher then?"

"Yeah, at Clark Literacy Center. How about you?"

He snorted with laughter.

"I've never had a job in my life, young lady. And I'm not about to give the United States government the satisfaction of taking part of my hard earned money and anyone who does is a damned fool!" he said indignantly.

"How do you live?" I asked, fascinated. I didn't really feel like hearing about the evils of paying taxes but, hey, Joy was right. I'm nosy as fuck.

"I get by just fine. They call me Handy Randy. I do odd jobs. I'm an excellent carpenter. I cut grass for people in the summer, fix small appliances, shovel snow in the winter, recycle bottles and cans, and run errands for old folks. People are happy to pay me under the table."

"Well, what about health insurance?"

"Don't need it. Never get sick. I only eat what I can grow in my garden. I don't touch none of that processed crap and no meat or dairy. I bake my own flat bread, make my own preserves and soap, even make my own wine, which I also sell. And I haven't had so much as a cold since I was eighteen," he said, proudly.

"Wow, I'm impressed." And I was even though his diet sounded like punishment to me.

"You come here everyday?" I asked to steer the conversation towards the night of Ramey's murder.

"Most afternoons when I'm not working. You'll find me right here. Why? You got any work needs to be done?" he asked hopefully. I suddenly remembered my mailbox that I'd killed the night before and told him about it. My landlady, Mrs. Carson, hadn't noticed it yet, and I wanted it fixed before she did.

"Sure thing. Sounds like an easy fix. I could do it for five bucks." We worked out the details and he got up to go. I stood up, too.

"Hey, did you happen to be here the other night when that gallery owner got killed up the street?"

"Left when the cops showed up. Hate cops."

Great. Even if he had seen the killer, would he be willing to tell the police what he saw?

"I was actually in the gallery when he got killed. I found the body. Scared the hell out of me. I bet I just missed running into the killer by minutes. He probably ran right out the side door. You may have even seen him," I said, hoping to jog his memory.

"No," he said, shaking his head. I never saw anyone run past me that night."

"You didn't see anyone at all?"

"Just rats—"

"No," I said, interrupting him. "I mean did you see a person coming from the gallery?"

"Just some real pretty black girl crying and talking on her cell phone. She came from the direction of that gallery and looked like one of those artsy types."

"Really?" He couldn't be talking about anyone but Pia Ramey.

"Yeah. Seemed pretty upset. Stood right over

there," he said, pointing towards a spot about fifteen feet away.

"Hmm. You happen to hear what she was saying?"

"Not really. Just a bunch of *daddy* this and *daddy* that and stuff I couldn't make out 'cause she was crying so hard. Sounded personal to me. I just minded my own business and she left and went back to the gallery. Good thing, too. She was scaring the birds."

"And you're sure you saw her go back into the gallery?" I asked.

It shouldn't have surprised me that Pia had lied about going to her art center after her confrontation with her father. Everyone lies. But I was annoyed because instead of proving she was no where near the gallery during her father's murder, thus ending my association with Joy, I'd just found out Pia could possibly be a killer.

"Why are you asking so many questions? You aren't a cop are you?" Randy asked. His eyes were narrowed to slits and his body was poised for flight.

I suddenly caught a whiff of something rank and sickly sweet smelling coming from his clothes that made me realize what else he was growing in his garden that would make him so nervous about the police.

"Calm down, Randy. I'm no cop. Just a nosy English teacher. And I wouldn't ask unless it was important."

He looked at me warily before breaking into a huge grin. His teeth were yellow and crooked. He may have no use for doctors, but he really needed to rethink a visit to the dentist.

"Yeah, she went back into the gallery," he said,

relaxing. "I watched her. Couldn't help it. Like I said, she was real pretty."

Graffiti Art Center was four blocks away on Hawkins Avenue. As recently as twenty years ago, Hawkins Avenue had been a decent street. I remember because I used to come here a lot with my grandfather when I was little. Mr. Daniel's, the barber who'd cut his hair for years, had his shop on Hawkins. There was also Filbert's Drugstore where he'd pick up he and Mama's prescriptions, Press N' Go Drycleaners, Dee Dee's Pizza shop, and Stucky's Ribs N' More, the more being pig feet and chitlins.

Today, Hawkins Avenue was rundown with abandoned buildings and empty trash strewn lots. Many of the businesses that had made their home here years ago had either gone through numerous incarnations, long since gone out of business, or moved to a more lucrative location. Only Stucky's was still here and it was only open when the late Marvin Stucky's son, Jermaine, was sober enough to come in, which was only about twice a week. Jermaine hadn't inherited his father's talent for cooking and his ribs were tough as rawhide. He mostly sold hot dogs and wings now to anyone willing to venture to this part of town.

Graffiti was located in what used to be Filbert's Drugstore. Filbert's moved across town ten years ago and hadn't looked back. The big picture window that used to say Filbert's in big black and gold letters now read Graffiti in a large, puffy, stylized lettering in multicolored paint. There rest of the window was painted an opaque white so passersby couldn't see inside, which was probably a good thing given the neighborhood. A bright yellow jeep, that I assumed was Pia's, was parked out front and I parked behind it. I pulled open the door and was almost run down when two teenaged boys in football jersey's and baggy jeans sagging off their asses came barreling out.

Inside, it was brightly lit and smelled like paint. Every square inch of the walls were covered in, what else, graffiti. And much of it was elaborate and exceptional. In a far carpeted corner were low round tables where a couple of kindergarten-aged kids were finger painting. Rows of easels were set up along a back wall with draped canvases occupying half of them. The center of the room was a small platform surrounded by a circle of easels. On the platform sat a saxophone propped against its case. There were ten kids ranging in age from about twelve to sixteen sitting at the easels sketching the saxophone. Another corner was decorated in pages from comic books and had desks where some grade school boys sat drawing and laughing. All the kids were so wrapped up in what they were doing, none of them paid me the slightest bit of attention.

"Wow. That's really good. Who is she?" I asked a chunky girl of about fourteen with pimples on her forehead who was hard at work on a drawing of a female superhero dressed in a red mask, with long, flowing, black hair wearing a purple cat suit and high-heeled, knee length gold boots.

"Me," she replied shyly. "Well, not really me,' she said, looking down at her lap. "She's who I wish I was when they pick on me in school. She don't take no mess from nobody."

"You're an amazing artist and I bet none of the

kids at school can draw like you," I said truthfully.

She simply shrugged and went back to her drawing. I'd obviously said something wrong and didn't know what it was. Not surprising since I'm not the greatest when it comes to kids. There's a reason why I work with adults.

"Is Pia here?" I asked the girl and she pointed to a closed office door in the back of the room.

I could hear voices as I approached the door. It was open just a crack and I knocked and pushed it open without waiting for a reply. Pia was sitting on the edge of her desk, which was actually just a large narrow wooden table. In front of the desk sat an older, thin, sickly looking, black woman, with sparse, close cropped hair dressed in a blue warm up pants that looked too big, a white Mickey Mouse sweatshirt, and dirty tennis shoes. The woman looked very ill. This must be Pia's aunt, Janette Ramey. Pia looked completely annoyed when she saw me in the doorway. Her aunt simply looked curious, and very tired. The dark circles under her eyes made them look big and feverish.

"Sorry to interrupt. Can I speak to you privately, Pia? It's important."

"If this is about what we talked about earlier, then it'll have to wait. I'm busy. My aunt and I need to go over details of my father's funeral before Lauren and Link have a chance to ruin it."

"Aren't you going to introduce me to your friend, Pia?" asked her aunt.

"This is Kendra Clayton, Aunt J., and we actually just met today," Pia replied, making no secret of the fact she didn't want me there. For a chick that needed all the help she could get, she sure was acting funky, or maybe she just sensed I wasn't buying her innocent act.

Janette Ramey smiled at me and held out her hand. I noticed her skin felt dry and papery when I shook it.

"Nice meeting you, ma'am. I'm sorry for your loss."

"Thank you, sweetie," Janette replied. "Now, don't let me keep you two. You go right ahead and talk. I'll just step outside," she said, struggling to get out of her chair.

"You don't have to leave, Aunt J. You're family. I'm sure whatever Kendra has to talk to me about, she can do it in front of you, right, Kendra?" Pia asked like she was tossing down a challenge.

"Sure, Pia, if that's what you want. I just needed to know why you lied to me about coming straight here after your argument with your father when you actually went to the park down the street and then went back to the gallery. And, if I could find something like that out, then the police can, too. Do you even realize how bad this makes you look?"

"How it makes me look? Are you for real? I don't care who you are or what Joy thinks. I didn't ask for your help in the first damned place, and I certainly don't owe someone I've known for all of two hours any explanations about anything. Now, get the hell out of here and leave me alone!"

"Pia!" said her aunt in a voice that was louder and stronger than I'd have thought a woman so frail looking could manage. "Don't be so rude and ungrateful. If this young lady is trying to help you, than you need to let her."

Pia shot me an embarrassed look and wiped a stray

tear from the corner of her eye.

"Fine," she said, walking around the table to sit down behind it. "When I left the gallery I just took off walking to try and calm down and ended up down the street in that park.

"Who were you talking to on your cell phone while you were in the park?" I asked and was pleased by the stunned expression on her face.

"That would have been me, Miss Clayton," Janette said. "I talked to Pia right after that ugly scene with her father. I was the one who told her to go back to try and reason with him. My brother and I had been on the outs for years. I knew how difficult he could be. But, he was the only father Pia had. I didn't want them to fall out, especially over me."

"So, you went back to the gallery and then what?" I turned to Pia.

"Then nothing. I went in through the side door and he was in his office on the phone arguing with someone. I waited for a few minutes and when it didn't look like he was about to get off the phone, I left and came straight here. The rest you know already."

"Could you tell who he was arguing with?"

"No."

"Did your clothes ever turn up?"

"No," Pia quickly replied. The sidelong glance she gave her aunt indicated Janette Ramey didn't know about Pia's paint stained clothes disappearing from the center's dumpster.

"What about your clothes?" Janette asked, looking from her niece to me in obvious confusion.

Pia filled her in and Janette let out a deep sigh and shook her head.

"Now, who would do some mess like that? Pia, didn't I tell you that you needed to watch yourself down here? Some of these kids will take anything that's not nailed down. You can hardly keep toilet paper and air freshener in the bathroom 'cause someone keeps taking it. Now they're taking trash, too? It's a damned shame."

"It could have been anybody, Aunt J. The dumpster is out back. There're a lot of homeless people around here. And besides, most of these kids don't know any better."

Janette snorted in disgust. "I've been poor all my life and I've never taken anything that didn't belong to me!"

She had barely finished her sentence before she was racked with coughs that shook her thin frame. Pia jumped to her feet to get her aunt some water from the dispenser in the corner and rubbed the older woman's back as she downed it.

"She had her chemo this morning. I need to get her back home so she can rest. Can we talk later, Kendra?" asked Pia, who was looking much more contrite and cooperative now that she had someone else's welfare to worry about.

"Yeah, sure, I'll be in touch. I hope you feel better, Ms. Ramey."

The older woman nodded at me over her paper cup as I walked out wondering why in the world Justin Ramey wasn't willing to pay for his sister's cancer treatment.

I was back at Estelle's a few hours later for my shift at the hostess station. Much to my delight, I hadn't seen the brown Chevy all day long. Maybe Harmon was right. Maybe I was overreacting. I called Willow Memorial Hospital and found out that Harmon's partner, Charles Mercer, was still in the hospital, and doing well, which was great. Only it meant that Trish Harmon, afflicted as she was with tunnel vision, would be focusing solely on Justin Ramey's murder. If the brown Chevy made another appearance, I was on my own. I bought a new can of pepper spray, with a childproof safety cap, to be on the safe side.

It was a slow evening at the restaurant and I spent much of it rolling silverware and napkins together, and dodging dirty looks from Gwen. My falling out with Mama had gotten back to her and Alex and she was making her disapproval of my behavior known with every rolled eye and heavy sigh she tossed my way. Alex wasn't thrilled with me, either, I could tell because, although he was speaking to me, it was only when I spoke to him and he wouldn't look at me. But I knew Gwen couldn't keep her mouth shut for too long and I was right. Finally, after two hours of the silent treatment, she sat down at the booth I was working at and starting helping me roll silverware.

"You know you're wrong, Kendra," she said, not looking up from the pile of napkins and utensils in front of her.

"Are you asking me, or telling me?"

"Why'd you have to get all up in Leonard's face like that, girl? Do you have any idea how upset Mama is?"

"Look, Gwen," I said, tossing down a napkin on the table. "First of all, I wasn't all up in Leonard's face. And if he said I was, he's lying. Secondly, this is between Mama, Leonard, and me. Thirdly, I'm sorry

Mama's upset. I'm upset too. And I'm tired of everyone treating me like I'm a child when I'm just concerned about the person my grandmother is spending so much time with. You don't know what I know about him, and if you did, you wouldn't be sitting there looking all high and mighty. You'd be worried, too."

Gwen looked taken aback, though I couldn't tell if was because of what I'd just said about Leonard, or because I'd basically told her to mind her own business. Either way, she kept right on rolling silverware in silence for a full ten minutes before she finally spoke again.

"I don't know what you know about Leonard, Kendra. And I'm not sure I even wanna know. But, if there's something not right about that man, it'll break her heart."

"I already know that, Gwen. I'm not trying to hurt her. But, I heard some stuff about Leonard that's really freaked me out."

"Then you need to be finding out if what you heard is true and not just some gossip before you go telling Mama tales about her man. And if you're so worried, how are you going to keep an eye on him when you and Mama are on the outs and you're not welcome in her home?"

Gwen had a point. Joy wasn't the most reliable source of information. I still remembered the wild goose chase she sent me on last spring when my best friend Lynette went missing days before her wedding. I needed to find out if what she'd told me about Leonard was true before I talked to Mama. Which meant as much as I didn't want to, I was going to have to bite the bullet and apologize to Leonard. It was the only way I could get close to him.

Gwen sat with me for a little while longer, though we didn't have much more to say. When Joy arrived half an hour later, she got up and left. She and Joy loathed each other, but then again, most people loathed Joy. Joy didn't pay Gwen's retreating form much attention as she made a beeline straight for me.

"Why'd you show up at Graffiti talkin' all reckless this afternoon? You didn't have no business callin' Pia a liar," she said, leaning down in my face so close I could smell the grape flavored Bubblicious bubble gum on her breath.

"Because she *is* a liar, Joy. She told me she went straight to Graffiti after the scene with her father, when she really —"

"I know all about that shit, Clayton. She already told me. That still don't make her a liar."

"Uh, hello," I whispered so Gwen and Alex couldn't hear us. "Yes it does and I'm sure the Willow Police department would agree." I stood up and tried to get her to walk over to the door with me for more privacy. She wouldn't budge.

"You supposed to be helping to prove what she didn't do, not where she went after she put her pops on blast. You trippin' Clayton," Joy said, pushing up on me and jabbing a finger in my face.

I couldn't understand why she was so upset. She had me backed up against the booth. Maybe it was because I was still feeling confident over standing up to Gwen, or maybe I was just sick of Joy's shit, but I shoved her out of my face so hard she fell and went sliding across the polished tile floor ending up under a nearby table. I bent down and shoved her back to the floor before she could get up.

"I'm not trippin, Joy. I'm finished with you and your friend Pia. Good luck proving her innocence."

"You owe me, Clayton! I warned you about Leonard."

"You don't want what I really owe you, Joy, and you didn't tell me about Leonard out of the kindness of your heart, you wanted something." I backed away from her afraid that if I turned around, she'd jump on my back.

She just sat there on the floor and I went back to rolling silverware. I finally looked over again to see her still sitting on the floor staring at me with big tear filled eyes. Was she crying?

"Are you okay?" I was unable to believe what I was seeing. I didn't think Joy's eyes had the ability to make tears.

"I really need you to help me, Clayton," she said in a husky voice and wiped her eyes with the back of her hand. "You know my mom's dead and I ain't real close to my aunt and my cousins. They only love me 'cause they have to. They don't really wanna know me. I've never been able to introduce any of my girlfriend's to them. From day one, when I first met her in junior high, Pia's always been cool with who I am. I've never been gay Joy to her, or weird Joy, or angry Joy. I'm just Joy, period. I gotta help her, man. She's the only one I go,t and she didn't kill her father."

Now, I felt like I'd just kicked a puppy—a mean puppy—but still.

"Okay, get up off the floor. I'll help you."

She came over and sat at my booth looking embarrassed to death and I quickly spoke up to fill the uncomfortable silence.

"Pia better not lie again, Joy. I can't help someone who won't tell the truth."

She simple nodded and didn't speak. She looked like a little kid in time out. Just then a man in a brown suit walked in triggering the bell over the door. I got up to greet him grabbing a menu from the holder on the wall.

"Hello, Sir. Will you be dining alone?"

"Are you Joy Owens?" he asked in a brusque no nonsense voice.

"No. She's over there," I said, pointing to the booth where Joy still sat.

He walked over to the booth and Joy stood up.

"Joy Owens?"

"Who wants to know?" she asked, looking the man up and down.

"Are you Joy Owens?"

"Yeah. Who the hell are you?"

"You've been served," he said, handing her a dark manila envelope and rushing past me out the door.

"What the fuck?" Joy looked at the envelope then tore it open. She pulled out a sheet of paper and read it, then burst out laughing.

I walked over and she handed the paper to me. It was a restraining order against Joy warning her not to come within five hundred feet of Link Ramey.

"I shoulda known his punk ass would do something like this," Joy said. She was still laughing.

"What did you do?" When it came to Joy, nothing would surprise me at this point.

"When I found out you went to the park and Graffiti, instead of goin' to talk to Lauren Ramey like I told you to, I decided to go talk to her myself. I went out to the house and she wasn't home. But Link was and I jumped all over his ass about bein' a shitty big brother to Pia and how he should be stickin' up for his little sister like a big brother should."

"And how'd that go?" Like I needed to ask.

"He started talkin' grimy about Pia. Sayin' she's always been a spoiled little bitch and now daddy wasn't around to save her, and she had to live in the real world with the rest of us. That's when I lost it and punched him dead in his grill. Knocked him right on his ass. You shoulda seen it," she said, cracking up with laughter.

"Oh, that's just great. That really helps me out a lot."

I went back to sit in the booth. I'd always known Joy had the people skills of a troll that lived under a bridge. Yet, I'd held out some dim hope that she'd be able to help me find some info to help her friend thus lightening my load. No such luck.

"What? He had it comin'."

"Just forget it. Promise me you'll stay away from the Rameys."

"Only if you promise you'll go talk to 'em."

"I have no choice now since I can't prove Pia wasn't near the gallery around the time her father died."

"What do you want me to do?" she asked eagerly, a little too eagerly.

That was a good question. What could Joy do without ending up in jail herself? It was a miracle Link Ramey hadn't filed assault charges against her. I wondered why he didn't?

"When I figure that out, I'll let you know," I told her.

"Make sure you do," she said, clearly back to her usual charming self again.

Later, after work, I was settling in front of my TV with my jammies on and another tin of chocolate chip cookies, when I heard the sound of a car idling outside. I went over to the window and saw the brown Chevy pull into a parking space across the street from my duplex and cut off its engine. That was it. I couldn't take this one minute longer. I flung open the door and the Chevy immediately roared back to life. I grabbed my car keys from my purse and ran out the door barefoot as the car took off.

I jumped into my own car and could see the Chevy at the corner as I started my car and headed off after it. When I got to the corner, I could see the Chevy in the distance about two blocks ahead of me stopped at a stop sign. Before I could reach it, the Chevy sped off. I stepped on the gas and my sweaty foot almost slipped off the pedal. I gripped the steering wheel tighter as my car accelerated to 60 miles per hour. When I was half a block away from the Chevy, the driver floored it, then sped through a red light and rounded the next corner on a hairpin. The light was turning green as I sailed through. I turned the corner the Chevy took, and had to slam on my breaks when a dog suddenly darted out in front of me. I was thrown forward in my seat almost cracking my head on the steering wheel. Thankfully I missed the dog. It trotted down the sidewalk oblivious to the fact that it had missed becoming road kill by mere inches. I sat back and watched the Chevy's taillights disappear into the distance and slapped the steering wheel in frustration, accidentally hitting the horn and scaring myself half to death.

When I got home I called Joy and was happy to discover I'd woken her up.

"It almost midnight, Clayton, what the hell do you want?"

"I've figured out what you can do," I told her. "Be at my place at 7:30 tomorrow morning and don't be late."

I hung up before she could say a word.

SIX

Joy was late the next morning just like I knew she would be. Knowing this I'd purposefully told her to arrive a half an hour earlier than I need her to. She was just pulling up in front of my apartment in her electric blue pick-up truck as I was walking out the door to go to work. And if I thought her attitude was foul during the day, it was nothing compared to first thing in the morning. She got out of the truck looking ready to kill someone.

"I ain't been up this early since I was in high school. This better be good."

"What about college, Joy? Are you trying to tell me you never had to take a morning class?"

"Just cause I registered don't mean I went," she said, sighing and rolling her eyes like I was stupid.

"Whatever. Look, Joy, I need you to start following me."

"Say what?"

"You heard me. I need you to follow me. I need

91

you to go everywhere I go and if you see any cars following me, I need you to get the license number."

"How's this help Pia?"

"It doesn't help Pia. It helps *me* so I can help Pia. There's been a strange brown car following me for the past few days and it's got me pretty freaked. I can't concentrate on helping your friend if I'm stressed out and constantly looking over my shoulder."

"Call the cops."

"I did. They need proof I'm being followed."

She sighed and leaned back against the hood of her truck.

"And nobody else who can do this?"

"Oh, trust me, Joy. If there was someone else I could ask, you'd still be in bed right now dreaming about Halle Berry."

"Make that Angelina Jolie. And how long I gotta do this?"

"Just for a couple of days. You may even be able to get the plate number today."

"Is this about that burnt up bitch that tried to kill you? That who you think is followin' you?"

"That'd be her."

"All right, I'll do it. And it better only be for a couple a days," she said. "But if your ass gets jumped, you're own your own. Me bein' a body guard ain't part of the deal."

"Like it ever could be," I muttered under my breath.

"Oh, and I'll need some coffee and a box of donuts every morning. Fresh brewed coffee, too, none of that instant shit. And I only eat Crispy Cremes, glazed. Got it?"

"Anything else?" I asked. I impatiently looked at my watch.

"Yeah, pretend you don't know me. I don't want people gettin' the wrong idea if they see me with you. I got a rep to uphold."

"Not a problem," I told her. I got into my car wondering what I'd just gotten myself into.

My morning went by quickly. Periodically, I'd look out the window to see if Joy was still parked in the lot. She was, which would have been fine if she hadn't also been sleeping half the time. But, there was no sign of the brown Chevy. At least there wasn't until I walked out of the literacy center at 11:30 to go to lunch. I spotted it parked in the back row of the parking lot. I looked over at Joy and saw her sitting in the bed of her truck laughing and talking on her cell phone. She didn't even see the car. I waved my arms to try and get her attention. She didn't see me. I was about to throw a rock at her when Margery Warfield, one of our volunteers, stopped me. She was carrying a big cardboard box and had a large tote bag hanging off of one arm.

"I'm sorry to bother you, Kendra. Could you help me carry this stuff to my car?"

Margery was one of our new volunteers. She was a retired teacher in her late fifties and lived with her mother. She volunteered at the center twice a week tutoring students. She was a really nice lady but a bit old fashioned sort of like the second coming of June Cleaver. She was also the one who brought in the tins of heavenly homemade chocolate chip cookies every week that I'd been gorging on almost nightly since Carl left. The cookies were so good, local restaurants, including Estelle's, bought them to sell.

"Here, let me help you," I said, taking the box from her arms and following her to her van.

"Just set it on the front seat," she told me pressing a button on her black key chain and unlocking the van. I sat the box on the seat and noticed a wheel chair in the back. I figured the chair must belong to her mother who was handicapped.

I glanced through the side window of the van and saw the Chevy pulling out of the parking lot while Joy was still obliviously yacking on her phone.

"Thank you, dear. Here you go," Margery said, handing me another tin of cookies from a box full of tins on her backseat. I gratefully accepted it feeling like a sugar addict getting a fix of cookie crack.

"You're spoiling me, Margery. I'm going to weigh a ton if I keep eating these." Margery cocked her head to the side and her shoulder length, blonde pageboy shone in the sunlight.

"Oh, don't say that, Kendra," she said in her husky voice as she pulled a pair of large, white framed sunglasses from her purse.

Margery was a big woman, tall, but not fat, and always looked immaculate in perfectly pressed skirts and silk blouses. It was like wrinkles were allergic to her clothes.

"Cookies are comfort food," she continued. "And there's nothing wrong with having a little comfort in your life, is there?"

Well, when she put it like that, I had no reason to feel bad.

Once Margery left, I headed over to Joy's truck and stared at her until she reluctantly ended her call.

"What?" she said.

"You didn't see that brown car parked in the back of the lot?"

She looked at me like I was crazy.

"That's the car that's been following me, Joy! It was parked in the back of the lot and you just let it drive off without getting the license number!"

"I didn't see no brown car and plus you said to watch out for any cars followin' your ass, which is what I did. You didn't say nothin' about cars that were parked."

"You really didn't see that car?"

"I wasn't payin' no attention and you need to be more specific. I ain't a mind reader."

"Well, now you know. It's a brown Chevy. So next time pay attention."

"What's that," she asked, pointing to the cookie tin in my hand. I offered her a cookie.

"I'll pass. And you need to step away from that tin your damn self, Clayton, before someone sticks one of those wide load signs on your ass."

After sending Joy home and telling her to come back when I got off, I sat in my car eating cookies and thinking about all the places I could hide her runty little body.

When Joy came back later that afternoon, she was in a fouler mood than usual. Pia had been brought in to the police station again for questioning and needed Joy to go check on her aunt Janette, who wasn't answering her phone. I decided to follow her to make sure everything was okay.

Janette Ramey lived in the Jefferson Park housing

project on the north side of Willow. I don't know why this surprised me but it did. Jefferson Park was an apartment complex of roughly a dozen nondescript brick buildings laid out around a central courtyard with cracked sidewalks, a rundown playground with broken swings, a rusted out jungle gym, and a basketball court where drug deals went down regularly. When we arrived there were several shirtless boys playing basketball, while a variety of teenaged girls, some of them with babies perched on their hips, sat watching and gossiping.

When we knocked on the door of Janette's third floor unit, I could hear the faint strains of gospel music coming from inside. We had to knock again before she finally answered the door dressed in a frayed, white terrycloth housedress and looking a little tired but otherwise okay.

"Oh come in, come in ladies. I was soaking in the tub. I didn't even hear you knocking 'til I was on my way to the kitchen," she said, ushering us inside the dimly lit apartment and looking genuinely pleased to have visitors. The enthusiasm was dampened when she heard why we had come.

"Why are they doing this to her? She adored Justin. She couldn't have done that to him."

In a show of tenderness I didn't know she was capable of, Joy helped Janette to nearby chair.

"It's okay, Ms. Ramey. We're not gonna let them arrest Pia. We're on it. Aren't we Kendra?" Joy asked with narrowed eyes that dared me to disagree.

"Of course," I replied. "We'll do all we can."

"It makes me feel so much better to know you girls have her back. I don't know what's wrong with that brother of hers. Pia and Link are going to end up just like Justin and me. My brother's dead now and I never got a chance to make up with him." She shook her head sadly. Joy rubbed her back.

Now that she knew Janette was okay, Joy left and went to the police station to wait on Pia. At Janette's urging, I stayed behind. I could tell she wasn't just worried about her niece. She was lonely, too. And to be honest, I was feeling a little lonely myself these days. She insisted on fixing me some iced tea and I looked around while I waited.

Janette's apartment was immaculate but shabby. The flowered sofa I sat on was faded and threadbare with bright silk pillows strategically covering the barest parts. The legs of the oval coffee table in front of it were nicked and there were a couple of cigarette burns decorating the top. But, it was polished to perfection, as were the end tables on either side of the couch, which held cheap brass lamps. A blue rug covered the center of the dingy living room carpet and brightened up the room. Her TV sat against a far wall and looked at least twenty years old with rabbit ears sticking out of the top. There were family pictures decorating the top and I got up to look at them.

The most recent picture looked like it had been taken more than a decade ago and showed a younger and heavier Janette dressed to the nines at what looked like a nightclub or a party. She was sitting at a table with a group of other well-dressed people I didn't recognize and was holding a drink in her hand. Another picture showed and boy of about five and girl who barely looked a year old sitting on Santa's lap. The boy was grinning. The girl was crying. It was Justin and

Janette as kids. There were other pictures circa the sixties of Janette with an older woman who she resembled that must have been her mother, and even more party pictures. But, there were no other pictures of Janette and Justin together. Janette saw me looking at the pictures when she came back into the room.

"Those were taken back in my glory days when I still had a shape. I know it's hard to believe since this chemo's got me so darned skinny. But, girl, I used to be stacked back in the day. All the brothers were after me." She laughed as she handed me a tall plastic tumbler of iced tea with a large wedge of lemon.

"I was noticing that Pia looks a lot like you," I said and could tell the comment pleased her. I could also tell from the pictures that Janette had been a party girl but I didn't comment on that.

"Pia's mama wouldn't want to hear that but it's true. That girl looks just like me."

I wouldn't go quite *that* far but there was certainly a family resemblance. I sipped my tea and sat down next to her on the couch.

"Can I ask you a question, Ms. Ramey?" I ventured and hoped she wouldn't think I was being too nosy.

"Sure, sweetie. What's on your mind?"

"What happened with you and your brother Justin? Why weren't you close?"

She settled back into the cushions of the couch and I could tell she was remembering better days.

"You know Justin and I used to be like this when we were growing up," she said, crossing her index and middle fingers. "But Justin was always different. Always wanted more from life than all the other folks 'round here. He could draw and paint the prettiest pictures and our mother was so proud. Would always put his pictures on the refrigerator to show 'em off. Then he got an art scholarship to Kingford. That's when he changed." She shook her head.

"What happened?"

"He went to Kingford and lived on campus. Everything was fine the first year. Then he stopped coming home on weekends and started going home for the holidays with those rich kids he met at school. Never brought any of them around for us to meet like he was ashamed of us. After he graduated, he got a job as a buyer for some fancy art gallery in New York City. We didn't see him for five whole years. He didn't call or write. When he finally did come home to visit he'd gotten married and brought his new wife Ingrid home for us to meet. He was just showing off so we could see how successful he'd gotten. He'd changed so much we didn't know him anymore."

"In what way," I prodded.

"He was arrogant and uppity and acted like he was doing us a big favor by coming home for a visit. Our mother was so happy to see him and he barely stayed a day. About ten years later, he moved back here and bought that gallery of his and that big fancy house out in the country. By then our mother was real sick. She had cancer, too. Died not long after Justin moved back home. He didn't even bother coming to the funeral. I went out to that fancy house of his and he was having a party. I couldn't believe it. I told all his rich friends he skipped his own mother's funeral."

"Wow, what'd he do?"

"He threw me out and we didn't speak for a few years until he had kids and needed a cheap babysitter and sweet talked me into doing it. I used to watch Link and Pia while Justin and Ingrid were at all their fancy parties. Ingrid and I never got along. She was an evil uppity heifer. We got into an argument and she fired me when she found out I was letting the kids watch Soul Train. Said it was lowbrow. Justin didn't stick up for me, either. He knew how much I need the money. That was the last straw. I walked out and never spoke to my brother again until a couple a months ago when I got sick and needed some money. I had hoped the years had changed him but he was still just as snotty. Had plenty of money and carried on like I asked him for a kidney."

"And Pia came to the rescue?"

"Yes, she did," Janette said proudly. "That's the only good thing that's come of all this. I finally have a niece."

"Are you close to Link, too?" I asked and Janette snorted in amusement.

"You kidding me? That boy is a chip off the old block and just as arrogant as Justin. But at least Justin had some talent to be arrogant about. Link is twenty-seven and still don't know what he wants to be when he grows up."

"I heard he used work with Justin at the galley until he got fired."

"Link is a shady little so and so. Do you know what he was doing?"

"Something about scamming clients?"

"Yeah, but not just clients. Pia told me he was scamming artists, too. Charging them bogus display fees to show their work at the gallery and then pocketing the money. He even burned one of Pia's friends. Pia told Justin and he didn't even blink an eye, which made Pia suspicious that he may have been in on it, too. Justin only fired Link and refunded the money after Pia's friend threatened to raise a stink."

"Really?" I said and stared at the ice melting in the bottom of my tumbler.

Was Joy the friend of Pia's who Link scammed? And if so, is that the reason why he didn't press assault charges against her. Was he afraid she'd file fraud charges against him in return? It also meant I'd just added another person to my suspect list because if Justin had indeed been in on Link's scam, then Joy could have had a motive for murdering him herself. I wondered if he'd tried to screw her over somehow the night of the showing. I tried to think if Joy had been absent at all during the showing but I couldn't remember. Neither Pia nor Joy had mentioned this to me when I'd had lunch with them.

"You want some more iced tea?" Janette asked and started to get up again to take my empty glass.

"No, I'm fine. Is there anything I can get you?"

"Yeah, sweetie, my glasses are on the kitchen counter can you get 'em for me? It's almost time for Wheel of Fortune."

I went into the kitchen and put my tumbler in the sink. I spotted the glasses on the counter next to the refrigerator and grabbed them when something attached to the refrigerator door with a Minnie Mouse magnet caught my eye. It was a copy of the Serenity Prayer, the one popular with members of AA. Given the party pictures sitting on the TV, I wondered if Janette was a recovering alcoholic.

What else had Joy and Pia not told me? I called Joy a

few times but she never answered. I figured she was still waiting for Pia, and since I was in no big hurry to run into Trish Harmon, I didn't bother going to the Willow Police Station to look for her. Instead, I went past the Ramey Gallery and was surprised to see that it was open. I parked and went inside, noticing that the shrine to Justin that had been piled in front of the door was now gone, with only a few drops of candle wax on the concrete to show that it had even been there.

Lauren Ramey was sitting on a high stool behind the counter with piles of receipts stacked in front of her. She was wearing a white, haltered, jumpsuit with wide, billowy, palazzo pants and a black belt cinched tightly around her middle. The white set off her deep dark tan. Her short, black hair was spiky with gel that made it shine like patent leather. She looked like a model. What she didn't look like was a grieving widow and she didn't even bother looking up when I walked in.

"Excuse me. Are you open?" I asked. Her head snapped up and she gave me a blank look, which had probably served her well in her modeling days.

"That's what the sign says," she replied and bent back over the receipts.

"Oh, yeah. I saw the sign. I was just surprised to see you open again so soon after the owner's death."

"Well, I'm the owner's widow and the bills aren't going to pay themselves just because my husband died," she said, getting down off the stool and coming out from behind the counter. She was wearing three inch, spike heeled sandals and that put her height at close to six feet tall.

"I'm sorry, Mrs. Ramey. I'm Kendra Clayton. I was the one who found your husband's body. I just wanted to express my condolences. I'm so sorry for your loss."

"You were a friend of my husband's?" She fixed me with a suspicious, appraising look. Either Lauren Ramey was a very insecure woman, or Justin had been stepping out on her.

"No," I said quickly lest she nail me in the forehead with one of her spiked heels. "Actually, I was working here that night. My uncle's restaurant was catering Joy Owens's art show."

"Oh, that," she said dismissively with a wave of her manicured hand. "I don't know what Justin saw in that girl's work. It looked like someone on a bad acid trip painted that crap. And that one with the crawling babies in the desert really creeps me out."

She'd probably be surprised to know that that was the exact effect Joy had been going for.

"Yeah, Joy's work is...different." It was the kindest thing I could say.

"Is there anything else I can help you with?" she asked in a voice that said she'd rather do anything but.

"Oh, no. I just stopped by to offer my condolences. Sorry to bother you." I started to leave and stopped. "Could I use your restroom?"

She pointed a long, red-tipped fingernail in the direction of the back hallway without even looking at me. Justin Ramey had sure found his soul mate in this chick, I though as I headed back down the same narrow hallway I'd staggered down blood-soaked and in shock only a few short days ago.

I wanted to check out something in Ramey's office and hoped they'd cleaned it. Since all the traces of my bloody hand and fingerprints had been washed from the hallway walls, I was hopeful. I stood at the bathroom door and looked down the hall towards the front counter. Lauren Ramey was busy with a deliveryman who'd just arrived. I quickly headed around the corner to Justin's office. Remembering the last time I'd been in this office, I hesitated a few seconds before opening the door.

Once inside, I flipped on the lights and slowly turned to look at the desk. It was empty, of course, and not just of a dead body. Everything that had previously sat on top of the desk was now gone. There was fingerprint powder all over the desk and chair and dark stains on the carpet next to the desk as well as underneath it. I could smell disinfectant and noticed that the walls and ceiling had been washed down as well. I took a deep breath, pulled the office door shut behind me, and headed towards the desk.

The cord from Justin's desk phone had been removed from the wall jack. The phone itself was sitting with the cord wrapped it around on his desk chair. I unraveled the cord and plugged it back into the jack. Then pressed the receiver to my ear to see if I had a dial tone. When I spotted dried blood on the underside of the phone that the cleaners had missed, my stomach heaved. I took a couple of calming breaths before pressing the redial button. Pia had claimed her father was arguing with someone on the phone when she'd come back to the gallery to talk to him. I wanted to know who it was and was hoping it was the last number he'd dialed. The phone started ringing.

"Kingford Inn. This is Lois, may I help you?" asked the pleasant voice on the other end of the line. I hung up, disconnected the phone again, and quickly left the office.

When I got back out to the front of the gallery, Lauren Ramey was using a large pair of scissors to try and cut thick purple twine from what looked like a large painting that had just been delivered. She was having trouble, which was no big surprised since her arms looked like tanned twigs and she couldn't have had much upper body strength. I, on the other hand. . .

"Need some help?" I offered.

"Knock yourself out," she said, handing me the scissors.

The twine was thick and I had to apply a little force. But I was able to cut the two pieces of twine that bound the painting. I noticed that the painting was addressed to Lauren Ramey and not the Ramey Gallery. I'd barely cut through the last piece of twine before Lauren started ripping off the brown paper covering it. When it was free of its bindings, Lauren propped it against the cash register to get a good look at it.

The painting was of a sunset at dusk and was done in vivid yellows, oranges, and browns. It was a nice painting but nothing spectacular. It looked like a picture someone in high school art class could have painted. It was in a black lacquer frame with a silver plate on the bottom center that read: Destiny. The painting was unsigned. I looked over at Lauren and was shocked to see all the color had drained from beneath her tan. She was staring at the painting like she was afraid it was going to bite her.

"Are you okay, Mrs. Ramey?"

My voice snapped her out of her trance and she immediately knocked the painting over so it was lying face down on the counter.

"I need to close up. You have to leave," she said and went over to the door and held it open for me.

Once I was out the door she locked it behind me and flipped the closed sign over. What the hell was that about? Why had an innocent painting of a sunset freaked her out so much? I headed back to my car and spotted the dumpster in the alley running next to the gallery. A though occurred to me and I headed over to the dumpster and stood on my tiptoes to look inside. All of the candles, cards, and flowers that had made up the shrine to Justin in front of the gallery door had been pitched into the dumpster, no doubt by Lauren.

Most of the stuff was strewn on top of the fragrant trash bags already filling the dumpster. One card in particular caught my eye only because it was crunched up like someone had balled it up before tossing it in the bin. I stepped up onto the side of the dumpster and leaned over the edge to try and grab it. I was teetering on my stomach with my legs flailing in the air behind me when I heard Lauren Ramey's voice.

Lauren was coming out of the gallery's side door and talking on her cell phone. If she turned her head she'd see me. However, when I tried to get down, I found my belt buckle was caught on the edge. I quickly rocked back and forth like a see saw to try and extricate myself to no avail. Lauren was now locking the side door and was about to turn when my belt buckle suddenly came loose causing me to do a forward flip right into the dumpster. The impact of my landing made the lid slam shut with a deafening clang.

"I think those damned rats are in the dumpster again. Can you swing by here when you get a chance and take care of it?" I heard Lauren say to the person she was talking to on the phone.

She also gave the dumpster a good kick, which made the smelly bags vibrate and the aroma emanating from them to intensify. I wasn't so much worried about the eye watering smell, as I was the possibility of rats. As I've mentioned in the past, Kendra don't do rats. I quickly scrambled to my feet, pushed the lid open and looked out just in time to see Lauren Ramey's Mercedes pull away from the curb. I spotted the crumpled card, grabbed it, and hoisted one leg over the side of the dumpster and was sitting on the edge about to jump down, when a hunter green Range Rover pulled into the spot Lauren had just vacated and Link Ramey got out, also talking on his cell. Crap!

I leaned backwards allowing myself to fall back into the dumpster. But the lid was still open. I could hear Link's voice approaching and was afraid he'd see me if I tried to reach for the lid. I burrowed further down amongst the foul smelling bags to hide and tried my best not to gag.

"Didn't I tell you I didn't know she was here?" I heard Link say. It sounded like he was standing right next to the dumpster. I didn't move a muscle.

Who was he talking about?

"No, I haven't seen her. Why would I? She didn't bother telling me she was coming," Link continued.

Suddenly everything went black as Link closed the dumpster lid. I heard the unmistakable sound of a lock clicking. Link had locked the dumpster lid shut.

"Alright, it's taken care of, Lauren. But I don't think locking the damned thing is going to keep the rats out. They'll always find a way in."

I remained silent as I heard his voice trail off into

the distance. Then once I figured he was gone, I frantically tried to push the lid open. No such luck. I was trapped in a hot, dark, stinking hellhole. I lay on my back on top of the bags and used my legs to try and kick the lid open. No such luck. If anyone passing by saw the dumpster violently shaking, they'd probably think it was a monster rat trying to get out and would run in the opposite direction. After a few minutes my legs started to hurt and I stopped kicking. That's when I heard the sound of someone fumbling with the lock on the lid and what I could have sworn was the unmistakable sound of laughter.

"Hello? Who's out there?" There was no answer. I could hear more fumbling with the lock. "Hey! Is anyone out there?" I called out again. "Can you help me?"

There was still no answer. After a few minutes, I heard a click, and the sound of something heavy hitting the ground. The dumpster lid came open a crack and I immediately pushed it open and looked around. The alley was empty. I looked down to see a large padlock on the ground. I scrambled out of the dumpster and picked it up. The lock hadn't been cut. Someone had picked it. The hair on the back of my neck stood up and turned to look down the alley towards the street, and saw the brown Chevy idling there. For the first time could see the silhouette of the driver through the dark tint on the windows. The person's shoulders were heaving. The asshole was laughing at me. I was about to run towards the car when a sound made me look into the dumpster. Rooting around amongst the bags was a big black rat. It climbed up on top of one of the bags holding what looked like a piece of broken cracker in its little paws. It was probably a cousin of the rats Handy Randy saw in the park the night of Justin's murder. I took off like a shot.

SEVEN

It's bad when you smell so foul that you make yourself sick. I smelled like a dead bird rolled in crap. My stomach was roiling as I headed home with all my windows down, while mentally making plans to burn my clothes and soak in a hot soapy tub for a week. I hoped I'd be able to get the smell out of my car. I was parked at the light when I remembered the crumpled up card in the dumpster. I'd stuffed it in my pocket and forgotten about. I pulled it out and unfolded it. It was a white card with two silver figures symbolizing a man and woman entwined in an embrace. There was no writing on the front. I opened the card and there was a handwritten message inside that read: *Didn't We Almost Have it All. All My Love Forever.* There was no signature.

I was right. Justin had been stepping out on Lauren. Only a lover would be busting out Whitney Houston lyrics. Lauren must have realized it, too, or she wouldn't have crumpled up the card. It must have been left at the shrine. That would also account for her attitude. Had Justin been planning to divorce Lauren for the other woman? Did Lauren kill him before he'd had the chance? If that were the case, what would Lauren have to gain if, according to Pia, all of Justin's money was going to KingFord College? More importantly, who had Justin been arguing with on the phone when Pia had come back to the gallery?

I made a left turn and headed to the Kingford Inn. My plan had been just to drive past. However, when I spotted Pia, Joy, and another woman I didn't recognize, walking down the Inn's wide front steps, I parked and got out. Those two had some 'splaining to do. When Joy spotted me and saw the look on my face, she rushed forward to try to intercept me before I got to Pia and the other woman. She must have realized I'd found out about what Link had done to her. However, she didn't get within three feet of me before my funk repelled her. Her hands immediately flew to her face to cover her nose.

"Jesus, Clayton! You smell like a port-a-potty at a sauerkraut festival!"

"Thank you, Joy. But, you've got a bigger problem than my smell to deal with. Why didn't you tell me about Link Ramey scamming you into paying a phony display fee to show your work at the Ramey gallery?"

She didn't say a word. Just kept staring at me with her hand covering her nose. I could see her eyes were also beginning to water. Pia and the elegantly dressed older woman with her came to stand next to Joy. The woman was wearing a blue sleeveless dress with a paisley scarf knotted around her neck. Her shiny chin length bob fell just short of her jaw line. Her skin was a flawless nut-brown color. If it hadn't been for the laugh lines in her forehead and around her eyes, I would have put her age at early thirties but she must have been at least in her mid-to-late fifties.

"Kendra, this is my mother, Ingrid Ramey-Dubois. She here visiting from Paris," Pia said.

This must have been the woman Link had been talking on the phone with Lauren about. The one who hadn't bothered telling him she was in town.

"Nice meeting you," I told her not bothering to shake her hand.

"We're on our way to dinner. Would you like to join us?" asked Ingrid, purely to be polite, I'm sure. I couldn't miss the horrified looks from both Pia and Joy. I knew that smelly or not, they wouldn't want me around.

Pia was trying to be polite and not hold her nose. Instead, she put her index finger right under it, like she was trying to keep the aroma from getting inside. Her mother was standing sideways to let the breeze blow the smell right past her. I realized my being stinky might actually work to my advantage. All I had to do was try and hug them and they might actually tell me the truth just to get rid of me.

"No thanks, Mrs. Ramey-Dubois. I don't want to hold you up, so I'm going to get straight to the point. Can I assume that you're the one your ex-husband was arguing with on the phone shortly before his murder?"

"Damn, Clayton! Show some respect," exclaimed Joy. Pia didn't say anything just bit her lip self-consciously.

"Are you with the police?" Ingrid asked, looking taken aback.

"No, just someone trying to keep your daughter from going to prison for killing her father."

"This is so ridiculous," Ingrid said, throwing up her hands. "Yes, I was the one he was arguing with."

"The only reason why I didn't tell you, Kendra, is because I didn't want the police thinking my mother had anything to do with my father's death," said Pia. Her mother reached down and squeezed her daughter's hand.

Pia had good reason the think the police would be looking at Ingrid if they knew about the phone call. The Kingford Inn was only two blocks from the gallery. She could have easily walked to the gallery, entered through the side door, killed Justin, and walked out unseen.

"What were you arguing about?" I asked eliciting more protests from Joy.

"If you must know," she replied haughtily. "We were arguing over a piece of art I left behind when I walked out on Justin. I inherited it from my father and its value has grown tremendously over the years. My second husband's death last year has left me cash strapped and I need it back so I can sell it. Of course, with Justin's unfortunate demise, I have no idea where it is. He refused to tell me. And I certainly wouldn't have killed him because now I'll never know what he did with it."

"Is it a painting?" I asked, thinking back on the sunset painting that got delivered to the Ramey gallery. It certainly didn't look valuable but what did I know?

"No. It was a sculpture, why?" Ingrid asked.

"No reason," I replied.

"You makin' me lose my appetite, Clayton. If that's all you wanna know, then we need to bounce. We got reservations." Joy put her hand on my back and started shoving me towards my car.

"Pia and her mother don't know about you assaulting Link and the restraining order he filed, do they?" I asked once we got out of earshot.

"Keep your voice down," she hissed. "They got enough on their plates. They don't need to know about it."

"You never answered my question, Joy. Why didn't you tell me about Link scamming you?"

"It ain't important, that's why. Justin agreed to give me my money back plus my own show to make up for what Link did. That was enough for me."

"Hmm. That's not what I heard. I heard he didn't do right by you until you threatened to make a stink. What happened, Joy, did he not give your money back? Did you get mad and bash him in the head with that pineapple? We both know you have anger management issues."

Joy jumped in my face, or as close to it as she could get being so short, and jabbed a finger in my face.

"Fuck you! By the time my show rolled around, Justin and me was cool. No harm no foul. Pia was the one who made sure he put Link's ass in check. And the only one raisin' a stink 'round here is you."

"Hey! Don't get mad at me. If you and your friend would just tell the truth in the first damned place, I wouldn't have to waste my time asking you stuff like this. Everything is important whether you think so or not."

"Is everything okay, ladies," asked Ingrid sounding concerned. We both turned to see Ingrid and Pia standing on the sidewalk by my car.

"Everything's cool," replied Joy still glaring at me. "Clayton has a date with a bar of soap and I don't wanna keep her waiting."

All three women laughed.

The next morning I rolled out of bed and ran straight to the bathroom to throw up. Once I pulled my head out of the toilet, I vowed to lay off the sweets. After taking a steaming, hour-long shower the night before, I'd polished off a spicy meatball sub, a bag of chips, plus half the tin of cookies. My stomach was aching as I cautiously stepped on the scales for the first time in more than a month. I wasn't surprised to see that I'd gained ten pounds. But, when I went to grab a towel, and spied an unopened box of tampons in my bathroom closet, I realized my period was at least two weeks late. With everything that had been going on lately, I'd completely forgotten about my period.

Could that be why I was eating so much and sick in the mornings? Could I be pregnant? It would make a lot of sense. It would also be poetic justice since my not being ready for kids was the reason for me not being able to accept Carl's marriage proposal. I went to the kitchen and looked at the calendar on my fridge to count back to the last time I'd been with Carl. It had been a week before he'd left for Atlanta, which had been roughly six weeks ago, give or take a week. It was certainly possible that I was pregnant. And the thought terrified me. I wasn't ready for a baby. I was feeling too out of sorts to go to work and called off sick. I went to the drugstore to get a home pregnancy kit and sat staring at it on my coffee table for an hour, too afraid to actually take the test.

Instead, I headed over to Mama's. I'd missed her terribly and needed some of her TLC. I was hoping that she'd missed me too and when she saw me she'd change her mind about not wanting me over. I pulled into her driveway and walked up to the house. I could hear laughter coming from the direction of the back porch. I rounded the corner and climbed the back steps in time to see Mama through the screen door still dressed in her night gown and robe, setting a glass of orange juice in front of Leonard, who was dressed in my grandfather's old navy blue terry cloth robe. He'd obviously spent the night. I stood there staring at them frozen to the spot with my mouth hanging open. This was moving way too fast. I had to do something.

"Morning," I said brightly as I walked into the kitchen uninvited.

They both froze, like they'd just been caught stealing, then Mama pulled her robe together self-consciously. Leonard stood up abruptly, almost knocking over his glass of juice, and put his arm around Mama's shoulders pulling her close. You'd think by the indignant look he was giving me that I was public enemy number one. He hadn't seen anything yet.

"Don't get up, Leonard, I didn't come by to start a fight. I came by to apologize for my behavior the other day. It was uncalled for and wrong. Mama can take care of herself and I had no right getting into your business. Can you forgive me?" I did my best to look sincere.

I could tell by the way Mama's eyes were shining that she'd bought the load of crap I'd just dumped on her kitchen floor. However, Leonard was looking less than convinced.

"Oh, Kendra, this means so much to us," Mama

said, coming over to give me a big hug. "Right, baby?" she said, over her shoulder to the man wrapped in my dead grandfather's robe.

My eyes met Leonard's and a thin insincere smile spread across his face. "Right, Stella baby. No harm done," he replied. "Come on over here, Ken, and give ole' Lenny a big hug." I detected a definite note of sarcasm at that Lenny part.

Mama stepped aside and Leonard and I engaged in the most awkward hug that two people who didn't want to touch each other could manage. But, Mama seemed to buy it.

"You want some breakfast, baby?" asked Mama heading towards the stove.

"Yes," Leonard and I said in unison each of us thinking she was talking to us.

While Mama was busy whipping up a batch of her famous homemade waffles, I sat in the TV room with Leonard and attempted to make small talk. I could tell he was still wary of me and I knew I really needed to turn on the charm if I was going to get close enough to get the goods on him.

"I really am sorry about the other day, Leonard," I told him. We were both sitting on the couch watching a rerun of the Golden Girls. Leonard just nodded without looking at me and didn't speak.

"It's just really hard for me to see Mama so happy with a man who isn't my grandfather. I really miss him." It wasn't a lie and I was surprised to realize I was about to cry. Wow, I really could be pregnant.

Leonard noticed the catch in my voice and looked over at me in surprise. "Oh, Ken, I'm not trying to take your grandpa's place." He reached out and squeezed my hand. It took everything in me not to pull away.

"No one could take his place, honey. Stella and I are just happy to have found each other. It's rare enough to find love once in this life. But, to find it twice, and at our age to boot, is pretty darned amazing."

"Well, you're the first man Mama has dated since my grandfather died. Was it hard for you to get back out there after your wife passed away?"

Leonard tensed up and let go of my hand. He turned back to the TV and I thought I'd blown it until he finally spoke up.

"My wife's been gone a long time, Ken. I try not to dwell on the past," he concluded.

I just bet he didn't. We were silent for a long time and could tell that the little bit of rapport I'd just built up with him was rapidly fading. I had to get him talking again. I had to get him to trust me. I glanced at the calendar Mama had hanging on the wall behind the TV and got an idea. I scooted closer to Leonard. He looked startled like I was about to molest him.

"Mama's birthday is next month, Leonard," I whispered so she wouldn't hear me. "I was planning a surprise party for her. Would you be interested in helping me plan it?"

I could see the look of relief wash over his face. "I think that's a mighty fine idea. I'd be happy to help you." He grinned.

Leonard and I agreed that I would come to his house after Sunday dinner to work out the party details, and by the time breakfast was ready, I felt I was well on my way to finding out if he was a murderer.

I spent all morning at Mama's and went home right

before lunchtime when Mama and Leonard left for their Tai Chi class at the senior center. The home pregnancy kit greeted me when I got back home. Realizing that putting it off wasn't going to make me any less knocked-up, if that were the case, I grabbed it from the table and went into the bathroom. After pissing on the test strip, I sat on the toilet and waited for a pink line to appear. I waited and waited and waited. Two minutes passed, then five, and then ten. No pink line. No blue line. No line, period. I slid off the toilet onto the bathroom floor in relief. I wasn't pregnant. I was just a pig.

Joy was obviously still mad at me. I hadn't seen her all day. I also hadn't seen the brown Chevy since the driver had picked the lock and sprung me from the dumpster. Whatever my stalker had in store for me, having me crushed in the jaws of a trash truck's compactor wasn't it. I had the padlock in my purse in a baggy. I was at the Willow police department waiting for Trish Harmon to grant me an audience so I could hand it over to her to be processed for prints, when Rollins came sauntering into the station. He looked yummy in a crisp white shirt that made his brown skin glow and a pair of black dress pants. When he spotted me he smiled and made a beeline straight for me.

"Hey," he said, plopping down next to me on the hard bench. "I came by to see you a couple of times to make sure you were okay. You've been busy."

He didn't know the half of it.

"Yeah, I've had a lot of running around to do. But don't worry, I'm fine," I assured him.

"You sure? Because you look a little peaked."

"Positive. I'm just a little tired."

He smiled and an awkward silence ensued. It didn't used to be this way. We always had plenty to talk about in the past. Back when I was still with Carl and he was the one alone. Now the shoe was on the other foot and I didn't like it. And it wasn't just the fact that he was dating Harmon, I didn't want to see him with anyone and that wasn't fair. I was being a bitch and it was about to cost me a friend. Time to do some damage control.

"I'm really sorry about the way I acted at the gallery, Rollins. Of course you have the right to be happy. I wish you and Trish all the best."

He had no idea how hard it was for me to say that, especially since I was being less than sincere. But the look of relief that washed over his face was well worth it.

"That means a lot to me, Kendra. Thank you." He swept me up in a big hug and I held on tight, not realizing how much I really needed that hug.

We were still hugging when Harmon finally came out. A hard look passed over her face when she saw the two of us wrapped in each other's arms. It would have been worth sticking my hand down his pants just to see her head explode. But I resisted the urge. When Rollins saw her, he gently pulled away from me, which made his girlfriend relax.

"I understand you have some kind of red hot evidence that you're being stalked?" she said sarcastically with bothering to greet me.

"This should have the prints of the person who's been following me on it." I handed her baggy with the padlock. "I'd appreciate it if you'd let me know what you find out."

I left of them standing there and when I got to the station's revolving door, I looked back to see them laughing and talking, I'd been forgotten already.

I went to the grocery store and wandered up and down the aisles. I made a brief stop near the produce section and put lettuce, tomatoes, and carrots into my cart with every intention of starting a diet the next day. By the time I got to the frozen food section, my resolve had vanished and I added a gallon of chocolate chunk ice cream to my cart next to the box of Ho Ho's I'd picked up along the way. I headed to the check out counter and saw our new volunteer, Margery Warfield in the medicine aisle. I headed down to say hello.

"Hey, Margery, how's it going?" I asked but could tell by looking at her that things were not well. She looked pale, and tired, with red-rimmed eyes. Her usual immaculate attire replaced by polyester pants and a ratty looking T-shirt. She had one hand over her stomach and in her other hand she was holding a bottle of Pepto Bismo.

"I've been better," she replied setting the bottle in her cart. "I've been sick with some kind of stomach bug. My mother's got it, too. It hit us last night and I'm just now feeling well enough to leave the house."

"Sounds like you had what I had. I've been feeling kind of sick for about a week now. Must be something going around."

"Must be," she said, turning her cart to face the opposite direction.

"I hope you feel better," I told her retreating form and she waved.

I was in the parking lot loading groceries into my

truck when I saw Lauren Ramey across the street in the parking lot of the Willow Savings & Loan. She was decked out in her I-used-to-model-and-still-wear-a-size-0 attire of super skintight jeans, a black tube top, and sky high-heeled sandals. She was talking to, or rather arguing, with a muscular man with thinning blond hair and a bushy mustache. He was wearing a white suit with a peach colored shirt and a big gold chain around his neck. He was smoking a cigar.

I could only hear about every other word of what they were saying. But deduced from the words: go away, I told you no, and leave me alone, from Lauren, that the guy must be hitting on her. When I heard the words: think about it, lots of money, studio, and comeback, from the guy with the mustache, I realized I was mistaken. He wasn't hitting on her. It sounded like he was trying to hire her. He pulled out a card and handed it to her before getting into a yellow Corvette and driving off. After he was gone, Lauren tossed his card on the ground, hopped into her Mercedes and drove off.

When she was gone, I bolted across the street and picked it up off the ground. The card was white with gold lettering that read Elton Paul, Venus Studio with a phone number and address in the outskirts of Willow. I wondered if Venus Studio was an art gallery and if this Elton Paul was the one who sent Lauren Ramey the painting that had freaked her out so much. When I got back to my car, I wrote the painting's title, destiny, along with the word sunset on the back of the card and put it in my wallet. I planned to pay Mr. Paul a little visit.

I was surprised to see Joy pulling up behind me when I got home. She hopped out of her truck wearing a baseball cap, sunglasses, and a grim look. Normally I'd be irritated at the sight of her. But I was still so happy not to be pregnant even the sight of Joy didn't phase me one bit. When I gave her cheery hello, she took off her sunglasses looking surprised like it was the sign of the coming apocalypse.

"What brings you by?"

"I been followin' your ass all morning. Ain't that what you wanted me to do?" she replied looking annoyed.

"Where were you? I didn't see you following me." I said my cheerful mood starting to evaporate.

"That's 'cause I got skills. I was always a few cars behind you. Followed you to the drug store, your granny's crib, the police station, and the grocery store. I even saw you run across the street and pick up that trash Lauren Ramey dropped in the bank parking lot. You're a regular Woodsey the Owl, Clayton," she said, chuckling.

"Who?"

"You know that damned cartoon owl from back in the day. Give a hoot, don't —"

"Pollute. Yeah, I remember. Very funny." I handed her a bag and she followed me into my apartment.

"I'm surprised you showed up, Joy. Figured you still be pissed about yesterday."

"I understood what you were tryin' to say. I just get tired of everybody thinkin' the worst of me. Damn! I got feelings, too. I didn't kill Justin Ramey."

"I was simply pointing out what the police might think," I said not wanting to get into it again. "So, did you see the brown Chevy?"

"Naw. No brown Chevy. But there was a grey Ford Taurus with tinted windows followin' you. You didn't see it?"

I was so wrapped up in my thoughts I hadn't noticed anything. My stalker must have ditched the Chevy and was using another car.

"No. Did you get a plate number?"

"Sorry," she said, and then opened my frig and helped herself to a can of Pepsi. "All I saw was the back plate and it was smeared with mud."

"Well, what happened with Pia at the police station yesterday?"

"Oh, yeah, you pissed me off so bad I forgot to tell you that the cops got a hold of a copy of Justin's will and Pia gets it all: the house in the country, the gallery, and all the money, including the life insurance. He didn't leave Lauren, Link, or Kingford College a dime. So you know how that makes Pia look, right?"

"Like she found out about the will and killed him before he could change it?"

"Bingo."

"And did she know about the will?"

Joy shot me a pissy look. "Didn't she tell you the other day that she thought Kingford would get it all? She's just as surprised as the cops were."

I wondered just how surprised Pia really was. I also wondered if Pia's cash strapped Mama knew her little girl was about to be flush with cash and if that's why she hadn't bothered to tell her son she was in town. Was she sticking close not only to the child with the money, but the child most likely to share it with her? From what I'd overheard in Link's conversation, it didn't sound as if there were any warm fuzzy feelings between he and his mother. But the bigger question was, why did Justin cut Link and Lauren out of his will?

"Do Link and Lauren know about Justin's will?" I asked but figured that Lauren wouldn't have been pouring over receipts at the Ramey gallery if she knew it now belonged to Pia.

"They know now. The will was read at his lawyer's office this morning. Man, I wish I could have been a fly on that wall," Joy said with a smirk. "So, when you gonna go talk to them?"

"Soon, Joy, soon."

EIGHT

I was sick to death of being followed by both my mysterious stalker and Joy. After Joy went to sit in front of my apartment to keep an eye out for the grey Taurus, I slipped out of my house while she was on her cell phone. I cut through the backyard to the alley and caught a city bus into town where I rented a car. I was planning on renting something sleek and sporty but all they had left was a station wagon with a loud muffler, which I figure was on par with the rest of my life. I headed out to Justin Ramey's house in the country. If Justin had changed his mind about leaving everything to Kingford College, instead leaving it all to his daughter, he must have done it to punish Link and Lauren, and that would certainly be a motive for murder.

The Ramey house was just off of Willowdale Pike down a narrow paved road that you'd easily miss if it weren't for the red mailbox with and R on it next to the turnoff. I turned down the narrow road and drove for about a half a mile finally coming upon a large, red-brick, three-story Georgian style house with black shutters, and a portico supported by four large white pillars. There were two chimneys on either end of the roof. The house sat behind a high, black wrought iron fence. Surprisingly, the front gate was open and I drove through and parked behind Link Ramey's Range Rover in the circular driveway.

The station wagon's loud muffler must have signaled my arrival because Link Ramey was standing on the portico steps looking at me like I was a country cousin. He was dressed in preppy drag. His knife creased navy Dockers, crisp white Polo shirt, and highly polished Italian loafers making him look like he'd be more comfortable on some Ivy League college campus instead of Ohio. The only thing detracting from his buppy swagger was his swollen left eye where Joy punched him. She must have clocked him good.

"This is private property. I'll have to ask you to move your vehicle. If you're having car trouble, they can help you at the Marathon station down the road," he said, coming down the steps and nodding towards the station wagon, which was now dripping oil onto the pristine driveway.

"Oh, I'm not having car trouble," I said, walking over to where he stood. He was still looking at me like I was dirt in a way only a Ramey could manage. I'd have thought it was genetic if Lauren Ramey wasn't also endowed with this ability to belittle with a mere look. "I came by to see you Mr. Ramey. And before you ask, no, you don't know me. But you know my sister."

"Your sister?" he said, looking momentarily taken aback. "Oh, I don't think so." He glanced at the station wagon again and shook his head. "You need to leave.

You've got the wrong guy." He turned and walked back up the portico steps. I followed him.

"You don't know my sister, Joy? You know, Joy Owens, also known as the chick who busted you in the eye?" He stopped dead in his tracks and turned to face me.

"What do you want?"

"Just to thank you for not pressing assault charges against my sister."

"She's damned lucky I didn't sue her ass for slander over all the crazy accusations she was throwing around. That little bitch accused me of killing my father."

"No, I'd have to say you were the lucky one, Mr. Ramey. My sister could have sued you and the Ramey Gallery for fraud. I know all about you scamming her with those bogus display fees. What was up with that? You live in this big house. Your father had money. But you're scamming folks?"

Link at least had the decency to look embarrassed. He held up his hands and took a step back. "Hey, that was a big misunderstanding. She got all that money back and my father gave her own showing. She's got nothing to complain about."

"Maybe not," I said and sat down on a stone bench under the portico indicating that I wasn't ready to leave just yet. "But it's hardly behavior I'd expect from Justin Ramey's son." I shook my head.

"You don't know me," he said, looking me up and down. "Now are you finished because I've got better things to do?"

"Like pack?" I blurted out without thinking. Link squared his shoulders and gave me a contemptuous look. "Sorry, I heard about your father's will and Pia getting everything. I guess this is her house now, huh? That's gotta be rough."

Link shrugged like he didn't care but the tick in his left eye gave him away. "My father always knew I was the strong one. He knew I didn't need the money. I'm a man. I can make my own way. I've got my own gig and soon I'll have all the money I'll ever need."

"Really?" I waited for him to elaborate on this new gig but he didn't.

"Besides, it all depends on what happens with my father's murder investigation. Pia may never get a chance to move into this house or spend any of Dad's money. She may be living in an institutional setting," he concluded smugly.

"You really think Pia had something to do with your father's death?"

"I think the person who benefited the most from my father's death is the one who killed him and that's obviously not me, is it?"

"Link Ramey! Don't you talk about your sister that way! She's your own flesh and blood!"

Startled, we both turned to see Janette Ramey standing in the doorway. She was leaning heavily on a cane and was looking even thinner and frailer than when I'd seen her last. Pia claimed the chemo was working but if that was the case, it was draining her dry in the process. She made her way slowly towards us. I was surprised to see her. I looked at Link and his expression was fixed and unreadable. He went to help her over to the bench I was sitting on.

"Auntie Janette, you need to rest. Let me get you something cold to drink," Link said in a flat voice. I got the feeling I wasn't his only unwanted visitor.

"Some lemonade would be nice. Why don't you go fetch us some while I sit and visit with Kendra. And don't think you and me won't be talking about your sister later."

Only a slight lifting of his eyebrow showed Link's surprise that I knew his aunt. But he quickly disappeared into the house.

"I'm surprised to see you here, Ms. Ramey. How are you feeling?" I grabbed her hand and squeezed it.

"Well, I'm still here, thank the good Lord. Can't complain about that, can I?" she said with a big cheerful smile I didn't know if I'd be able to manage if I were in her shoes. "Thought it was high time the Ramey's started acting like a family again. I caught a cab and came over here to talk some sense into that knuckle headed nephew a mine. He and Pia need to pull together and put all this nonsense behind them before they end up like Justin and me."

"How's it going?" I asked.

She shrugged her thin shoulders and smiled. "It's not. Link's always been jealous of Pia. It was Justin and Ingrid's fault. Pia came along at a time when Justin and Ingrid thought they couldn't have any more kids. She was born premature and was sickly the first few years of her life. Justin and Ingrid treated her like a China doll. I'd never tell Pia this but Link has a right to be angry. After Pia was born, he never got much attention from his parents."

"Yeah, but he's like twenty-seven, isn't he? Shouldn't he be over that by now?"

"Well, Kendra, some wounds go so deep they never really heal." She had a faraway look in her eyes that I couldn't decipher.

Link returned with only one glass of lemonade. I took that as my cue.

"I really need to get going," I said and stood up to go. "Oh, Link," I said turning back around. "I met your mother Ingrid the other day. It must be comforting to have her around since your father's death."

Link didn't respond. Just stared into the lemonade glass with a grim expression. Janette was the one who reacted.

"You didn't tell me Ingrid was in town," she said angrily to Link.

"Why do you care?" he replied, leaning heavily against a pillar.

"I don't care," snapped Janette sounding highly put out. "I just would have liked to have known that's all."

I wasn't surprised by the anger in Janette's voice. I got the feeling it wasn't just because Ingrid, the woman who fired her, was in town. It was because she'd been trying to pull the family together and been completely left out of the loop. Link glared at his aunt.

"I'm surprised my sister didn't tell you since you two are so close now," Link said laughing spitefully. "Guess that means you've got some competition for my sister's inheritance."

Looking hurt, Janette got up and went back into the house without a word. I felt bad for the woman and wondered why she was even bothering. Link was a lost cause. He started to follow her then remembered I was still standing there.

"Unless Joy wants to share a cell with my sister, make sure she stays the fuck away from me. And get that piece of crap out of my driveway." He sauntered into the house.

"You mean Pia's driveway, don't you?" I called out to his back. He didn't bother turning around, just held his middle finger up.

Ten minutes later, I was at the Marathon station up the road from the Ramey house getting gas and oil, when I saw Link's Range Rover fly past. Wondering where he was in such a hurry to get to, I hopped into the station wagon and followed him all the way through downtown Yellow Springs, finally stopping at a farmhouse between Yellow Springs and the neighboring city of Xenia.

Link turned into the farm's dirt driveway and drove past a small farmhouse and parked in front of a large barn. There were at least fifty other cars parked in a large paved parking area. The barn was huge and looked more like a house, and was at least two-stories, with three rows of small narrow windows. It was painted red and trimmed in white with a black, slanted, peaked roof. Two sets of large barn doors were in apparent disuse as they had no way to open them and the only indication there'd even been a doors there were the white arches around them.

There was a smaller door on the side that Link disappeared through and over the door in gold curly cue lettering were the words: Venus Studio. I pulled Elton Paul's business card that I'd retrieved from the ground earlier out of my wallet and sure enough, the address was the same. This was the same Venus Studio. What was Link doing here? I sat in my car, which was parked two rows behind Link's and waited for him to come out. I watched as a variety of men and women of all races both scantily attired and dressed in business casual came and went and I wondered just what type of a place Venus Studio was. Link finally emerged almost an hour later, hopped into his car, and took off. I waited until he was gone and got out of the station wagon and went inside.

There was a long counter to my right being manned by an overweight woman with hair the color of egg yolk and a flowered muumuu. To my left was a large, noisy, waiting room crammed with people. A long hallway in front of me led to what must have been a suite of offices. An overly tanned young woman with long bleached blond hair; bee stung lips coated in pink gloss; giant boobs stuffed into a tight black leather halter top, a silver micro mini skirt; and feet contorted by four inch Lucite platform heels emerged from one of the rooms down the hall.

An enormous black guy in a black T-shirt and jeans wearing shades and a grim expression followed her. He looked like a bodyguard. I won't say what she looked like. As they walked past, all conversation in the waiting room ceased instantly and people were craning their necks to get a good look. One young, muscular guy jumped out of his seat to run to the entrance of the waiting room.

"I love you, Tastee! I'm Charlie Dickens! I hope we get to work together!" he yelled. The blonde didn't acknowledge his existence and a scowl from the bodyguard made Charlie shut up and take a step back.

"Tastee?" I mumbled under my breath.

"She's my idol. I'd love to work with her," wistfully exclaimed the young woman standing next to me.

She looked like a clone of the blonde only with long, dark, curly hair and in addition to the enormous chest; this chick also had an ass that looked like a beach ball was under her skirt. Both women had the same plastic artificial look. In fact, as I looked around the waiting room, I noticed that all the women looked like this. And all the men had physiques like action figures. What the hell was going on? This obviously wasn't an art studio.

"Who is she?" I asked. The girl's head snapped around.

"Who is she?" she said like I was the village idiot. "You don't know who Tastee Cummins is? What rock do you live under?"

"The rock I'm about to hit you with," I mumbled under my breath as I watched her flounce off to the waiting room. The Charlie guy who yelled at Tastee got up and gave her his seat. Apparently, chivalry still lived. Who knew?

I turned to the woman behind the counter and before I could even ask her if Elton Paul was in, she handed me a clipboard.

"Fill this out and then have a seat in the waiting room. Make sure you complete the section on your medical background. This is just a preliminary interview. You'll need to submit to an HIV test if you get a callback for an audition." She pointedly looked me up and down and added, "If you're applying for the fluffer job, make sure you list all of the actors you've worked with and their contact info. We're running behind so be prepared to wait."

Fluffer? HIV test? Audition? What the hell?

"Um, I'm just here to talk to Elton Paul. Is he

available?" I asked.

"You and all those other people in the waiting room, sweetie. You'll have to wait your turn like everyone else."

She shoved the clipboard across the counter at me and I grabbed it and stalked over the waiting room. All the seats were taken, and unlike Beach ball Butt, none of the guys jumped up to offer me their seat. I ended up sitting on the hard floor just inside the waiting room entrance. I sat the clipboard next to me on the floor and noticed the movie posters on the far wall of the waiting room that I'd been unable to see from the reception counter. All the posters were of nude, freakishly endowed men and surgically enhanced women in various explicit sexual positions under movie titles such as: *Beverly Hills Cock, India Jones and the Temple of Boobs, King Dong,* and *Free My Big Willy*, which had the tagline of: *a "touching" tale of a man named Moby and his dick*. I finally got it now, and mentally kicked myself for being so stupid. This wasn't an art studio. This was a porn studio!

For the next two hours I waited along with the porn star wannabees who either talked nonstop on their cell phones to their agents, bragged about the movies they'd been in, or gossiped about the actors they'd worked with. I found out quite a lot while I waited. For instance, Chance Cockran was dumped by his studio because he gave herpes to the entire female cast of his last movie. Misty Blowford was only doing girl on girl movies because she just got married, which I imagine would also call for a name change. And one of Keke French's breast implants exploded during a book signing in Reno where she was signing copies of her autobiography entitled, *Humpin: The Life and Loves of a Porn Star*.

I also found out that the movie they were all there to audition for was *Star Whores II: The Nympho Strikes Back*. The coveted role of Princess Laidalot had already been given to Tastee Cummins, who didn't even have to audition, grumbled some of the "actresses". The rest of them were there to try and snag the remaining roles of Jabba the Slut, R2-DoubleD-2, Handjob Solo, and Luke Skyfucker, though I overheard many of them say they'd be more than happy if they were cast as Sex Troopers. Everyone assumed I was there for the fluffer job. I didn't want to admit I had no idea what a fluffer was.

Almost three hours later, I was finally called back to an office down the hall. When I got in there the only person in the room was Elton Paul still dressed in the same cheap and cheesy white suit and peach shirt he had on when I spotted him arguing with Lauren Ramey earlier. Up close I could tell that despite the fact that it looked like he took good care of his body, he wasn't a young man. I'd have put his age at somewhere over fifty. He was sitting behind a long white folding table and was smoking a cigar. The room was filled with smoke that made my eyes water. Even Elton Paul had to wave away a mushroom cloud of smoke just to see me.

"Could you do me a favor, honey, and turn on that fan in the corner," he asked and pointed to a large round fan sitting on the floor. It was the kind that rotated.

I bent to turn it on and when I turned back around could tell by the way he'd sat back down abruptly that he'd been leaned over the table checking out my ass.

"What's your name, honey?" His voice was low and gravelly and he'd leveled his question at my chest.

"Kendra Clayton. I'm here to. . ."

"Sounds a little tame to me. That your real name?" he asked, stubbing out his cigar in the ashtray in front of him.

"Of course it is. Mr. Paul, I need to. . ."

"Change that name if you wanna break into the adult film industry," he said, lighting up another cigar. "And lose some weight. You've got nice tits but way too much meat on your bones, unless, you wanna break into fetish films. If that's the case you'll need to gain a lot more weight. There's a market for fat girls. Believe it or not, there are a lot of guys who like flab. Personally, I don't get it. But to each his own I always say."

"No. I'm not here for that. I need to..."

"Good. Now just take off your top so I can get a better look at your tits. They look pretty good but the real test is what they look like out of your bra."

"Mr. Paul!" I yelled to get the sleaze bag's attention. He finally shut up and took the cigar out of his mouth.

I pulled out the business card he'd given Lauren Ramey from my wallet and tossed it on the table. He picked it up and squinted at it in confusion.

"Do I know you? How'd you get my card?" Before I had a chance to answer, he turned the card over and saw the words I'd written on the back and burst out laughing. "Don't get me wrong, honey, you're cute and all. But you'll never be another Destiny Sunset."

Sensing my confusion he gestured to the row of

movie posters on the wall behind me that I hadn't paid any attention to when I'd walked in. All of them depicted the same nude young woman with long red hair. And though she barely looked out of her teens, was a good twenty pounds heavier, and had a slightly crooked nose, I could tell I was looking at Lauren Ramey aka Destiny Sunset. Her specialty was going down, according to the tagline on all the movie posters.

"Did Lauren Ramey's husband know his wife was an ex porn star?"

"I have no idea who you're talking about," said Paul, leaning back in his chair and putting his hands behind his head.

"Really?" I said, leaning on the table. "Well, I know for sure that a couple of those girls out there in the waiting room are underage? And I bet the cops would love to know that, too."

He glared at me for along minute and looked at the gold Rolex on his wrist. "Alright. You've got two minutes. Whaddya wanna know?"

"I want to know how Lauren Ramey became Destiny Sunset."

"You mean how little Lunell Scaggs became Destiny Sunset?"

"Yeah, whatever. Just tell me."

"I met Destiny. . .er. . .Lunell when I she was nineteen and auditioned for a part in an adult film I working on. I was just a lowly cameraman back then, but I knew a star when I saw one and Lunell had the goods, greats tits and long legs that could wrap around you twice, and a mouth like Kim Basinger. She didn't get the part, though. The director gave it to his coked out girlfriend. I tracked Lunell down and told her if she listened to me, I'd make her a star. She had an affinity for oral sex. I swear that girl could suck the chrome off a bumper. So I changed her name to Destiny Sunset. It was the start of a beautiful friendship. That was sixteen years ago and Destiny's movies are still among my biggest sellers."

"What happened?" I asked. He shrugged and puffed on his cigar.

"Who knows? We'd only made six movies when she up and retired. Just walked away. Left town. I didn't see her again until a few years later when I was sittin' on the can flippin' through one of my wife's magazines and saw her in a fashion spread for some French designer. She was skinny as hell and had chopped off her hair and dyed it black, even got her nose fixed from when her old man kicked her in the face and busted it when she was twelve, but I knew it was her. I'd know that mouth anywhere. She was going by the name Lauren Frangelico like she was Italian or somethin'. Only Italian she had in her was when she banged Tony "The Bull" Bonaducci in her last movie Raging Cock," he said, chuckling.

"How'd that make you feel when you found out your little money maker had gone legit?"

"I was happy for her," he said, puffing on the cigar. I gave him a skeptical look and he leaned forward in his chair. "No. Really. I was happy for her. By then I had my own studio and a whole roster of actors. Business was booming. I didn't begrudge Destiny her success. I had no hard feelings."

"When did you see her again?"

"Ten years later. Her modeling career was over and she was broke and living back at her mother's place and looking for rich husband to take care of her."

"And she found Justin Ramey?"

"Eventually, she started with the son first."

"Link? She dated her husband's son first?" Elton
Paul nodded and smiled. "How'd she go from the son to
the father?"

"Link Ramey doesn't have what it takes to keep a
woman like Des. . .I mean Lauren happy. She needed a
man with money and all Link had was an allowance.
After she found out Link's lifestyle was being financed
by his daddy; she joined the country club and started
playing tennis just to meet Justin Ramey. And if she's
half as good a fuck as she was when she was nineteen,
then Justin Ramey never had a chance."

"Did Justin know about Link and Lauren?"

"Hell, I don't know."

"Well, is Link Ramey is in business with you?"

"Link fancies himself a budding film maker. Seems
to think he can get his feet wet in the porn industry and
move on to Oscar winning movies," he said with a
laugh. "What a joke. Don't get me wrong. There's good
money to be made in porn. But you can forget
respectability. People turn their noses up at us and treat
us like trash but you'd be hard pressed to find a person
who hasn't watched at least one porno in their lives.
And once you start here, you get stuck here. But, I'm
hardly gonna tell a guy who's offering to invest in my
new movie to get lost."

"Where's he getting the money to invest in your
movie?"

"Beats the shit outta me. I don't ask where it comes
from. I just cash the checks. And your two minutes
were up two minutes ago." He stood up and headed to

the door to call for his next audition.

"Wait! Just one more question."

He paused at the door and waited.

"If business is so booming, then why were you trying to get Destiny to make a comeback?"

"Because in my book you can never make too much money."

"Are you the one who sent Lauren Ramey that painting?" He looked at me like I was crazy.

"That was two questions," he said, opening up the door. "Next!" he shouted.

I left and was halfway down the hall he called out after me.

"We're always lookin' for fluffers if you ever need a job."

"For the love of God what the hell is a fluffer?" I yelled.

Laughter broke out in the waiting room and the yellow haired receptionist rolled her eyes and waved me over. She whispered in my ear and my faced flushed hotly. I left in a hurry. And I'm too embarrassed to repeat what she said.

NINE

When I left Venus Studio, I headed straight for the Ramey Gallery. When I arrived, Lauren Ramey was struggling with the lock on the front door. I parked a little way up the street and got out. By the time I got to the gallery, Lauren had gone from pulling on the door to kicking it.

"Is everything okay?" I asked.

"No! Everything is not okay! My dead husband's daughter had the locks changed and I can't get in. She and that bitch of a mother of hers think they're going to screw me out of everything. But I'll be damned if I'm going to end up empty handed!" She gave the heavy wooden door one last savage kick causing it to rattle in its frame.

"Can't you go back to modeling?" I asked, figuring it was a perfectly reasonable question. However, Lauren suddenly realized she was venting to a stranger. I couldn't tell if she remember me from when I'd been there the day before.

"I've got more important things to do than spill my

guts to some nosy nobody asking questions." She headed back to her Mercedes.

"Hey, Lunell!" Lauren froze. "They're holding auditions at Venus Studio for a new movie. I'm sure your old friend Elton Paul would love to give Destiny Sunset her old job back," I called out after her.

She looked around wildly to see if anyone had overheard me, then walked over to where I was standing and towered over me in her four-inch heels.

"Who the hell are you! And don't give me any of that bullshit about this being about you finding my husband's body. You want something. What is it, money? Because if you were fucking him then you've already gotten the little bit from him that you're ever going to get," she said and laughed spitefully. How could Justin Ramey not have known he was married to such a snake?

"I wasn't screwing your husband, Lauren. Sounds like you had that covered from every angle," I replied and was pleased to see her flinch. "I'm a private investigator," I said, letting the lie slip from my lips with an ease that scared me. "And I'm looking into Venus Studio's finances. "Did you know your ex, uh, I mean stepson Link was an investor in Venus Studios?"

"Of course I knew. Who do you think gave him the money to invest in Venus Studios in the first place? I'm not stupid. There's a lot of money in porn. And I don't mind having my fingers in the pot just as long as I don't have to do it on my back."

"You might want to tell that to Elton Paul. He's wants his little moneymaker back. Seems the half dozen movies you made are still big sellers after all these years."

Lauren looked a little stunned, but quickly replied, "Elton's a fool if he thinks Destiny Sunset is ever going to make a comeback. My days of fucking on film were over a long time ago."

"Did your husband know about you and his son's involvement in the porn industry? I know you didn't have any money of your own, so I'm guessing you must have been investing Justin's money in Venus Studio. Wouldn't that have ruined your husband's respectable image if it got out that his wife and son were involved in porn?"

Lauren bent down and poked a long, red tipped fingernail in my chest. "It was his own fault for being so damned stingy. And I'd be very careful if I were you," she hissed at me. "Justin found out all right and wanted his money back. Elton wouldn't give it to him and he threatened to go to the media to embarrass Venus Studio's investors. And look where it got him."

"So Venus Studio's investors have a lot to lose if their names got out and you think that's why your husband was murdered?"

"I guess you're not as dumb as you look," she said with shit eating grin.

I wanted to smack the gloss off her lips but Karma has a way of intervening at the most appropriate times. A red truck pulled up and parked in front of Lauren's Mercedes. It looked like a normal truck in front but had a short bed in the back with towing apparatus. A man jumped out of the passenger's side, checked the car's license against the clipboard in his hand, and attached the apparatus to the front end of Lauren's car. By the time Lauren realized what was happening, the guy with the clipboard had already jumped back into the driver's side and his friend gunned the engine and took off.

"Hey! That's my car and it's paid for you bastards! Come back here!" she shrieked.

"Not according to Willow Savings and Loan!" shouted clipboard guy out the window.

Lauren tried to run after them but one of her spiked heels got caught in a rut in the sidewalk and sent her sprawling. It was time for me to go.

I headed to the Willow Police Station to tell Trish Harmon about my conversation with Lauren Ramey, though I knew it would be as welcome as fire ants at a nudist colony, not because it wasn't relevant information, but because it was coming from me. I pulled into the station's parking lot and saw Harmon's unmarked Crown Victoria pulling out. I followed her figuring that even if she was going to some kind of rendezvous with Rollin's, I could kill two birds with one stone, telling her about what Lauren said, and horning in on her date.

Filled with a renewed sense of purpose, I continued to follow Harmon all the way through town and out to the Weenie Hut on route 40. Harmon parked in the crowded lot and got out. The place was crawling with groups of teenagers hanging out and older couples looking for a nostalgia fix. The Weenie Hut had been around since my parents were kids. They had the best root beer floats and chili cheese dogs on the planet. Figuring she was just getting a late lunch, I started to get out and join her when I saw her bypass the order window and head around to one of the benches out back. A muscular black man was leaning against one of the tables sipping on a soda.

I couldn't tell exactly how tall he was, but guessed he was about six two. He wore wired-rimmed glasses and was bald. His skin was the color of honey. He was clean-shaven and like Rollins wore an earring in his left ear, though his was a tiny hoop and not a diamond stud. He was wearing a white button down shirt that did nothing to hide his muscular arms and chest, and black slacks with creases ironed into knife's edges. He looked like a superhero disguised as a really buff accountant. He was actually pretty damned sexy. Was Harmon stepping out on Rollins? I crept closer and sat with my back to them at a bench just around the corner. From the snatches of conversation I could hear, they were arguing about something the buff guy lost. I slid further down the bench so I could hear them better.

"How the hell did you let this happen?" I heard Harmon ask. She sounded highly aggravated.

The buff guy's voice was much deeper than Harmon's and he was speaking more quietly. I couldn't hear what he said but whatever it was really pissed Harmon off and her voice rose making it easy for me to hear what she said next.

"You're not getting paid to think, Mason. You're getting paid to baby sit Kendra Clayton! And if anything happens to her, you'll have hell to pay. So, you'd better get back out there and find her!"

I couldn't believe it. Harmon had someone tailing me? I got up and snuck back around front and looked into the parking lot. Sure enough, there was a grey Ford Taurus with tinted windows parked in the very first row. My mysterious stalker had been revealed. I could feel a head of steam building up. Harmon had known how scared I'd been of the person following me, and she hadn't said a damned thing to me. Instead, she'd treated me like I was crazy and paranoid.

I heard the sound of Harmon's voice coming closer and ducked back around the corner. Harmon and the guy she'd called Mason, came around the corner and stood by the Ford Taurus talking. I couldn't hear what they were saying but could tell by Harmon's red face that she was still pissed off. But she wasn't nearly as pissed as I was, not by a long shot. If Harmon had one of her people watching over me, then that could only mean that Stephanie Preston must have been spotted somewhere in the area. It was information I should have been told about and wasn't.

A few minutes later, Harmon and Mason got into their separate cars and drove off. Once they were gone, I ordered a chili cheese dog, a large root beer float, and sat down at one of the benches out back to eat and think. In retrospect, it was probably a good thing that I hadn't talked to Harmon about Venus Studios. For one thing, I was way too mad. I also knew that once I got back home and started driving my own car, that Mason guy would start following me again and reporting everything to Harmon. She'd know that I'd gotten myself involved in one of her investigations, again, not that she wouldn't know soon enough. But I didn't want to rush things. Instead, I called Joy.

"Where the hell you at, Clayton? I was sittin' in front a your crib for two hours. Two different people came by lookin' for your ass and when you didn't answer, your landlady got worried cause your car was still parked out front and used her key to get in. How'd you get past me?"

"That's not important. I had somewhere to go and

didn't need any extra company."

"Thanks a hell of a lot for tellin' me. That's two hours of my life I'll never get back. You know what? I quit! Find someone else to be your shadow."

"I'm sorry, Joy. And you don't need to follow me anymore. I found out the person following me is with the Willow Police department. I also found out something that might help Pia, but it would be best if you told Detective Harmon. I'm not exactly her favorite person."

I quickly filled Joy in and she was uncharacteristically silent.

"Are you still there?"

"I'm here. I just can't believe it. Link and Lauren both knew about this Venus Studio shit and neither of them said jack to the police. They just let Pia twist in the wind."

"I know. It's pretty disgusting," I said.

"And just where am I supposed to tell that detective that I got this hot tip from?"

"I don't know. Make something up. It's not like you don't know how to lie. Just don't tell her it came from me, okay?"

"Whatever," she said and hung up.

I called the car rental place and told them I'd be keeping the car for another day and snuck back home to get some clothes. If Stephanie Preston was in Willow, she'd just have to look for me along with that Mason guy from the Willow PD. When I got home, I climbed through my kitchen window to avoid Mrs. Carson who was probably sitting on her front porch and waiting for me to come home to administer some choice words. I packed clothes for two days and snuck back through the window and across the backyard to the alley, where the rental was parked, and took off.

I checked into the Kingford Inn. It was a little pricey but I figured what the hell. If I was going to hide out, I might as well do it in style. The Kingford Inn was a converted, three-story Victorian Mansion and very popular with the wealthy parents of Kingford College students and visiting professors. Fall quarter at the college was in full swing so parents dropping of their kids were long gone, which meant there were plenty of rooms at the inn.

"How long will you be staying with us, Ms. Clayton?" asked Virgie Trent, the owner of the inn.

Virgie was fiftyish and plump as a mother hen. I could tell by her flowing Laura Ashley print dresses and all the complicated floral arrangements, which were all over the inn's cozy living room and front entrance, that she must worship at the alter of Martha Stewart.

"Oh, just a couple of days. My apartment is being painted and the smell makes me sick."

"I understand completely," she said with a smile. "If you need anything you can call the front desk and we even have a mailing service if you need packages mailed." She gestured towards the counter in back of her to a pile of small packages all neatly wrapped in brown paper and tied with purple twine, just like the painting Lauren Ramey had received. Another mystery solved.

"I have a friend staying here as well and we're supposed to meet for dinner. Could you please tell me what room Ingrid Ramey-Dubois is staying in?"

"Oh, I just saw Mrs. Ramey-Dubois not ten

minutes ago out back having tea in the garden."

"Thanks," I told her and then headed up to my room on the second floor.

Each room was named after a flower. I was staying in the daffodil room. It was large and airy with pale yellow walls, a shiny hard wood floor, and a queen sized sleigh bed with white satin spread and a mattress so high it had a small footstool by the side of the bed so you could climb in. A vase of fresh daffodils sat on a tall bureau next to the small bathroom. I looked out the room's one large window and saw that it overlooked the garden. The center of the garden was an octagonal paved section with about six small round tables where a few people were having tea. There was an elderly couple at one table and Pia's mother, Ingrid Ramey-Dubois, sat at another table with her back facing away from me. I sat my overnight bag on the bed and went out to join her.

"Mrs. Ramey-Dubois, hello," I said when I got to her table. She looked up abruptly and I could see she'd been crying. She quickly dabbed at her eyes with a lace handkerchief. "I'm sorry. I didn't mean to startle you."

"That's okay. It's Kendra, right? You're the one helping Pia."

"That's right. Mind if I join you?"

I could tell she did mind but I could also tell she was a woman bound by good manners. She nodded her head towards the empty seat opposite her. I sat down. Today she was dressed in dove grey slacks, and a long, white, silk tunic. A double stand of black freshwater pearls encircled her neck.

"Would you like some tea?" she asked, lifting the blue ceramic teapot.

"No thanks. And don't worry. I won't take up much of your time. I just needed to ask you something and I hope you'll be honest with me because it's important."

"As long as it helps Pia, I'm happy to answer any questions." We'd see about that.

"I know you're the one who sent Lauren Ramey that sunset painting. How'd you find out about her past?"

"Well, anybody into pornography would know all about little Ms. Destiny Sunset. She was quite the star at one time," she replied, shocking me.

"And you're into porn?" I asked, looking at the classy elegant woman in front of me.

"When you're married to a Frenchman almost twenty years older than you, who needed a little extra help getting aroused, you'd be surprised at the things you'd be willing to do to please him. So if he wants you to watch porn with him, you watch porn with him, especially if you want to stay married," she concluded sourly.

I looked over and saw that the elderly couple was looking at us completely appalled. They quickly got up and left. I imagine the wife didn't want her husband getting any ideas.

"You recognized her from one of the movies you watched with your husband?"

"Not at first. She'd been a model in Paris at one time and is still a minor celebrity over there. One of my husband's friends loaned him all her videos swearing it was her. I wasn't as convinced. But by the time we'd made it through her entire repertoire of films, I knew it was her."

"And you told your ex-husband?"

"Not right away. I was happily married. I had a good life in Paris. Justin's marriage was none of my business."

"What changed?"

"I got a call out of the blue from Justin a month ago. I hadn't spoken to him in years. He'd caught Lauren and Link in bed together and was devastated and needed a friend to talk to. My second husband died last year and by the time I paid off all his debts, I was broke. And I never really stopped loving Justin. I wanted him back. He was trying to decide whether or not to file for divorce. I wanted to give him a little nudge and sent him one of her videos. *Party in Her Pants*, I believe was the title," she said with a humorless laugh. "But it did the trick. He was planning to divorce her. He had already spoken to a divorce attorney to draw up the papers."

"You weren't really arguing on the phone with him about a piece of art right before he died, were you?"

She shook her head and tears filled her eyes. "No, we weren't. In the month that he'd been crying on my shoulder about his marriage, we'd become close again. I thought that meant he wanted me back. Then I came to town to surprise him and found out he'd changed his mind about divorcing that trashy bitch. He still loved her and thought counseling would help them. I couldn't believe it. I was so furious!"

"Furious enough to kill Justin?"

"No!" she said, shaking her head vehemently. "I loved that man. I'd have never done anything to hurt him. It was Lauren I wanted to kill. I swear I could just wring that whore's neck."

"That's why you sent her the painting?"

"I wanted her to know that her dirty little secret was out and she wouldn't be able to go back out to the country club and get a rich new husband. I was hoping to run her out of town so she wouldn't contest Justin's will."

"You already knew he'd changed his will and left everything to Pia?"

"I'm the one who encouraged him to do it. He swore me to secrecy. Didn't want to have to deal with how mad Lauren and Link would be if they found out. Of course, he wasn't planning on them finding out quite so soon," she said in a flat voice.

"You encouraged Justin to change his will even when you knew your own son would be left without a dime?"

Ingrid took a long sip of her tea before answering. "Link isn't my child, Kendra. We adopted him when he was two. He took to Justin right away, but he never bonded with me. I bent over backwards to please that child. But nothing I did was ever enough. After Pia was born, I just stopped trying."

"I had no idea," I said. "I guess that's why he and Pia aren't close then?"

"Justin insisted we not tell them about Link being adopted. He thought it might just make things worse between them, though I can't see how. Link has always resented Pia's closeness to Justin."

"You think maybe he or Lauren could have found out about the will and confronted Justin?" I asked.

"What you really want to know is if Link or Lauren could have killed Justin, right?" I nodded. She shrugged. "When you get to be my age, you realize you never really know anybody. Nothing surprises me anymore," she said with a grim smile.

After my chat with Ingrid, I went back up to my room and took a long nap. I woke up around eight. It was just getting dark outside and I changed into jeans and a black sweatshirt. I waited around until after nine and then headed to Venus Studio. My plan was to break in and get a copy of their list of investor's, which I would then send anonymously to Harmon.

When I arrived I parked my car on the road and walked down the farm's dirt driveway. Lights were on in the farmhouse. I crept past and headed towards the big barn out back. I was relieved to see that there weren't any cars parked in the lot. There were also no lights on in the barn, at least not that I could see. I didn't bother trying the doors. I knew they'd be locked. Instead, I walked around to the back of the barn where I found a row of windows about a half story up. But I was way to short to reach them to even see if any were open. I looked around and saw some large round bales of hay along the fence behind the barn.

I went over and grabbed one, thinking it would be easy to lift and pulled a muscle in my shoulder when I found out otherwise. That sucker was heavy. I ended up having to roll it underneath one of the windows and set it up on one end. I climbed on top of it and still wasn't quite able to reach the window. But my hands could reach the sill and I pushed against the window. To my surprise it opened, swinging inward. I was able to brace my feet against the side of the barn and hoist myself up onto the windowsill. It was dark inside and I couldn't see a thing. I tentatively lowered one leg down and could feel nothing but empty air. I had no idea how far up I was.

I tried to turn my body so I could lower myself down into the room, thus lessening the impact of my landing, but a sharp pain in my shoulder caused me to let go of the sill. It felt like I was in free fall forever when I finally landed hard on my side on top of what felt like a box spring. I must have fallen a good five feet and my hard landing knocked the wind out of me. But other than that, I was okay. I lay still for several long minutes until my eyes adjusted to the darkness then pulled my keys from my pocket. There was a penlight on my keychain. It didn't give off much light but I could see that the room I was in was crowded with boxes and rack after rack of cheap skimpy costumes. There was also a full bedroom set, living room set, dining room set, lots of office chairs, a couple of desks, bookshelves, cordless phones, and lots of other household crap. I was in the prop room.

I got up, rubbing my sore shoulder, and searched for the door. When I found it, I pressed my ear to it but didn't hear anything outside. I slowly opened it and saw that I was two doors down from the room where Elton Paul had been auditioning for his film. The hallway was dark but I could see a faint glow of a light coming from the receptionist's station. I crept down the hall and saw that the light was florescent and coming from underneath the counter. I searched the receptionist's desk drawer and found nothing but a package of Kleenex, a dried out tube of Chapstick, hand lotion, a brush with yellow strands of hair in it, a phone book, and an a black leather appointment book filled with names I didn't recognize.

There was a large filing cabinet behind the receptionist's desk and I immediately started pulling on the drawers. They were all locked. There was a push in lock at the top of each row that locked all the drawers in that section. I searched the desk to find something to pry open the locks but could find nothing except some plastic paperclips. I gave up and turned to the Dell computer sitting on the desk. I pressed the on switch and the computer made a loud humming noise like a refrigerator that made me jump. Since the cabinets were locked up tight, I'd expected there to be a login to access the computer files but there wasn't.

I started opening random files and found movie scripts with laughable dialogue, invoices for bulk condom and KY Jelly purchases, boilerplate studio contracts, Venus Studio letterhead with a logo featuring the Venus De Milo with a boob job, receipts for travel expenses and camera equipment, and financial statements showing just how much money Venus Studio had made in the past year. When I saw the figure my jaw dropped. Elton Paul hadn't been kidding when he said there was money to be made in porn. Venus Studio had raked in over five million dollars in video sales just in the past six months alone. But company expenses, and actor and employee salaries had eaten much of that up. Elton Paul was earning a whopping 750,000 a year even the cameramen and the receptionist were earning high five figure salaries.

I didn't find anything that listed investors until I came upon a document labeled Board of Directors. I opened the document and saw a list of about twenty names including Lauren and Link Ramey. But there were other names I recognized such as a prominent

Willow judge, a congressman, a college dean, and a former professional athlete turned minister. Each name had a dollar figure next to it. Link and Lauren's names each had ten thousand dollars next to it. But some of the names had two and three times that much listed. None of these people could afford any negative publicity. Any of them could have killed Justin Ramey if they knew he was trying to expose Venus Studio's investors.

I printed out the list on the laser printer next to the computer and stuffed it in my pocket. I was heading back towards the prop room when heard a noise coming out of the back hallway. The noise sounded like something spinning and dragging. I hesitated at the prop room door torn between getting the hell out of there and finding out what the noise was. In the end my curiosity got the better of me and turned and crept down the hall. It was short hallway with only two doors. One was marked projection room and the other storage. The sound was coming from the projection room. I don't know why but I knocked softly on the door before opening it a crack.

It was dark inside the room save for a beam of light coming from a portable film projector sitting on a cart in the back of the room projecting onto a large screen in front of the room. The room was large and carpeted with three rows of four black high-backed leather chairs in the center. The noise was coming from the broken film still spinning inside its reel causing the ends to make a flapping sound. I switched off the projector and started to leave when I noticed a tuft of hair sticking up over the top of one of the leather chairs in the front row. I froze.

"Hello. Is someone in here?" I said in a voice

kicked up a good five octaves by fear. No answer. I crept closer. "Mr. Paul, is that you?" Still nothing.

I got close enough to reach out and touch the chair. I gave it a hard push from behind and it swung around revealing Elton Paul with a dark, round bullet hole in his forehead. Blood spatter stained the white suit he was wearing. I turned and pushed my way through the chairs to get to the door. I pulled the door open and saw a shadowy figure out of the corner of one eye. Before I could turn, I heard a crackling sound and felt a jolt of electricity course through my body. Then everything went black.

TEN

It was déjà vu when I woke up on the floor outside the projection room. Just like Justin's murder scene, a paramedic was tending to me. The projection room was filled with police. I tried to sit up.

"What happened?" I asked, feeling weird and out of it. The paramedic, a big burly man with hairy forearms, pushed me back down.

"Don't move, ma'am. I need to check you out." He pressed a stethoscope to my chest to listen to my heartbeat.

"But what happened?' I asked again.

"From the marks on your arm, it looks like some used a stun gun on you." I immediately touched my left arm and felt two small, raised marks that hurt like hell.

"She okay?" came a deep voice from the projection room doorway. I looked up to see Mason the buff guy Harmon had met at the Weenie Hut, the one who'd been following me. Up close he was even better looking. I could see he had a cleft in his chin like an action figure.

"Heartbeat's steady and strong and no other injuries. She should be fine," declared the paramedic. I slowly sat up. And then the paramedic and Mason helped me to my feet. I was unsteady and leaned against the wall for support.

"You feel well enough to answer some questions?" Mason asked with his hand on my shoulder.

"She'd damned well better be," said Trish Harmon coming out of the projection room looking like she could chew nails.

"How did you know about Mr. Paul?" I asked. "I didn't call the police."

"We got an anonymous tip that a major drug deal was going down here this evening. We get here and find you unconscious on the floor not twenty feet away from a guy with a bullet in his head. How do you explain this, Ms. Clayton?" Harmon was livid but so was I.

"How do you explain not telling me you've had one of your officers following me? You knew how scared I've been about that car following me and you treated me like I was a paranoid idiot!"

Harmon's face flushed but she said nothing. We glared at each other.

"Actually, I'm Detective Blake Mason, Ms. Clayton. I'm Detective Harmon's new partner. And I didn't mean to scare you."

"Partner? Oh my God! Did Mercer?" I let the question hang in the air.

"Mercer's fine. He's retiring for health reasons," replied Harmon. "Now, can you please tell us what the hell you were doing here at this time of night?"

"I came to get this." I reached into my back pocket

for the list of Venus Studio's board of directors but my pocket was empty. I checked all my pockets but the list was gone. Whoever killed Elton Paul must have taken it.

"Get what?" asked Harmon.

I told her about my conversation with Lauren Ramey and the possibility that one of Venus Studio's investor's could have killed Justin, as well as about the list of Venus Studio's Board of Director's I found on the computer, and watched her face go from pink to a deep mottled red.

"And you thought you'd just trot on out here and break in and get this list yourself instead of informing me?"

"Would you have listened?"

"I guess we'll never know now will we?" she snapped.

"What's the big deal? All you have to do is print out another copy of the list. It was on the receptionist's computer up front."

"Before or after I arrest you for breaking and entering?"

"That's enough!" Mason said making Harmon and I jump. "We don't have time for this. Now, Ms. Clayton can you please show us what computer you're referring to?" he said, guiding me passed Harmon and out to the receptionist desk.

"It's right. . ." I stopped cold and looked at the empty space in the desk. The printer was still where it had been but the computer was gone. "It was right here, I swear. It had all of the studio's financial records and everything on it."

Mason and Harmon exchanged glances.

"I'm not lying," I said.

"We know," said Mason. "We're just trying to piece together what happened. Can you tell us if these file cabinets were like this when you got here?"

The file cabinets behind the desk looked like they'd been broken into. The drawers had been pried open and there was a crowbar on top of the cabinet. It also looked like all of the files that had been inside were gone.

"No. They were still locked when I got here."

"So, when we dust it for prints, I'm guessing we'll find yours, too, right?" asked Harmon. Her voice dripped with contempt. I didn't answer and she threw her hands up in disgust and stalked off in a huff.

"I messed up, huh?" I said to Mason.

"Well, you sure haven't helped matters. Paul must have been dead when you got here so you've contaminated the crime scene. We've also got an empty wall safe," he said, gesturing towards the waiting room where I could see that one of the movie posters was hinged along one side and had been opened outwards revealing an open safe in the wall behind it. "We've got a dead body, missing computer, missing files, missing money and your prints all over the place."

"The person who did all this was still here hiding when I got here. So technically speaking, I walked in on a crime in progress, which makes me a victim and not a suspect."

Mason didn't look convinced. "I get the impression from Harmon that you do this kind of thing a lot?"

"Depends on your definition of a lot," I said unable to look him in the eye. He burst out laughing. I changed the subject.

"Has Stephanie Preston been spotted in Willow? Is that why you're following me?" The question wiped the smile from his face.

"Honestly, we have no idea where she is. There hasn't been any new sighting of her in weeks. Harmon figures better safe than sorry, especially since according to her, you have a knack for getting into trouble."

"Detective Harmon exaggerates," I said.

"And you're forgetting that I'm the guy who sprung you from that dumpster. Following you around may not have been the most challenging job I've ever had, but it sure as hell wasn't boring." He walked off to join Harmon and I stuck my tongue out at his retreating back.

On Harmon's orders, Mason followed me back to the Kingford Inn where I collected my things and went home. I thought he was just going to resume his vigil in his car outside my apartment. Instead, he followed me inside and parked himself on my couch.

"What are you doing?"

"Making sure you stay out of trouble, which means no more following you around in my car. From here on out, I'm your shadow. And just in case you get anymore bright ideas to sneak out again, I'm sleeping on the couch." He kicked off his shoes and propped his big feet up on my coffee table.

"For how long?"

"I'd say at the very least until the Ramey case is solved. Harmon wants you out of her hair. In case you haven't noticed, you bug her. And when she's annoyed, she takes it out on everyone else, including me. After that, I'm sure an officer will be assigned to baby sit you until Stephanie Preston is caught. But, in my opinion, if she was smart, she'd be long gone by now."

"And I don't have any say in this?" I suddenly didn't think Mason was quite so sexy anymore.

"Nope," he said, taking off his gun and holster and setting it on the table. I started to walk away when he called out after me. "Hey, can I at least get a pillow or something?"

"Check the hall closet," I said without looking back. I went into my bedroom and slammed the door.

The next morning the smell of food drove me from my bedroom. I was planning on hiding in there all day to avoid Mason but could ignore the gnawing sensation no longer. I put on sweats and went to see what he was doing in my kitchen. Mason was at the stove dressed in his T-Shirt and boxer shorts. His back was to me and I could see the bulging muscles in his shoulders, back, and calves. Even his ass looked like you could bounce a dime off of it.

"Morning," he said without turning around.

"Morning," I replied and headed for the coffeemaker where Mason already had a pot brewing.

I glanced into the living room and saw that the blanket he'd used was neatly folded and sitting in my rocking chair with a pillow laying on top of it. I poured myself a cup of coffee and liberally heaped sugar and creamer into it. Mason turned to watch me and shook his head in disapproval. The look I shot him kept any comments he might have been about to say from coming out of his mouth. He set a plate in front of me.

"What's this?" The plate contained what looked like an omelet made from egg whites, with green peppers, onions, and mushrooms in it, along side a small bowl of oatmeal and a half a grapefruit.

"What's it look like?" He sat down at the table opposite me with his own plate and dug in.

"It looks like a diet plate. Where's the egg yolk and the cheese in this omelet? Where's the toast dripping with butter and jam? Where's the bacon? And more importantly, where'd you get all this crap? None of this stuff was in my frig."

"I know," he said, grimacing. "I couldn't find a single thing in there that wasn't a contributing factor to a heart attack and diabetes. I had to go to the store."

"You mean you left me all alone to go to the store? What would Harmon say?" I asked sarcastically. I tasted a forkful of the omelet. It wasn't bad for something cooked in vegetable spray. But I wasn't about to let Mason know that.

"It was a chance I was willing to take for the sake of my cholesterol count," he said, spooning a section of grapefruit into his mouth.

"I thought cops were supposed to be into pizza and donuts. I thought it was a job requirement."

"Well this cop is an ex marine and that overrules everything else. I'm still the same weight I was when I left basic training ten years ago. And I plan to stay that way."

"Good for you. But I'm just a civilian," I said, getting up and pulling a box of frozen waffles from my freezer and popping three into the toaster.

Mason reached over and took my plate and scraped the contents onto his own. Ten minutes later, I sat back down with a plateful of hot waffles dripping in butter and syrup.

"What's going on with the Ramey case? Is Pia Ramey still a suspect?" I asked around a mouthful of waffles. They weren't nearly as good as the ones Mama made. But they hit the spot.

"How would I know that? I've been too busy following you."

"Everyone else is working the Ramey case and you're stuck following me? How'd you get so lucky?"

"I'm the new guy, which means I get the jobs no one else wants. Plus, I think Harmon is holding out hope that Mercer will change his mind when he's feeling better and come back."

"And Harmon hasn't told you a single thing about the Ramey case?"

"Nothing I'd tell you," he said bluntly.

That pretty much ended the breakfast conversation and after I ate, showered, and dressed, I returned to my room to grade papers and get away from Mason. Every half an hour or so, I'd come out and peek into my living room to see him reading quietly, watching baseball, or snoozing. After three hours, I was getting punchy and was seriously contemplating sneaking out my bedroom window and shimmying down the tree outside my window, when I heard a loud commotion coming from outside. I flew to my front door to see Mason with his knee jammed into the back of a scrawny white man, with a long, grey ponytail, wearing a tied dyed T-shirt who was lying on his stomach. Mason had a gun to his head.

"Hey, man, what gives! I'm just trying to earn a living!" shouted the man I now recognized as Handy Randy. I'd forgotten that today was the day I'd arranged for him to fix my mailbox.

"What are you doing? Get off him, Mason. He's my handyman."

"You know this dude?" he asked, reluctantly easing his knee from Randy's back and tucking his gun back into its holster.

"Yes! Now get off of him!" Mason stood up and pulled Randy to his feet.

"Sorry. I thought you were trying to steal Kendra's mail."

"Like I said, I'm just trying to earn a living. I'll take this back to my place and pound it back into shape," Randy said, grabbing my dented up mailbox. "I'll bring it back tomorrow."

"Thanks, Randy. Sorry about that," I said to his rapidly retreating form. He wasn't exaggerating when he said he didn't like cops. Then again, he did reek of weed.

"Good work, Detective," I said sarcastically to Mason and went back into my apartment when I heard my phone ringing. I took the call in my room. It was Joy.

"Well?" she said when I answered the phone.

"Well what, Joy?"

"Don't you read the paper? Some serious shit went down last night at Venus Studios, which means the cops will find out about the connection between the studio, it's investor's, and Justin's murder. You can thank me later, Clayton."

I groaned. "Are you the one who called the police and told them there was a drug deal going down there?"

"Damned straight! I made an anonymous call. Figured if they thought drugs were involved they'd confiscate all the studio's files and shit and find the connection to Justin's death without me having to explain where I got the info."

I had to admit it was pretty smart. Too bad it didn't accomplish anything except getting me into trouble. I filled Joy in on what happened the night before and about the computer and files being stolen. She cursed and promptly hung up on me.

Around four o'clock I emerged from my room and Mason was watching a movie. I walked past him and down my steps without speaking and got into my car. Before I could start my engine, Mason was knocking on my window. I rolled it down.

"Where do you think you're going?"

"Don't worry. I'm just going to my grandmother's for dinner. I eat there every Sunday. I'll be back in a couple of hours." I started the car and Mason ran around the passenger side and got in.

"What part of me being your shadow aren't you getting?" he asked irritably. I bet he'd be in a better mood if he had more sugar and fat in his diet.

"I'm just going to my grandmother's for diner. I'm not going to sneak off. There's no need for you to tag along."

"Yeah, like I trust you. I saw you run off to your room when you got that phone call. Either I go with you, or you don't go," he said not budging from the passenger seat. I slapped the steering wheel in frustration.

"Fine," I said and started the car. "But don't you dare tell my grandmother you're a cop or that you've been assigned to protect me or she'll flip out. Got it?"

"Whatever you say," he replied with a devilish grin.

"Dr. Mason, how long have you and Kendra been dating?" asked Mama as she passed Mason the bowl of green beans.

"Just a couple of weeks, ma'am. I can't believe she hasn't mentioned me," he said, giving me a big smile and spooning a big helping onto his plate.

I was sitting next to him with a stiff smile pasted to my face. When we'd arrived at Mama's I was barely through the door before Mason introduced himself as Dr. Blake Mason, my new man. Everyone in the room was falling all over themselves to make him comfortable. Everyone except Leonard, who was uncharacteristically quiet and subdued. I figured he was just mad because an extra guest meant less pie for him.

"What kind of medicine to you practice?" asked Gwen, who hadn't taken her eyes of his biceps since he walked through the door. If he really were my man, I'd have been annoyed.

"He's a proctologist, aren't you baby," I blurted out and then turned to smile at my man whose fork had frozen inches from his open mouth.

"Bet that makes you the butt of a lot of jokes, huh?" commented Alex, who wasn't appreciating the way Gwen was openly admiring Mason's physique.

Mason didn't answer, just glared at me and shoveled more food into his face. Even with the table laden with Mama's good cooking, Mason had limited himself to chicken breast—with the skin pulled off—and not a single roll, while gravy-free mashed potatoes, and a heap of green beans rounded out the rest of his plate.

"You must be a doctor, honey. You eat so healthy,"

said Mama. "I guess I won't be able to tempt you into having a piece of my peach cobbler, will I?" Mama set the steaming pan of cobbler in the middle of the table along with a tub of her homemade honey vanilla ice cream.

"Maybe just a little," Mason said, cracking under the pressure in a major way. Just a little turned out to be four helpings of cobbler sans ice cream earning him a hearty stamp of approval from Mama.

Leonard had been so quiet during dinner I'd almost forgotten he was there. But I hadn't forgotten that I was supposed to go to his house to plan Mama's surprise birthday party.

"Are we still on for tonight?" I asked him when he carried his cobbler bowl into the kitchen where I was washing dishes. Mama, Gwen, Alex, and Mason were in the living room. Leonard looked at me like he didn't know what I was talking about.

"Huh?" he replied absently.

"You know, Mama's party? We were supposed to meet at your place tonight to plan it, remember?"

"Oh, yeah," he said, smacking the palm of his hand lightly against his forehead. "I'm gonna have to take a rain check on that, Ken. I need to visit a sick friend this evening."

"Oh, I'm sorry to hear about your friend. Maybe tomorrow then?"

"Maybe," he said and walked away leaving me to wonder just who this sick friend was and how I could sneak away from Mason to follow Leonard tonight and find out.

Mason was quiet on the drive home and when I looked

over at him, I could see his face was drawn and tight.

"What's wrong with you?"

"Stomach's bothering me," he said, grimacing.

"What do you expect? You ate four helpings of cobbler."

"You should talk. You hung in there like a champ yourself and you're not sick," he said.

"I eat like that all the time. You're just a lightweight," I said, though I was wondering why my stomach wasn't hurting like it had earlier in the week because I certainly hadn't cut back on food.

"I'm sure I'll be just fine once I spend some quality time in your bathroom."

"Just make sure you spray. There's air freshener under the bathroom sink," I replied, wrinkling my nose.

"That's not the kind of quality time I was talking about," he said and clutched his stomach.

When we got home, I went straight to my bedroom and Mason made a beeline for my bathroom. I could hear him in there retching. I felt kind of bad for him. He sounded really sick. He finally emerged looking sweaty and weak.

"You got any peppermint tea? It's a natural anti-inflammatory great for stomach aches."

I shook my head. "Sorry, all I've got is Pepto. But I can run out and get you some tea," I said hopefully, figuring I could swing back by Mama's so I could wait for Leonard to leave and follow him.

He fixed me with a hard look. "Nice try but I'm not letting you out of my sight. I'll take some Pepto."

"It's in the bathroom cabinet," I said, and stalked back to my room.

I didn't care what Mason said. I was determined to

find out who Leonard was going to see. And I didn't have much time to get out of the house, either. Leonard usually hung out at Mama's at least until nine. Then he went home to let Queenie out. It was now 8:27.

I went into my kitchen under the pretext of getting a can of Pepsi and peaked into my living room. The TV was on and Mason was lying on the couch in his boxers and undershirt. His eyes were closed and I watched the rhythmic rise and fall of his chest. He was sleeping. I looked at the clock on my microwave. It was 8:36. It would take me less than ten minutes to get back to Mama's. But I had to leave now. There was no way I could get out my front door without waking Mason up. I had no choice. I'd just have to sneak out my bedroom window.

I closed and locked my bedroom door and turned on the TV. Then I went over to the window next to my bed, unlocked it, and quietly pushed it open. There was a screen behind the window and it was rusted shut. I had to pry it loose with a nail file before I could open it and even then it would only open halfway. I pushed with all my might until it opened another few inches. Thankfully, it was enough for me to get through. I climbed out the window and turned to straddle the sill. Had it only been last night that I'd done this same thing at Venus Studio? I was just happy that sneaking out of my own home wasn't a crime.

I grabbed the largest tree limb and pulled my lower half out the window. I must have been about ten feet from the ground and my tennis shoes kicked against the trunk of the tree, until they came to rest on a lower limb. I steadied myself against the trunk and sat down on the lower limb. Then in a move I remembered from my grade school days of playing on the monkey bars, I reached down and grabbed a thick branch further down on the trunk with the intention of swinging down and jumping to the ground. I swung myself down all right. However, instead of jumping to the ground, I jumped straight into the waiting arms of Detective Blake Mason.

"Going somewhere?"

His big arms were around my waist and we were looking into each other's eyes. His were soft and brown behind his glasses. There was nothing at all soft about his body. He was still in his boxers and I was pressed closely enough to feel that his biceps weren't the only rock hard part of his body. My face flushed hotly and struggled to free myself.

"Let go of me!"

He loosened his grip and I slid down the length of his body, almost falling when my feet hit the ground. He caught me before I landed on my ass and then effortlessly slung me over his shoulder and carried me kicking and screaming back up the steps and into my apartment.

"You aren't nearly as slick as you think you are," he said as he carried me to my bedroom, pausing in the living room only long enough to grab something from his pants pocket that I couldn't see.

"What are you doing? What have you got?" I tried to see what he had in his hand.

"You'll see," he said and tossed me onto the bed. "I should have done this as soon as we walked through the door." He grabbed my right wrist and clamped a handcuff onto it then cuffed the other end to my bedpost.

"You have got to be kidding me!" I pulled on the cuff trying hard to free myself. "This is against the law! You can't do this to me!"

"Yes, I can. My job is to protect you by any means necessary and since you've already proven that you can't be trusted, I have no other choice but to restrain you."

"Come on, Mason! This isn't necessary!"

"Good night. Sleep tight. I hope the bedbugs bite," he said and started to shut my bedroom door.

"Wait!" I called out. He paused in the doorway looking impatient. "I had a very good reason to sneak out and it has nothing to do with the Ramey case, I swear."

"I'm waiting," he said, leaning against the door jam.

I quickly filled him in on my suspicions about Leonard, my fears for my grandmother, and my desire to find out who Leonard was going to see that night. The entire time I was talking, I could see the skepticism manifesting on Mason's face by the way his eyebrow shot up and the corner of his mouth lifted into a smirk.

"You really think that little old dude at dinner is a stone cold killer who ran over his own wife and left her for dead?"

"That's what I'm trying to find out if you'll unlock these handcuffs," I said pulling on the cuffs.

He turned and left.

"Mason! Get back here and unlock me or I'm filing police brutality charges against you! Mason!"

He came back a few minutes later and was fully dressed, which wasn't a good sign. "Pipe down. I had to put my clothes back on." He unlocked the cuffs. I got up and immediately grabbed my purse and keys.

"Where do you think you're going?" I asked as he proceeded to follow me out to my car.

"Like I said, I'm not letting you out of my sight. So if you're going on some wild goose chase, I'm riding shotgun, end of discussion."

ELEVEN

When we got back to Mama's house Leonard's car was already gone. It was nine o'clock on the dot. He must have left early leaving me no choice but to go to his house. Leonard lived in a half double on Oakleaf Avenue. As I pulled onto his street, I could see Leonard in his front yard with Queenie on her leash. She was sniffing round the yard looking for the perfect spot to do her business. I parked four doors down from his house and turned off the engine.

"What are we waiting for?" asked Mason.

"He told me he couldn't plan Mama's birthday party with me this evening because he was visiting a sick friend. I want to know if he's telling the truth or if he's stepping out on my grandmother."

"If he is, don't you think that should be between the two of them? Maybe they're not an exclusive couple."

"My grandmother is almost 73. She's old fashioned. She not into man sharing."

"Ever thought maybe you're the problem? And that

he just doesn't like you and lied so he wouldn't hurt your feelings."

My head whipped around. I started to say something smart aleck but could see that Mason was in pain. Beads of sweat had formed on his forehead. He was clutching his middle.

"Is your stomach still hurting? I thought you took some Pepto?"

"I did and it worked for all of ten minutes."

"Maybe I should take you back to my place."

"Don't even think about trying to ditch me. Besides, the suspect is on the move," he said, pointing at Leonard's house. Leonard's car was pulling away from the curb.

I started my car and followed him. He was a very slow driver and I had to purposefully hang back so he wouldn't notice me behind him. He stopped at a gas station and got gas, then to the liquor store. Each stop I had to figure out where to park so he wouldn't see me. Tailing people wasn't as easy as it looked. We finally ended up on the north side of Willow. Leonard pulled into the Jefferson Park housing project, parked in front of a building I was familiar with, and went inside. It was Pia's aunt Janette's building. I stared up at Janette's third floor window. The light was on and the curtains were open. I could see Leonard standing in her living room. He hadn't lied after all. He was visiting someone sick. I was relieved and annoyed at the same time. I didn't wonder how they knew each other. In Willow everyone was just a person away from knowing everyone else.

"What's he doing?" asked Mason.

"Visiting a sick friend," I said grudgingly. Mason

let out a pained laugh.

I looked up at the window again as I started up the car to go and saw Leonard handing Janette the bag of liquor he'd bought along with what looked like a big wad of cash. The scene reminded me of the one I'd witnessed of Mama giving Leonard money. Was this fool giving Pia's aunt my grandmother's money? Janette snatched the money out of Leonard's hand and immediately started counting it. He was staring at her with an expression that was very close to hatred. It definitely wasn't a look you'd give a friend, especially a sick one. I turned off the ignition and Mason looked over at me.

"I need to go inside. Are you coming?"

"Why? I thought you said he was just visiting a friend?" Mason said, trying to sit up.

"Yeah, but there's something off about this. I want to go see if I can listen to what they're talking about."

Mason once again tried to sit up but the effort was too much for him and he fell back against the seat.

"Damn, this gastritis is kicking my ass. You'll have to go without me," he said, shaking his head. He was sweating even more profusely.

"You look awful, Mason. I need to take you to the emergency room."

"No!" he said, putting up a hand. "We're already here. So just do what you need to do and hurry up so we can get out of here." Mason must really be in pain to allow me to go forth and snoop with his blessing.

"Are you sure?"

"Go! And if you get caught, pretend you don't know me," he said. I got out of the car.

I looked up at Janette's window and saw that she

and Leonard were gone. They must be in another room. Janette's apartment only had four rooms and going by the look of loathing he'd been giving her, I doubted seriously they'd gone to the bedroom. I was hoping they were in the kitchen. I walked around to the back where an ancient rusted out fire escape zigzagged up the back of the building. One of the landings was right next to Janette's kitchen window, which was open about two inches. Though the kitchen curtains were closed, I could see the silhouettes of two people next to the window.

I started up the steps of the fire escape and it creaked ominously and swayed a little bit. Heading up to the third story landing probably wasn't such a good idea. But if I wanted to know what Leonard and Janette were talking about, I had no choice. I climbed the remaining steps, practically hugging the building as I went. I finally reached the landing next to Janette's window and knelt down so I could hear.

"This is the last time, Netty," I heard Leonard say.

"That's what you said the last time, and the time before that, and the time before that," Janette replied and then laughed. "Sure you don't want some of this?"

"That stuff's what got me into this mess in the first place and if you was smart, you'd give it up, too. It's nothing but trouble."

"What the hell happened to you, Leonard? You used to be so much fun back in the day. Now, you're always preaching to me like you of all people got room to talk."

"You know damned well what happened. You know better than I do what happened since I still can't remember much about that night."

"All you need to remember is how I helped you out. And that's all you need to remember. You owe me."

"And what about this other mess you got cooked up? How can you do what you're doing and still look at yourself in the mirror?"

"The same way you get up and look at yourself in the mirror everyday for the past fifteen years. Don't you dare judge me, Leonard Duncan! I'm doing what I've got to do."

"No, Netty, it ain't the same, and you know it. What I did was an accident. You're hurting people on purpose."

"All I'm doing is robbing Peter to pay Paul. And if you ever loved anyone but your damned self, you'd understand that. As for that accident shit, well, if that's what gets you through the night, baby, then you go ahead and keep thinking that. But don't forget that I was there and I saw what happened and it sure as hell wasn't an accident."

I felt a burning sensation in the pit of my stomach as I realized they must have been talking about the night Leonard's wife had been killed. Joy had been right. Leonard had killed his wife, run her down in cold blood. And Janette Ramey must have been in the car when he'd done it. She'd helped him cover it up. Was that why he was giving her liquor and money, to keep her quiet? The fire escape creaked and swayed again as I leaned forward to try and hear more. But I couldn't hear anything else. They must have moved to another room. I'd heard enough anyway. I headed back to my car.

I could hear loud retching noises as I approached

my car. Mason wasn't in my passenger seat. I ran around to the other side of the car to find him violently vomiting into the bushes. A sour stench hit me in the face as I knelt down next to him and touched his arm. He looked up at me and his pupils were dilated. He was drenched in sweat and fell over onto his side. I thought he'd passed out.

"Mason!" I yelled, shaking him. He groaned but didn't open his eyes. "Can you stand?" I said, putting my hands underneath his armpits and trying to lift him to his feet. He was dead weight and all I succeeded in doing was turning him onto his back.

"Mason, can you hear me? I need you to help me out here. I need to get you back into the car so I can take you to the emergency room."

Mason groaned then reached out and grabbed the back door handle of my car and made an attempt to pull himself to his feet. With me pushing him up from behind, I was finally able to get him upright enough to shove him back into the passenger seat where he promptly passed out.

I rushed him the hospital. Two emergency staff members were able to get him out of my car and onto a stretcher. I jogged along side as they quickly wheeled him into the hospital.

"I think he might have food poisoning," I told the young freckled face female doctor attending him.

"Vomiting and diarrhea?" she asked while she checked Mason's vital signs.

"Vomiting, yes, but I don't know about diarrhea," I told her.

"Thanks for the info," she said brusquely.

"Will he be okay?" The doctor didn't answer me.

Instead, a nurse blocked my path as I tried to follow the stretcher into the examining room.

"Sorry, ma'am, but I'll have to ask you to wait in the waiting room. Someone will be out to speak with you shortly.

I watched them wheel Mason away unable to shake the feeling that somehow this was my fault.

The next morning I was up bright and early to head back to the hospital before work. I'd gotten home from the hospital around midnight. The only thing they'd tell me about Mason was that he'd had his stomach pumped and would have to be admitted. They'd asked me what he eaten that day. Aside from breakfast, we'd eaten the same thing. So what ever made him sick he must have eaten earlier in the day? I bagged up everything that he'd eaten for breakfast and took it with me to the hospital. I arrived to find Harmon waiting outside Mason room talking to a doctor, a different one from the one who'd treated him in the emergency room.

"What the hell happened last night?" Harmon growled at me. The doctor looked down at the floor and wisely walked away.

"Mason has food poisoning. Didn't the doctor tell you?"

"I don't know where you're getting your information from but detective Mason does not have food poisoning. He's been intentionally poisoned with some kind of toxin."

The bag of food I was carrying slipped though my trembling fingers and fell to the floor. "Poisoned," I whispered. "But we were together all day long. How could he have been poisoned?"

"That's what I'm asking you."

"How would I know?" I snapped then realized what she was getting at. "You think I had something to do with this?"

Harmon jumped in my face. "All I know is that a police detective is in critical condition after spending the day with you. Are you sure you didn't slip him a little something to make him sick so you could sneak away from him and stick your nose in police matters that don't involve you?"

"Go to hell!" I said and was about to push her out of my face until I saw the look in her eyes.

She wanted me to put my hands on her so she could arrest me for assaulting an officer. I stepped back and took a deep breath. I bent down and picked up the bag and shoved it into her arms.

"We had the exact same things to eat and drink for dinner at my grandmother's and neither me or my family is sick. This bag has what he ate for breakfast. I didn't see him eat or drink anything else but if you want to send someone to check out my apartment, knock yourself out. I've got nothing to hide."

Harmon looked down at the bag and back at me then did something that signaled the coming apocalypse. She apologized.

"What did you say?" I asked, leaning forward. I couldn't have heard her right.

"I'm sorry," she said again louder this time and then shook her head like she was trying to clear it. "I know you didn't poison Detective Mason. I've had about two hours of sleep in the past forty-eight hours and I'm dead on my feet."

Now that I had a chance to get a good look at her I

could see that she was exhausted.

"That's okay," I said, feeling a little uncomfortable to be seeing this side of her.

"You'll be happy to know that your friend, Pia Ramey, is off the hook for her father's murder."

"Seriously?"

Harmon nodded and then went to sit down in the waiting area across from Mason's room. I joined her.

"We picked up Lauren Ramey this morning trying to board a flight to Mexico. She had almost three hundred thousand dollars in her suitcase and the gun she used to kill Elton Paul was in a car she rented that we found in the airport parking lot. Seems Paul had cheated her out of sixteen years worth of royalties for her videos. We're talking millions of dollars. When she confronted him about wanting her money, he told her she'd have to earn it on her back as Destiny Sunset. She snapped and shot him then cleaned out the safe and ran."

That explained why Lauren looked so stunned when I'd told her about her movies still being moneymakers. She had no idea Paul owed her money and her being broke only added to her desperation. I bet she made a beeline straight for Venus Studios right after she talked to me.

"You find the stun gun she used on me? I'd like to file assault charges against her."

"We're still looking for it along with the computer and files."

"Has she confessed to murdering her husband?"

"No. It's only a matter of time before she does. The threat of the death penalty usually works wonders."

"Well, if she had a gun, why didn't she just shoot

Justin? Why bash him over the head with a pineapple sculpture? It's so messy. That doesn't seem like her style. Plus, she has the upper body strength of a two year-old," I said, remembering how hard it had been for Lauren to cut through that purple twine on the painting Pia's mother sent her.

Harmon sighed wearily. She was getting exasperated. "Three words, Ms. Clayton, crime of passion. If you're angry enough, you can do just about anything. She probably found out she'd been cut out of her husband's will and confronted him about it. After she killed him, and found out about Justin Ramey's argument with his daughter Pia, all she had to do was sit back and let Pia take the blame."

It still didn't sound right to me. If Lauren had known about being cut out of Justin's will the night he died, then why would she have been at the gallery sorting through receipts days after Justin's death? If she already knew the gallery hadn't been left to her, why bother? If she knew the gallery didn't belong to her, why bother having Link come over to lock the dumpster to keep the rats out? And if Lauren had just wanted the money Elton Paul owed her, why would she take the computer and files? I didn't think Harmon was in any mood to have her theories questioned so I kept my doubts to myself and got up to go.

"Can I see Mason before I leave?"

Harmon shook her head. "He's in intensive care and can't have visitors."

"Will you keep me posted on how he's doing?"

"Of course." She stood up and walked off down the hall with the bag of food.

I was on my way to the parking lot when Pia's yellow Jeep pulled up in front of the hospital. I could see her aunt Janette sitting in the front seat. She must be dropping her off for her chemo treatment. I headed over to say hello.

"Hey, Kendra," said Pia when she spotted me. She actually looked happy to see me for once.

"I was here visiting a sick friend and heard from Detective Harmon that you're off the hook for your father's murder. I'm so happy for you."

"Thanks for everything you did, Kendra," Pia said, coming over to give me a big hug. "I know I acted like a spoiled brat. But I was just scared."

"No harm done," I said. "I'm just glad it's over."

"I knew that skinny heifer was no good," said Janette as Pia helped her out of the car. "I hope they put her butt under the jail for what she did. Justin and I may not have been close, but he was still my brother. He didn't deserve to die such a horrible death."

Neither did Lila Duncan, I thought, thinking about the conversation I'd overheard between Janette and Leonard. Had she really helped Leonard cover up his wife's murder? Knowing what I knew, I wasn't quite able to look Janette Ramey in the eye.

"Call me when you're ready, Aunt J., and I'll come back and pick you up."

"That won't be necessary, honey," said Janette, squeezing Pia's hand. "I've got some errands to run when I leave here. I can get a cab home."

"It's no problem. I'm not busy today. I can. . ."

"Pia, I'm not helpless! I said I could get a cab home!" Janette snapped. Pia looked startled but didn't argue.

"I'll see you two later," I said. Pia gave me and embarrassed smile and Janette simply nodded.

I watched the two of them head inside the hospital and went to my car. By the time I got in and started the ignition, Pia was back in her Jeep and pulling off. I started to pull off too when I spotted Janette Ramey peaking out from inside the hospital's front entrance, watching her niece leave. I turned off the ignition and watched Janette. She watched until Pia's Jeep was completely out of sight, and then left the hospital and walked down to the bus stop. A minute later, the bus pulled up and Janette got on. Where was she going? I quickly started my car and followed the bus for about six blocks before it stopped across the street from the Spotlight Bar and Grill. Janette got off and went inside. I started to go inside, too, when I realized I was almost late for work.

Work was chaotic that day. I was so busy I barely had time to breathe let alone wonder just what Janette Ramey was up to and why she had skipped her chemo treatment. Was that why she didn't look like she was getting any better and was still so thin and frail looking? Was she skipping her treatments so she could go drink? I wondered if her drinking was affecting the potency of her medication. I toyed with the idea of telling Pia but figured it was none of my business. I had other worries, namely Detective Blake Mason. I was worried to death about how Mason was doing. I hadn't heard a word from Harmon all morning. And when I finally called the hospital to check on him, they wouldn't give me any info other than that he was still in ICU.

"I'll be glad when Margery comes back to work," commented my coworker, Rhonda Hammond.

Rhonda taught math at the literacy center and since most of our students needed a lot of math help, Rhonda had been relying on Margery to help her grade math assignments when she wasn't tutoring. When Margery wasn't there it doubled Rhonda's workload.

"Are you missing her or her cookies?" I asked absently. My thoughts were elsewhere.

"Both," she said and we laughed.

"Any idea how long she'll be out?"

"Whatever stomach bug she and her mother had last week really hit her mother hard. Margery's fine but her mom's still really sick," Rhonda said.

"Where do they live? Maybe I should go out and check on them," I said.

"Oh, I wouldn't go out there, Kendra. They live in that trailer park out by the fairgrounds. That neighborhood is really dicey. Those people out there are kind of scary," said Rhonda like she had a bad taste in her mouth.

"Really," I said, giving her a hard look and wondering if she meant they were scary because they were poor.

I liked Rhonda a lot but being an affluent doctor's wife had turned her into a bit of a snob. She seemed to have forgotten that she'd come from a humble background and had grown up in a dicey neighborhood in a little house that was only a step above a trailer.

"Well, let me know if you decide to go out there and I'll go with you," she added quickly when she saw the look on my face, then got busy grading papers.

When lunchtime rolled around, I headed back to

the hospital to check on Mason and was happy to learn that he'd been moved to a regular room. But I still couldn't see him because I wasn't a family member and since he'd been poisoned, he was under police guard. I left and drove past the Spotlight Bar and Grill in time to see Janette Ramey lurch out of the bar and stumble across the street to the bus stop. I couldn't believe she'd been in there drinking for four hours. I pulled up to the bus stop and rolled down my passenger side window.

"Ms. Ramey, do you need a ride home?" She looked good and toasted and leaned inside the window squinting at me.

"Hey, girlfriend! How you doin'?" She hollered filling my car with the smell of alcohol. If I lit a match we'd go up in flames.

"Just Fine, Ms. Ramey. Why don't you get in so I can take you home?"

"Aw, you so sweet," she said, flinging my car door open so hard it almost hit the pole of the stop sign.

She got into the car and threw her arms around me. "You so nice. Thank you, girlfriend, thank you," she slurred. I gently pushed her away. She reeked of liquor, sweat, and cigarettes. It took me five minutes to get her settled into the seat so I could fasten the seat belt. She was as squirmy as a toddler.

Once we were on our way, I figured now would be a good time to ask her some questions. "Ms. Ramey, do you know a man named Leonard Duncan?"

"I know lots a men, honey child," she said, trying to wink but closing both eyes. "I used to be stacked back in the day. All the men were after me."

I was about to ask her if she knew Lila Duncan when she burst into her own loud, off key rendition of

Brick House by the Commodore's.

"*I'm mighty mighty just lettin' it all hang out! I'm a brick. . . do. . . do. . . do. . house! Yeah! That was me, back in the day! I was built like an Amazon! I was a brick . . do. . .do. . .do. . . house!*" she yelled out the window.

I wished I had a brick to shut her up and quickly pressed the button to close the window. She was still singing and humming when I pulled into the parking lot in front of her building. I had to help her out of the car. Once the fresh air hit her, she stopped singing and started dancing.

"Ooh, girl, and I could dance, too, back in the day. I could do the bump," she said, bumping my hip with her bony one. "And the double bump, and the robot," she said, stopping mid step, stiffening up, and moving her arms in jerky robotic motions. "And the hustle." She spun around and tried to clap, missing her hands by a mile and losing her balance. I had to catch her before she hit the ground. "And the funky chicken!" She flapped her thin arms like a chicken and shook her narrow tail feather.

"That's good, Ms. Ramey," I said, stifling laughter as I guided her towards the entrance to her building.

She fumbled in her purse forever before finding her door key. All the singing, dancing and drinking must have worn her out, because once we were through the door, she made a beeline straight for the couch where she lay down and fell fast asleep. Before I even closed the apartment door she was snoring loudly and filling the small apartment with the smell of her breath. There was a quilt draped over the back of the couch and I covered her up with it.

I should have just left and gone back to work since I only had about twenty minutes left on my lunch hour. Instead, I snooped around. In my book there was always time to be nosy, especially when it involved a potential murder cover up. Janette didn't have much to snoop through in the living room. I looked through the kitchen drawers an only found expired coupons, menus for take out, past due bills, old batteries, broken pens, an assortment of rubber bands and bobby pins, and half empty spools of thread. Her cabinets held canned soup and vegetables, and her fridge was mostly bare except for a carton of milk, a half a dozen eggs, and a dried up pork chop on a plate.

I checked to make sure she was still asleep on my way down the hall to the bathroom. She was still out like a light. Janette's bathroom was lime green with a fuzzy white cover on the toilet lid, a fuzzy white rug in front of the bathtub, and a green plastic shower curtain trimmed in white tassels. The cabinet under the sink was filled with toilet paper—the cheap one ply variety—soap, and cleaning supplies. It was the cabinet above the sink that I found the most interesting. It wasn't what was in the cabinet that was so telling, as it was filled with the usual Band-aids, toothpaste and toothbrush, and deodorant. It was what *wasn't* in the cabinet. There was no medicine. None. No cough syrup, no antacids, no high blood pressure medicine, no aspirin, and more importantly, no cancer meds. No wonder Janette had skipped her chemo treatment. She didn't have cancer.

TWELVE

Janette Ramey was faking having cancer. That was what Leonard had been talking about the night before when he'd asked her how she could look at herself in the mirror. She was playing on Pia's sympathies to get money out of her. How sick. And Pia had no idea. Justin Ramey must have known what was up and that's why he refused to give her any money. But what was she doing with the money? Drinking it up? From the looks of her apartment she sure wasn't spending it on material things.

I heard Janette moan and stuck my head around the corner to see her turning over in her sleep. I went next door to her bedroom. Like the living room it was sparsely furnished with dingy looking beige carpet, a large bed with a cheap blue spread, and a chest of drawers that was propped up on one side with a phone book and had a small TV perched on top of it. There was nightstand next her bed that had a phone sitting on it. It also had a framed photo sitting next to it. I picked it up.

It was a picture of Janette when she was much younger. She had a little boy who looked about three years old perched on one hip. I recognized the kid as Link. He was even dressed in little Dockers and a Polo shirt back then, poor kid. Janette was smiling but Link was crying. There was a large house in the background. It was Justin Ramey's house. I knew Janette used to babysit for Link and Pia and figured this must have been taken before Pia was born.

I hunted through the drawers of the nightstand looking for anything to connect Janette and Leonard to Lila's death and came up empty. Next, I turned my attention to the chest of drawers. The first five drawers contained clothes and underwear. The bottom drawer was empty. I went over to the closet, which was full of outdated clothes and shoes from the seventies. There was an assortment of hats and purses on the top shelf. One large hatbox in particular caught my eye and I pulled it down. Inside were Janette's high school diploma, and the rental agreement for her apartment. There were also insurance papers listing her as the sole recipient of a ten thousand dollar life insurance policy of a Gloria Ramey—who must have been her mother, and the title to a 1982 blue Cadillac. Bingo!

The reason why the police were never able to find a Cadillac registered to Leonard Duncan was because legally it wasn't his car. The Cadillac had belonged to Janette. She helped him out by not saying a word about the car being in her name. I heard movement in the living room and held my breath as I watched Janette stumble down the hallway into the bathroom. I quickly stuffed everything except the title to the car back into the hat box and noticed another piece of paper was stuck to the back of her diploma. It was a birth certificate, a birth certificate for a baby boy born in 1971 listing Janette Ramey as his mother. The father was listed as unknown. The baby's name was Lincoln Kennedy Ramey. So, Link was Janette's son.

I heard the toilet flush and hurriedly put the box back. I rushed out of the bedroom but stopped when I heard loud snoring coming from the bathroom. I pushed the door open and saw Janette Ramey still sitting on the toilet fast asleep with her skirt pulled up around her waist and her panties rolled down around her ankles. Talk about an image I didn't need burned into my retinas. I closed the bathroom door and went back to work. Along the way, I wondered what happened to the Cadillac? If she'd sold it, there'd be a record of it at the Clerk of Courts title office. But that would have been risky since the police would have been on the look out for any transactions involving blue Cadillacs.

If a new owner had wanted to get the damage from the hit and run fixed, it would have raised red flags since Lila's murder would have been all over the news. The sale could have easily been traced back to Janette. The easiest thing to do would have been to wait until everything died down, and then scrap the car for parts. There was only one place to go in Willow where old cars go to die, Boo Boo's Junkyard. My little blue Nova now resided at Boo Boo's. Maybe it was time to pay my old car a visit.

An old curmudgeon named Nipsy Sheepshanks owned Boo Boo's Junkyard. To be fair, I'd be pretty pissed off all the time, too, if that were my name. And when I say Nipsy Sheepshanks is a curmudgeon, I'm not talking about an irritable, yet lovable old man, who was gruff on the outside but deep down inside, had a heart of gold. I'm talking about a mean old bastard who made Ebenezer Scrooge look like Mr. Rogers. In other words, Fred Sanford he was not. My uncle Alex still likes to tell the story about when he and his late best friend, Jesse Milton, were teenagers and used to torment Sheepshanks beloved Doberman and business namesake, Boo Boo, by standing just out of the dog's reach so they could watch him run snarling and growling towards them only to be jerked backwards off his feet when he reached the end of his chain. Cruel, I know, but Sheepshanks more then got back at them.

One day when Alex and Jesse showed up at the junkyard for their favorite sport of Boo Boo baiting, they were surprised and shocked to discover that Boo Boo's chain had been lengthened. Alex was the one who ended up with an ass full of Doberman teeth. And he was the lucky one. Jesse thought he'd gotten away free until he climbed back over the fence and jumped down on top of a wasp's nest that Sheepshanks had set under it. He ended up in the hospital covered in stings after almost dying of anaphylactic shock. After that, no one bothered Boo Boo again.

I headed out to the junkyard after work thinking about that story and wondering why in the hell I was going out to Boo Boo's. Sheepshanks was barely civil to anybody and was even less so to women, who he thought were stupid. To add to the fun of dealing with him when my car had been trashed back in the spring, I had to endure him asking me endless questions about the state of Alex's ass. But on the plus side, Boo Boo died years ago never to be replaced.

I pulled into the junkyard's lot and got out. Most of the junk in Boo Boo's junkyard was made up of old cars, and car parts, which were piled in sky-high mounds all over the lot. Sheepshanks lived in an aluminum trailer at the back of the property and could usually be found sitting in a lawn chair in front of the trailer chewing tobacco and spitting it into an old coffee can. And when he had an unwanted visitor, as in anyone who came onto the lot, he'd aim at their shoes instead. I was just going to take a quick look around, and since I wasn't buying anything, I hoped I wouldn't have to see Mr. Sheepshanks.

Upon getting out of my car I was immediately struck by the acrid stench of burning tires. It was so strong it made my eyes water. I could feel the smell seeping into my clothes and hair. There was thick black smoke coming from somewhere in back of the lot near Mr. Sheepshanks trailer. Everyone knew that once a month Nipsy Sheepshanks got rid of excess tires on his lot by burning them earning him the eternal scorn of local environmentalists, who unwisely picketed in front of the junkyard once, only to be pelted with flaming bags of crap. Whether it was human or animal excrement has always been a topic of debate. Happy that the old buzzard would be too busy releasing carcinogens into the air to harass me, I took a look around.

The junkyard was at least as big as a football field maybe larger and it was easy to get lost. There seemed to be no rhyme or reason as to how it was laid out. There were paths that weaved in between the rows and rows of junk leading all the way back to Sheepshank's trailer, and some paths that went in circles, or led to dead ends. Older junk was piled towards the back of the lot, while the newer stuff was up front. Since the last time I'd been here, he seemed to have acquired a good many more totaled cars. I didn't even want to think about where Janette Ramey's blue Cadillac could be after fifteen years, if it was even here.

I walked a good fifty feet and the only Cadillac I'd seen so far was a white, rusted out, 1980 Bonneville. I walked another ten feet and saw a sight that almost broke my heart. It was my little blue Nova sitting up on cinderblocks minus all its tires and front windshield. It looked so sad and forlorn I could have cried, or would have cried had I not spotted something else that made me freak out. It was the biggest Doberman Pincher I'd ever seen perched on top of an old station wagon. The dog was growling deep in his throat with his lips pulled back over his teeth. He was wearing a black collar with spikes on it. He seemed poised to lunge for my throat. I turned to run and ran right into Nipsy Sheepshanks. Great!

"You damned fool! Didn't anyone ever tell you not to run from a dog unless you wanna be chased?" He pulled a treat from his pocket and threw it over the dog's head and it jumped down off the car and disappeared. The dog must have been a new acquisition from my last visit.

Sheepshanks was a tall, hulking, round-shouldered man that reminded me of a more verbose version of Lurch from the Addams Family. He was wearing a torn white tobacco stained T-shirt and dirty jeans. He was carrying a tire. His face arms and hands were filthy and that, combined with his brown teeth and pungent smell of sweat, tobacco, and body odor, made him someone I wouldn't want to run into in the daytime let alone at night, yet here he was.

"What kind on an idiot would stand around and let them self be mauled by a vicious dog?" I snapped back.

"Whadaya want? I'm busy." He spit a slimy brown hocker at my feet and I jumped back.

"Do you have any 1982 Cadillacs here?"

"Do you see all this shit?" he said, gesturing around him. "You think I remember every dang blasted car on this lot?"

"Well what else have you got to do?" I mumbled.

"I heard that. And since you wanna be so sassy, next time Boo Boo 2 has ya cornered, I'm gonna let him have your ass. How 'bout that?"

Boo Boo 2? "All you have to do is answer a simple question, Mr. Sheepshanks, and I'll be out of your hair," I said, forgetting that he had no hair and was apparently very sensitive about it.

"You makin' fun a me? You tryin' to be funny? Is that it?" He rubbed his baldhead with a dirty hand.

"No! All I want to know is if you've got any 1982 Cadillacs."

"Try out back by the fence and steer clear of Boo Boo 2 unless you wanna end up with a chunk tore outta of your ass like your uncle." He walked away chuckling and mumbling to himself.

With the can of pepper spray from my purse clutched in my hand to ward of Boo Boo 2, I wandered around that smelly lot for almost two hours with no luck. In all that time, I found ten Cadillacs, three black, three silver, two brown, one gold, one pink, no blue, and none of them from 1982. Tired and disappointed, I was headed back to my car when I spotted a storage unit facility across the road. I'd seen it there before but never paid it much mind. There were six rows of twelve units. Each unit was the size of a small garage, the perfect place to hide a car.

I drove across the road and parked in front of the small office of SSSS, which stood for Storage Solutions Self-Storage Units, and even had a green snake as the logo. I went inside. There was a woman who looked about fifty behind a counter wearing a brown shirt with the company's snake logo on the front pocket. The walls to my left and right had small built in post office boxes. Each box was numbered. There was a fan on full blast sitting on the counter that did little to alleviate the stifling heat in the office or the acrid stench coming from across the road. I wondered why anyone would open a business across from a junkyard.

"Can I help you?" asked the woman. She was short and stocky with long white hair pulled into a ponytail. She squinted at me heavily behind glasses with thick lenses.

When she walked up to the counter I could see she had something thick and greasy smeared all over and underneath her red bulbous nose. She was also missing a front tooth. She noticed me looking at her nose and laughed.

"It's Vicks VapoRub. It's the only way I can survive that bastard Sheepshank's tire burning day. Otherwise, I'd have to close and lose a day's worth of business. What can I help you with? You need a unit?"

"No. But my aunt has a unit here and she's been sick. She needs me to get something for her and was supposed to call to see if it would be okay for me to get into her storage unit?"

"Depends. Anyone besides the owner who needs access to a unit needs to be included in writing on the rental agreement. What's the name?"

"Janette Ramey."

She went to a large, green metal file cabinet underneath the office's one large window and riffled through some files holding some of then up to her face so she could see the names and finally pulling out a folder and opening it. She carried it over the counter tripping over a step stool and falling against the counter and knocking the fan to the floor almost on top of my foot. I jumped back just in time.

"Shoot!" she exclaimed in embarrassment. I'm blind as a bat. That fan didn't get you did it?"

"I'm alright. It's okay." I assured her. She slapped the file onto the counter.

"Sorry, only person listed on the rental agreement as having access to Ms. Ramey's unit is Ms. Ramey. If she wants you to have access, she'll need to come out here in person and add your name to her rental agreement."

"Thanks. I'll let her know," I said and turned to go feeling quite satisfied with myself. Janette Ramey must have hidden the Cadillac Leonard used to run over his wife in her storage unit. Now, how could I get in there to find out for certain?

"You sure I can't interest you in a unit? We're running a special. Sign a year long lease and get your first two months for free."

"How much does it cost to rent a storage unit?" The woman pointed at a sign on the wall of rental rates based on the size of the unit and I was stunned to see that the cost per month of the largest unit was almost as much as my rent. I let out a low whistle.

"Just think of it as an investment," said the woman. Yeah, right. If I paid that much per month for a storage unit the only thing I'd be investing in is being broke.

"I'll have to think about it. Thanks for you're help."

"The special ends tomorrow and I'll be here until seven if you change your mind."

Next, I headed to a place I really didn't want to go but had no choice. I needed info on Janette Ramey and the only other place I knew I could get it was the Spotlight Bar and Grill. Most of the people, who frequent the "Spot" as it's known around town, had been drinking there for years. Janette was most likely a regular, and since she was a friend of Leonard's, he'd probably been one too. I just hoped I could find someone who may have remembered seeing one or both of them in the bar the night of Lila Duncan's murder.

I was halfway back into town when my cell phone rang. It was Harmon and she had baffling news.

"What do you mean the food I gave you tested negative for poison?"

"I'm just telling you what the tests revealed. Now, please think. Are you sure you didn't see Detective Mason eating anything other than what you described?"

I thought hard but came up empty. But just because I didn't see him, didn't mean he couldn't have eaten something else. "When I woke up yesterday morning, he'd already been to the grocery. He could have stopped somewhere on his way to or from the store." I heard Harmon sigh and then added. "Is Mason conscious? Can't you ask him what he ate?"

"He's in and out and what he's saying doesn't make sense. He keeps babbling about ten horses."

"Ten horses?"

"We have no idea what he's talking about and when we try and push him for further info, he gets very agitated. I'll let you know if anything changes," she said and hung up.

When I arrived at the Spot, business was just starting to pick up with people just getting off from work, mainly factory workers who got off between 3:30 and 4, and were still dressed in their uniforms. From the few times I'd been there, I knew the hardcore patrons wouldn't be in until later. The Dells' *"Stay in My Corner"* was playing on the ancient jukebox when I walked in and the air wasn't nearly as thick as it usually was with cigar and cigarette smoke. I sat down at the bar and ordered a Pepsi. The bartender, a sixtyish bald black man with a thick white mustache and muscular forearms sat it on a coaster in front of me. I smiled when I noticed he'd put a cherry in it.

"Don't think I seen you in here before, young lady. This your first time?" His voice was a deep velvety baritone that made me wonder if he sang.

"Nope. I've been here a few times before."

"Really," he said, giving me an appraising look. "Humph. Musta been on my day off," he said with a flirty wink.

"How long have you worked here?" I took a sip of the Pepsi. It was ice cold.

"Oh, I'd say off and on 'bout twenty years. I took early retirement from Wright Patt when I was fifty and started working here permanent part-time. Don't pay squat but it keeps me busy and in pocket change."

"If you've been here that long, I bet you'd know a friend of mine," I said.

"I know everybody, honey. Who's your friend?"

"Leonard Duncan."

"You know Lenny? Man, I haven't seen Lenny Duncan in years. How's he doin'?"

"He's fine," I said. "He's dating my grandma," I added truthfully just in case he wondered how I knew Leonard.

"Well good for him. I haven't seen that cat since his old lady got killed in that hit and run. Course his runnin' buddy old drunk Netty Ramey is in here everyday proppin' up the bar and runnin' her dang mouth. Poor Netty," he said, chuckling and shaking his head.

"Why poor Netty?"

He chuckled again and wiped a wet spot on the counter. "Netty was the life of the party back in the day. Good lookin'. I mean she was built like a brick shit house. No offense," he added quickly.

"None taken."

"That girl could dance her behind off and drink every dude in here under the bar."

"Sounds like she was a lot of fun."

"She was," he said then topped off my Pepsi. "But comes a time when the party's over and you got to go home. Ain't nothin' sadder than a party girl who stayed at the party too long. And that's Netty Ramey right down to the ground."

"And she was friends with Leonard?"

"It was all she could be. See, we all grew up together out in Jefferson Park. Lenny used to hang with my older brother, Hank, and they'd let me tag along. Netty was younger than all of us but she set her sights on Lenny Duncan early on. Followed him around like a puppy," he said, laughing.

"Was the feeling mutual?"

"No. Lenny thought Netty was real cute. Kinda like the little sister he never had. But he never had the hots for her. Always said he needed a woman who he could take home to his mama and Netty was too wild. When he married Lila Jones it broke Netty's heart. But she didn't give up."

"You mean she kept chasing him after he was married?"

"Yep. Course after a few years married to Lila, the barracuda, Lenny welcomed the attention, which was just plain wrong if you ask me."

"He was cheating with Netty?"

"Don't know that for a fact, young lady. So, don't get me to lyin'. But Netty always reminded me of one a those kids from school who used to give other kids candy to play with 'em."

"She used money to buy affection?"

"That's Netty. She was a beautiful lady and had everything going for her, but when it came to men she thought she had to have something more to keep 'em. And they'd stay for a while but when Netty's dough ran out. They'd be in the wind."

"She did this with Leonard, too?"

The bartender nodded his head. "That's what I thought was so messed up. Lenny didn't love Netty but he took money and gifts from her. Whenever they were in here he never had to pay for a single drink. She always paid. Whenever Lila wouldn't let him spend money to buy a new fishing pole or a bowling ball, Netty gave it to him."

"Wow. Where was she getting this money?"

"From her rich brother Justin. That cat had some stacks and made sure his baby sister always had what she wanted. Was always that way even when we were kids he looked out for her. He tried to get Netty to go to college and make something of herself the way he did. And she went to college for a hot minute but got kicked out 'cause she was too busy partyin' to study."

"Can I get some service up in this mutherfucka?" shouted a man at the end of the bar. I looked around to see that the bar was starting to fill up, which meant I should probably go. But I had a few more questions.

"Excuse me, honey, while I take care of this drunk fool," said the bartender before I could ask him anything else.

While he was tending to other patrons, I had time to think about what he'd told me about Justin always looking out for Janette. That sure wasn't the picture Janette had painted of her older brother. And if that was the case, what had happened to change it? They were certainly estranged at the time of his death and had been for years. Was it because of her drinking? And how was Leonard able to hide from his wife that Janette had bought him a car? Wouldn't she have wondered where he'd gotten the money? Is that why he ran her down? Did Lila Duncan find out and demand he give the car back? It was a good fifteen minutes before the bartender came back.

"Still here, I see," he said, smiling. He poured me another Pepsi and I popped the cold cherry into my mouth.

"So, I guess Leonard doesn't come in here anymore, huh?"

"Not since the night his wife died."

"He was here the night she died? I didn't know that. He doesn't like to talk about his wife's death."

"Can't blame him for that. I know how I would feel if I was up in some bar drinkin' with another woman when my wife is layin' dead in some parkin' lot? I bet you wouldn't wanna talk about it, either."

"He was with Netty?"

"He was always with Netty when he was here 'cause she was the one buyin'. Lila wouldn't let him spend any money so if he wanted to drink, he had to bring Netty with him. And Netty knew this, which is why she paid. It was the only way she could get Lenny to spend any time with her."

"That's so sad," I said.

"No. What's sad is Netty had a nice guy who was crazy 'bout her and could of settled down and had a nice family of her own. But she thought he was a square from nowhere and dumped him. Now she's kickin' sixty in the butt and all she has is memories, a monthly welfare check, and a bad liver."

People were starting to press against the bar for drinks and I could feel the heat from their bodies on my back. It was time to go. I pulled out a ten-dollar bill and slid it towards the bartender.

"Leavin' so soon? And I was just getting' started. You the only one interested in hearin' my stories." He looked genuinely disappointed.

"Yeah, and you told me everything but your name."

"Name's Ray. Ray Wallace," he said, holding out

his hand. I shook it.

"Kendra Clayton. And thanks for the stories, Ray. It was great meeting you." I started to get down off the stool then quickly asked another question before he got too busy.

"Hey, Ray?"

"Yeah?"

"Did Leonard and Netty leave together the night Lila died?"

"Of course they did. Netty didn't drive. Leonard was her ride. But Leonard was stinkin' drunk that night. Could barely even walk. I started to call them a cab 'til I had to break up a fight. By the time things settled down, they were gone. Next day, I read about what happened to Lila in the paper and I never saw Lenny in here again."

THIRTEEN

I just had enough time to go home shower and change before having to be at Estelle's for my shift. The place was bursting at the seams with college students and the rush didn't die down for two solid hours. I was leaning against the hostess station, to give my sore and aching feet a break, when in walked Pia, her mother Ingrid, and a subdued looking Joy.

"We're here to celebrate, Kendra!" exclaimed Ingrid Ramey-Dubois flinging out her arms dramatically to hug me and bathing me in the scent of her Shalimar perfume. "We'd like a bottle of your best champagne."

"We don't have champagne. How about a nice bottle of wine?" I asked, noticing that whatever they were there to celebrate, Joy wasn't looking too pleased about.

"As long as it's your best," she replied.

I showed them to a table and once they were seated, Pia and her mother started talking excitedly while Joy sat there looking sad and sulky. When I brought out the wine I noticed Joy had left and neither woman seemed to have noticed.

"So, what are you guys celebrating?"

"We'd rather not say just yet," said Pia. "It's really just in the idea stage right now."

"Don't listen to my baby girl, Kendra," said Ingrid dismissively. "This idea will soon be a reality if I have anything to say about it."

"I have responsibilities here, mother. Once those are taken care of then maybe we'll see," Pia concluded firmly and then took a big sip of wine.

Ingrid's eyes narrowed. "I hope you're not talking about that crone, Pia. You don't owe that woman a thing."

"You know how I feel about you talking down about aunt J. she's family, mother. And she doesn't have anyone else."

"Bull shit!" Janette slammed her wine glass down on the table and wine splashed onto her silk shirt. "See what you've made me do. The mere mention of that woman's name is bad luck. Where's the restroom, Kendra?"

I pointed Ingrid in the right direction and went back to the hostess station feeling uncomfortable in Pia Ramey's presence knowing what I knew about Janette. She really needed to be told that her aunt didn't have cancer but I needed to find out a few other things first, namely, if Janette was hiding a blue 1982 Cadillac in her storage unit. A few minutes later, I looked up to see Ingrid walking past on her way to her table with a wet spot on the front of her shirt.

"Mrs. Ramey-Dubois?" I said, stopping her.

"Yes?"

"I hope you don't think I'm intruding on family business, but I really needed to talk to you about your former sister-in-law."

Ingrid rolled her eyes. "What about her?"

"She's Link's real mother, isn't she?"

Ingrid looked stunned. "How did you know?"

"Just a guess. Was her drinking the reason she couldn't take care of him?"

Ingrid glanced over at the table where Pia sat nursing her wine glass and pulled me to the side. "Why do you need to know about this? It's ancient history."

"Because Janette may have been mixed up in something that happened fifteen years ago that concerns a man my grandmother is seriously involved with."

"Oh," said Ingrid, a sly smile tugged at the corners of her mouth. "In that case, yes, Janette's a lousy drunk. Has been for years. When Link was eighteen months old Janette was arrested for child endangerment. She was so drunk one night she passed out on the couch and forgot to shut her apartment door. Link wandered outside and was out on the playground playing all alone in the twenty degree weather wearing nothing but a dirty diaper."

"She lost custody of him?"

"Not that time. But by the time he was two, he was living with us."

"Didn't your ex-husband ever try to get her any help?"

"Justin didn't think his sister had a problem. He just thought she was immature and would grow out of it. And if I ever tried to bring it up, he'd get very angry and tell me I just wasn't giving her a chance."

"Janette told me that she and Justin weren't close

because he forgot where he came from and was ashamed of his poor relations."

Ingrid's head jerked back like I'd hit her. "That lying little. . . No! Justin never forgot where he came from. Yes, he could be arrogant and a snob. But he adored his sister and mother and never abandoned them. Any extra money he had he sent home to his mother. He offered to pay Janette's way through college but she messed up and got kicked out. She was even too hung over to go to her own mother's funeral. Showed up at our house for the post funeral gathering and acted a fool like we were having some kind of party and she hadn't been invited."

"She said she used to baby sit Pia and Link and you fired her."

"Justin made the mistake of letting her baby sit once because she cried and said she wanted to spend time with Link. We came home to find her and a houseful of her lowlife friends dancing and smoking marijuana. They emptied our liquor cabinet. There were cigarette burns all over the furniture. I put my foot down and told Justin I didn't want her around the kids anymore."

"What changed his mind about her? What caused them to fall out?"

Ingrid sighed and ran her fingers through her hair. "Well, it certainly wasn't because of anything I said that made him finally see the light," she snorted in disgust. "We were already well on our way to being separated when they had their falling out. I was sleeping in the guest suite one night and was walking past Justin's room and heard him on the phone. I thought he was talking to some other woman and listened at the door. He was on the phone with Janette and he was crying and telling her she'd gone too far and even he couldn't help her this time. I never found out what she'd done. But whatever it was broke Justin's heart. A month later I filed for divorce and he didn't even put up a fight. I only did it to shake him up. But he called my bluff. After the divorce I moved to Paris."

"Did Pia tell you Janette has cervical cancer?"

Ingrid burst out laughing. "Cervical cancer? You're kidding me, right?

I shook my head.

"Janette had to have a total hysterectomy right after Link was born."

"Oh," I said quickly. "I must have misunderstood. But surely Pia told you she was sick, right?"

"I knew something was wrong with her but I didn't know exactly what. I just figured all her hard living finally caught up with her. Pia knows the best way to piss me off is to bring up that woman's name so we rarely talk about her. And why my daughter feels such an obligation to a woman she barely knows is beyond me."

"Is Link close to her?"

"He's embarrassed by her but if she's got so much as a dollar to give him, he'll take it. It's usually the only way she can get him to spend any time with her."

"Do you know who Link's father is?"

"I don't even think Janette knows who Link's father is. She's slept with half of Willow. When she's drunk, anything goes."

I thanked Ingrid and she rejoined her daughter. Everything that she and Ray the bartender had told me had finally fallen into place. I had a pretty good idea what happened to Lila Duncan. I just had to be able to prove it.

After work I headed over the hospital where with Harmon's permission, I was finally able to see Mason. He looked like he'd lost a little weight and connected to an IV drip. His lips were dry and his face was covered in stubble. Without his glasses he looked younger and more vulnerable. I was hoping he'd be awake when I arrived but he was down for the count.

"Do they have any idea what kind of poison he ingested?" I whispered to Harmon.

"Whatever it was has managed to leave no trace behind." Despite her hard image, I could tell she was worried.

"Does his family know? Is there anyone who should be notified?"

"The truth is, I don't know much about Detective Mason. He mentioned once that both his parents are dead and there's no one listed in his file as an emergency contact."

"What's his prognosis?"

"The doctor said he'd probably be fine. The question is whether they'll be any lasting affects."

Harmon left and I sat with Mason for a while until an announcement was made that visiting hours were over. On impulse, I kissed him on the forehead before I left and he stirred and opened his eyes.

"Mason? It's Kendra. How are you feeling?"

His eyes looked feverish and unfocused and his voice was barely audible. I had the lean close to hear him.

"What did you say?"

"Ten horses," he said in a raspy whisper.

"Ten horses? I don't know what that means, Mason." He got agitated and grabbed my wrist. Even sick his grip was strong.

"Ten horses." He let go of me and fell back asleep. But I could still feel the pressure of his fingers on my wrist.

If I was going to get into Janette's storage unit, I was going to need the key, which meant I'd have to get back into her apartment to get it. I was at the bus stop in front of the Spot the next day waiting for her on my lunch break when she came stumbling out. When she spotted me she broke into a big grin.

"You need a ride, Ms. Ramey?" I asked, holding open the passenger side door for her.

"Aww, you gonna give me another ride, girlfriend? You so sweet." She clumsily patted my cheek and fell into the car.

Once we were on our way, however, Janette promptly fell asleep. When we reached Jefferson Park, I tried to nudge her awake but she just shifted positions and snored even louder.

"Ms. Ramey? Ms. Ramey, we're here. Wake up."

She shifted around and opened her eyes for a second then let out a loud fart and promptly fell back to sleep.

"Good Lord!" I said and immediately put my window down as a pungent odor of rotten eggs filled the car. "What have you been eating, road kill?"

I nudged her in the shoulder one last time with no luck then got out of the car and went around to the passenger side door and opened it. I leaned down next to her and put her arm around my shoulder and tried to lift her out of the car. Despite the fact that she didn't weigh much, she was dead weight and when I tried to pull her out of the car, she woke up long enough to jerk out of my grasp and close the car door. Before I could open it again, she hit the button that locked the passenger side door.

"Ms. Ramey!" I pounded on the window. "Open this door!" She actually stuck her tongue out at me.

I ran around to the driver's side just in time to see my window going up. Janette had her finger poised on the switch to lock all the car doors.

"Don't. . . you. . . dare!" I punctuated each word with a stab of my finger in her direction. I saw her laugh and then slap the button. A soft clicking sound indicated that I was now locked out of my own car.

"Ms. Ramey! What are you doing? Open the door!"

Then I saw something that made me realize being locked out of my car was the least of my problems. My keys were still in the ignition. Janette followed my gaze and saw them too. A grin split her face wide and her eyes lit up with excitement.

"No!" I yelled, pounding frantically on the glass then watched as she scooted her narrow behind into the driver's seat. "Are you crazy?"

She fumbled with the keys and tried to start the car but wasn't turning it far enough in the ignition.

"Stop it! Ms. Ramey! You can't drive you're drunk! Get out of my car!"

"Bye. Bye," came her slurred, muffled voice from inside the car. She waved and then pressed her lips against the inside of the window in a loud slobbery kiss.

I ran around to the front, stood in front of the car and put my hands on the hood as the car roared to life. She was putting her foot on the gas but since the car was in park, it wouldn't move. But she soon remedied that and put the car into reverse sending it flying backwards about four feet and almost hitting another parked car.

"No!" I screamed and ran forward waving my arms. "Stop!"

She did stop but only long enough to put the car into drive sending it flying forward. It came straight at me and I was rooted to the spot until a firm hand grabbed my arm and pulled me out of the way a mere second before impact.

"Kendra, what the devil is going on?" asked Reverend Morris Rollins. I was too busy watching my car speed out of the lot to register Rollin's presence, let alone thank him for saving my life.

"Where's your car?" I asked, grabbing the front of his shirt. "We have to follow her. She's pissy drunk and she's got my car!"

"Okay, Kendra. Now calm down," he said, ever the irritating voice of reason, but when I spotted his gold Mercedes across the lot, I ran towards it with Rollin's in tow. We jumped in.

"Did you see which way she went," I asked as he was pulling out.

"Left. I think," he said, navigating the turn. I couldn't see a trace of my car in the distance. "Are you going to tell me what's going on? Why is that woman in your car?"

I quickly explained about giving Janette a ride

home from the Spot and what led up to her stealing my car, careful not to mention that I was planning to search her apartment. I looked over at Rollin's and saw that he was struggling hard not to laugh.

"It's not funny! She's in no shape to drive!" All I could imagine was Janette wrapping the car around a tree, killing herself in the process, and me being held liable.

"I know that, Kendra," he said, laughing outright now. "But you've got to admit that this is the kind of stuff that only seems to happen to you."

He had a point, especially since he'd once rescued me from a locked casket, but that still didn't make it funny. "Just drive," I snapped.

"Okay," he said still grinning. "No need to get testy."

I let out a big breath. "I'm sorry. I'm just so damned mad. I can't believe she took off in my car. And what were you doing at Jefferson Park?" I asked as an afterthought.

"Checking on one of my sick parishioners."

"I didn't know you made house calls," I said, while scanning the side of the road and the fields for my car.

"When folks can't come to church, I'm more than happy to bring church to them," he said.

We rode on but there was still no sign of my car. Surprisingly, Janette could drive pretty well for someone so liquored up. And that fact sent a chill down my spine.

"There she is," said Rollins. We'd just come over a big hill to see my white Toyota Celica parked at the bottom in the middle of the road.

We pulled along side and it appeared that no one

was in the driver's seat. I jumped out and looked inside to see Janette slumped to one side fast asleep again. I practically sagged against the car in relief.

"She okay?" asked Rollins as he got out of his car.

"Yeah. Can you help me get her into the passenger seat?"

With Rollins's help we got a still sleeping Janette back into the passenger seat and strapped her in. I got behind the wheel and tried to start the car. It wouldn't start. It was out of gas. The needle was on E. I slapped the steering wheel in frustration. There were a couple of cars behind me blowing their horns impatiently. There was a tap on my window. It was Rollins, still laughing. I glared at him and put the window down.

"I'm guessing you need another ride?"

"You think?"

Twenty minutes later, after pushing my car to the side of the road with the help of Rollins and some Good Samaritan's, we finally got Janette home and tucked into her bed. I sat down on her couch to catch my breath and to wait until Rollins left so I could snoop. But Rollins wouldn't leave and sat down on the couch next to me.

"That was almost like old times again, wasn't it?" he said, stretching out his long legs.

"Almost," I agreed and realized just how much I'd missed Rollins' friendship.

"You know, just because I'm dating Trish doesn't mean we can't still be friends, Kendra."

"I'm not the one who stopped calling and coming around, Rollins," I said, looking down at the floor. "And I'm not so sure your girlfriend would want you spending time with me."

He didn't disagree and an uncomfortable silence ensued.

"Well, I'm going to stick around for a little while to make sure she's okay," I told him.

He gave me a skeptical look.

"What?" I said irritably.

"What are you really up to, Kendra? How do you even know that poor woman?"

"She's Justin Ramey's sister and I'm not so sure she deserves your sympathy."

I quickly explained about Mama dating Leonard, his wife's hit and run murder, Leonard's connection to Janette. Rollins let out a low whistle.

"Wow. So when are you going to tell Trish about all of this?" he asked with complete seriousness. Someone clearly didn't know his girlfriend very well.

"Are you serious? No offense, Rollins. But your girlfriend isn't exactly one of my biggest fans. I have to practically beat her over the head with evidence to get her to take anything I say seriously."

"But she still needs to know. The wheels of justice may turn slowly but they still turn," he concluded in a rather self-righteous tone.

"Well, in the case of Detective Trish Harmon the wheels fell off a long time ago."

Rollins abruptly stood. "Okay, it's time to go Kendra. I've got more parishioners to see and you probably need to get back to work."

I didn't budge from the couch. "I told you. . ."

"I know what you told me but we both know you're lying. I'm not going to let you snoop through this woman's apartment or whatever it was you were planning to do. Let's go before you get yourself into more trouble."

I stared up at him in astonishment. I couldn't believe I was hearing this.

"I'm not going anywhere until I find the proof I need. If you don't like it, Rollins, you can leave."

A noise from the hallway caught our attention and we turned to see Janette, butt naked, stumbling down the hall and into the bathroom. We quickly looked away.

"We have no right being here without her permission, Kendra," Rollins whispered. "If you don't follow me out that door right now, I'm calling the cops and reporting a break-in."

I continued to sit on the couch and Rollin's pulled out his cell phone and began pressing the buttons.

"So much for friendship, huh, Rollins," I said angrily as I got up to go.

"I just don't want to see you get into trouble," he said, following me out the door.

"You just don't want me showing up your precious girlfriend," I snapped. "And if she weren't so unwilling to listen to anything I have to say, I wouldn't have to do things like this." I stormed out into the parking lot with Rollins hot on my heels.

"Where are you going? Don't you need a ride back to your car?"

"What I need, Rollins, is to prove who killed the wife of the man who's dating my grandmother and since your loyalty to your girlfriend prevents you from helping me do that, then I don't need anything from you!"

I spotted the bus coming down the street and ran to the stop to catch it. Once I was settled into a seat, I looked back and saw Rollins in the parking lot staring after the bus with his hands on his hips.

I only took the bus as far as the nearest gas station where I bought a gas can and walked the mile back to my car. I was an hour late getting back to work and was hot, sweaty, and pissed off when I arrived. I noticed Margery Warfield's van parked in the lot and knew Rhonda would be happy she was back and wouldn't have to accompany me to Margery's dicey neighborhood. But when I walked in and saw Margery's drawn face and bloodshot eyes, it was clear that all was not well. She was standing in the far corner of the classroom talking to Rhonda, who was patting her shoulder.

"Hey, Margery, welcome back. How's your mother doing?" I asked. Rhonda shook her head and Margery burst into tears and rushed out of the room.

"Her mother died last night," she whispered.

"Oh, my God." My hands flew to my mouth. "But I thought she just had the stomach flu?"

"She was in poor health to begin with and couldn't fight off the infection. She took a turn for the worse last night," said Rhonda.

"What's Margery doing here? Shouldn't she be with her family?"

"I think her mother was all she had. I think she came in so she wouldn't be alone."

"I had no idea," I said, looking into the supply room to see Margery wiping her eyes. "I'm going to go check to see if she's okay."

When I walked into the small room, Margery quickly thrust the wadded up tissue she used to wipe her eyes into the pocket of her denim jumper, and bent down to pull a ream of yellow copier paper from the cabinet. I closed the door.

"I'm really sorry about your mother, Margery. It there anything I can do for you?" I hugged her but she pulled away.

"Not unless you can raise the dead," she snapped.

I wasn't quite sure what to say or do and had my hand on the doorknob to leave when Margery suddenly turned around looking embarrassed and contrite.

"I'm sorry, Kendra," she said in a flat voice. Her hair was pulled into a ponytail. Her bangs looked limp and her jumper, which was trimmed with dancing sheep on the hem, was stained down the front. She took a few steps forward which put her almost nose-to-nose with me.

"It's just that she meant so much to me and now I'm all alone."

"Don't you have any siblings or relatives?" I took a step back and found I was pressed against the door.

"It was just mother and me. I was married for twenty years but we split up this past spring. We're still friends, mind you," she added quickly, a little too quickly, making me wonder if her ex considered them to still be friends.

"Would you like me to contact your ex for you? Would he be able to come here to be with you?"

Margery gave me an odd look. Her eyes looked far off and dreamy. "Oh, but he's with me all the time, Kendra. He's always in my heart even if he's no longer my husband legally. He'll always be my husband spiritually."

She picked up the ream of yellow paper and left the

room, leaving me staring after her and feeling like I'd just made an unscheduled stop in Looney Ville. Grief sure did strange things to people.

"You didn't tell me she used to be married," I said to Rhonda while Margery was busy out in the hallway copying worksheets.

"Oh yeah, for like twenty years. He up and left her three months ago for another woman. She lost the house they lived in when he left, which is why she and her mom moved into that trailer park. I'm surprised she never mentioned it to you before. She talks about her ex like he's just away on vacation and will be back soon. It'd be sad if it wasn't so creepy."

"I guess you just never know what's going on in people's lives, huh?"

"You can sure say that again," replied Rhonda.

I spent the rest of the afternoon in a funk. I was furious with Rollins, worried about Mason, scared for Mama, and feeling sorry for Margery who was acting flakier by the hour. By the time quitting time came, I was more determined than ever to get into Janette's storage unit. I didn't care what Rollins thought about his precious girlfriend. I knew she'd never listen to me about my suspicions about Justin Ramey's sister and her connection to a fifteen year old hit and run, when she was too busy trying to get Justin's widow to confess to his murder. Once again, I was on my own. I was so lost in thought I almost ran a stop sign and hit another car. I slammed on the breaks and in doing so saw that something slid out from under my seat. I pulled over and picked it up. It was Janette Ramey's state ID card. It must have fallen out of her purse. I knew I'd have to return it. But suddenly I had a brilliant idea and pulled out my cell phone.

"I can't believe I let you talk me into this shit, Clayton!" said Joy as we pulled into the parking lot of Storage Solutions Self-Storage Units.

It was a little past five o'clock. I looked over at Joy and burst out laughing.

"This shit ain't funny," she snapped. But it was.

The only way I'd be able to get into Janette Ramey's storage unit was to bring Janette to the unit to add me to her rental agreement. Since I knew there was no way in hell that was ever going to happen, I had to improvise. I already had Janette's state ID. All I needed was someone to play Janette. That's where Joy came in. Only she wasn't quite feeling it.

"You owe me, Joy. I helped prove your friend didn't kill her father, remember?"

"And I told you about your granny's man. *That* was the deal. And forget about goin' to jail, if Pia finds out I'm illegally impersonating her aunt, she'll probably never speak to my ass again."

"How's she going to find out? It's not like anyone would recognize you in that get-up," I said and laughed again.

Joy was dressed in a hunter green polyester pants suit, a short, curly, brown wig, and fake teeth that made her lisp. It was my Halloween costume from the year before. The suit was way too big for her and hung on her like loose skin. I'd tried to make her look as close to Janette Ramey's ID picture as I could. The ID picture had been taken two years ago when Janette was heavier, and not pretending to have cancer. But if asked, the weight loss could be explained away by her being sick. However, there wasn't much I could do about Joy not looking like a woman in her fifties. I was hoping the clerk's bad eyesight would take care of that problem.

"Besides, don't you want to help me expose Janette? No telling how much money she's scammed Pia out of. Plus, she's hiding a car that was used in a hit and run."

"And that's the only reason why I'm doing this shit. So what the hell am I supposed to say?"

"Don't worry, I'll do all the talking. And remember, you're supposed to be sick and frail. So don't be acting all nasty and hateful."

"But I am nasty and hateful when I'm sick."

"Since when you do you have to be sick?"

"Keep it up, Clayton, and I'll run in there doing cartwheels and back flips."

"Just come on and don't screw this up." I headed up the steps to the office, said a prayer, and opened the door.

FOURTEEN

"How can I help you ladies?" asked the clerk. She'd been sitting behind the counter reading a newspaper, and holding it close to her face, when we walked in, which made me feel hopeful that we could pull this off.

"Remember me from yesterday? I needed to get into my aunt's storage unit. I decided it would be better if I just brought her out here instead. And she needs a new key. She lost hers."

"Oh, yeah," said the woman getting up and coming over to the counter. "I just need to see some ID and it'll be twenty-five dollars for a replacement key. What's the name?" she asked Joy. Joy was too busy looking around to respond. I gave her a hard nudge.

"What!" she snapped, then remembering she was supposed to be frail and sick, hunched over and clutched my arm for support. "What did you say?" she said in a high-pitched breathy voice.

"She needs to see your ID, Aunt Janette." I looked over to see the clerk squinting at Joy with her head cocked to one side.

"And don't forget the twenty-five dollar key replacement fee!" hollered the clerk.

Joy pulled me back by the door. "Why is that heifer screamin' at me. I'm supposed to be sick not deaf. And you didn't say nothin' about no twenty-five dollars," she whispered around the big fake teeth making spittle fly.

I grabbed Joy and pulled her up to the counter. "Don't worry, Aunt Janette, I'll take care of the replacement fee. You just show this nice lady your ID."

Joy reached into the large cloth handbag I'd given her, pulled out the ID, and flashed it at the clerk.

"Not so fast," protested the clerk when Joy tried to stuff the ID back into her bag. "I didn't even see it." She held out her hand and Joy scowled at me as she dropped it into the clerk's upturned palm.

The clerk brought the ID up to her face and then squinted at Joy. "You sure look a lot different."

"I've been sick, cancer," said Joy in a weak voice and then lapsed into a fit of fake coughing leaning against the counter for support.

The clerk jumped back like she was afraid whatever Joy had was contagious and immediately retreated to the file cabinet. Way to go Joy. I winked at her and she stuck her tongue out. The clerk fumbled around in the cabinet for a few minutes while I held my breath.

"Here we go, Ms. Ramey," she said, putting the folder on the counter and placing a form next to with the words, KEY REPLACEMENT typed on the top. "I just need for you to put your initials in the top box and sign on the bottom line for your new key."

Joy's jaw tighten as she signed the form and I

could almost hear the worry that she was going to be arrested for fraud swirling around in her head. It was time to get the key and get out of there. I pulled a twenty and a five from my purse and set it on the counter.

"Want a receipt?"

"No just the key," I said hastily, making the clerk squint at me. "Please," I added and smiled.

She turned to a cabinet on the wall and thrust her head inside perusing several rows of keys, which were hanging on hooks before finally pulling out a key attached to a cardboard square. She held it just out of Joy's reach as she stared at her long and hard like she was having second thoughts about giving it to her.

"Can I get that key, *today*," snapped Joy. The clerk jumped.

"Sorry," she said, leaning forward and dropping the key into her hand. I hustled Joy out the door before the clerk had a change of heart.

"Come on and let's do this. It ain't like I got nothing better to do," she snapped. I walked past her snatching the key out of her hand.

"Oh, keep you hair on. You can stay here if you want. I won't be long." I was already sick and tired of Joy and hoping she'd go back to the car. No such luck. She fell in step right next to me.

"You ain't leaving me here alone. That crazy ass Sheepshanks across the road might grab me."

"Only if he's wanting to add some angry lesbian to his dog Boo Boo's kibble. Otherwise, you're safe."

"Ha fuckin' ha. You ain't funny at all. Now let's do this thing," she said, clapping her hands. "What unit is Janette's?"

I stopped in my tracks. I had thought of everything and had the key in my hand. But had no idea where the actual unit was.

"You don't know?" Joy started laughing hysterically. "You pulled off your brilliant master plan and don't know what unit belongs to Janette?"

I looked down at the key in my hand, which was attached to a cardboard tag. The number 14B-2 was written on the tag in black marker.

"Unit B14 in row 2," I said, walking fast to get away from the grating sound of her voice.

"And which way would that be?"

There were six rows of twelve units. We were standing roughly in the middle. The row of units to my right were labeled C on the left was D.

"This way," I said and headed around the corner where I spotted B14 right away. "Here it is."

I bent down and inserted the key into the lock at the bottom of the green accordion fold door. It clicked and I tossed Joy a smug look as I turned the handle and pulled it up. Joy burst out laughing again. The storage unit was filled to the gills with boxes. And unless she'd cut it up into pieces and put each one in a separate box, there was no blue 1982 Caddy in Janette Ramey's storage unit. I'd wasted twenty-five dollars to look at some boxes.

"I can't believe I fell for this bullshit!" said Joy.

"It's not bullshit," I snapped. "I know she was involved in that hit and run and has that car hidden somewhere. I just have to figure out where."

"Yeah, just like you *know* Janette ain't got cancer, right?"

"She *doesn't* have cancer," I insisted. But I didn't

sound very convincing.

"All I know is this." Joy said, suddenly serious. "You better not be steppin' to Pia with this shit about her aunt unless you're 100 percent, got it?" She sounded just like Gwen and it annoyed the crap out of me.

"Whatever," I said before heading back to my car.

After dropping Joy off, I went home to be greeted by the sight of Handy Randy re-attaching my good as new mailbox. Today he'd shed his jeans and T-Shirt for a pair of paint speckled white overalls and a black sweatshirt. But he still reeked of his usual Eau de Mary Jane.

"Thank you, sir," I said, handing him a ten-dollar bill, which was all the money I had left until payday. We'd agreed on five dollars but I threw in the extra money because I still felt bad about Mason thinking he was a thief and pinning him to the ground.

"Where's your cop boyfriend?" Randy asked, looking around like Mason might pop out of the bushes at any moment.

"He's not my boyfriend and don't worry. He's not here."

"Glad to hear it 'cause I forgot to give you this. It was in your mailbox," he said, pocketing the ten and handing me a letter with my name on it. It was from Atlanta. I recognized Carl's handwriting.

"Thanks, Randy." I stared at the letter for a few long seconds before I stuffed it into my purse and headed into my apartment.

Instead of reading the letter, I called Mama. I was feeling frustrated and stupid and needed some of her special brand of therapy. Plus, I was hoping maybe she and Leonard had broken up.

"Want some company for dinner? Or do you and Loverboy want to be alone?" I asked. Mama chuckled.

"You must be feeling too lazy to cook otherwise you wouldn't want to be bothered with your old grandma during the week."

"Well can I come over? I don't want to intrude on you and Leonard."

"Since when have you ever worried about that before? And, yes, you can come over and help me eat this chicken potpie I made. Leonard's been tied up all day with doctor's appointments and I could use the company."

"He's not coming to dinner?"

"He might stop by afterwards for dessert, why?"

"No reason. I'm on my way," I told her and hung up.

"Where's that handsome doctor of yours tonight?" asked Mama as she spooned chicken potpie onto my plate next to a pile of homemade slaw.

"He's working tonight."

"Well, I'm glad to see you back in the dating game, honey." She reached across the table and patted my hand.

"Mason and I aren't serious, Mama. We're just friends. I'm not looking for another boyfriend." Carl's letter was burning a hole in my purse and I wasn't in any big hurry to read it.

"That's okay. I just don't want to see you sitting at home feeling sorry for yourself when the sea is full of other fish. And I'll tell you something else, too."

"What's that?" I asked, taking a big bite of crescent roll.

"I liked Carl, I really did. He was a good man, a real good man, and real smart, too. But he was a little stiff and boring, baby. I mean I don't think I ever saw him in anything but a suit. Mason seems like he might be a lot more fun. Is he?"

"Loads." Leave it to Mama to like a man who drove me crazy.

Leonard still hadn't shown up by the time Mama and I had our dessert of pineapple upside down cake and real whipped cream, not the store bought stuff. And though Mama didn't say a word, I could tell by the way she kept looking at the clock on the wall that she was wondering where he was.

I was on my way out the door at half past eight when Mama's phone rang. She was waving goodbye to me as she answered it and I was already out the door and halfway to my car when Mama came flying out the door.

"Kendra! Wait!" Her eyes were big and she had her big black pocketbook swinging from one arm.

"What's wrong?" I asked as she jumped into the passenger side of my car.

"I need a ride to the police station! That was Leonard on the phone. He's been arrested!"

"For what?" I asked. My hand was still on my car door.

"Assault!"

"Assault? Who'd he assault?"

"I don't know! Just get in the car!" she snapped impatiently.

It wasn't until we'd gotten to the Willow Police

department and talked to the female officer at the front desk that we found out that Leonard had been arrested for assaulting Janette Ramey, who'd been found badly beaten and unconscious in her apartment by her niece Pia Ramey. After regaining consciousness in the hospital, Ms. Ramey named Mr. Duncan as her attacker.

"I don't know who this Janette Ramey woman is but I don't believe a word of this mess!" exclaimed Mama indignantly.

"Doesn't he have an alibi?" I asked, not wanting this to be true for Mama's sake, but given what I knew about Leonard and Janette figured it was. "I thought he was at doctor's appointments all day?"

"That's right," said Mama to the officer behind the desk. "He has an alibi!"

"If the two of you will have a seat, someone will be right out to talk to you."

The officer, looking like she'd heard it all before, gestured towards the hard wooden benches in the station's lobby. I was already very familiar with those ass-numbing benches from having sat and waited on them when my sister had been arrested.

"Come on, Mama. There's nothing else we can do but wait."

An hour later, Harmon finally came out to talk to us and Mama was all over her the minute she saw her.

"What is this nonsense, Detective Harmon? Leonard Duncan is a close personal friend of mine and he'd never hurt a fly!"

"We have one very badly beaten woman in the hospital that would disagree with you, Mrs. Mays," replied Harmon calmly. Harmon knew better than to smart talk my grandmother the way she usually did me. So I let Mama do all the talking.

"But he has an alibi. He had doctor's appointments all day. Didn't he tell you?"

"He's yet to tell us anything, Mrs. Mays. And when he was picked up this afternoon he wasn't at the doctor's office, or his house. He was drinking at the Spotlight Bar and Grill."

"What!" we both said.

"I thought he stopped drinking?" I blurted out before thinking. Both Mama and Harmon looked at me.

"I could have sworn someone told me he hasn't had a drink since his wife died," I said, tugging nervously on my earring.

"What do you mean he's not talking?" Mama asked.

"He's not confirming or denying he assaulted Ms. Ramey. He claims he blacked out and doesn't remember."

Mama looked stunned and for the first time uncertain of the man she'd grown so fond of. I felt bad for her.

"What's his bail?" she asked, looking deflated.

"He won't be going anywhere tonight, Ma'am. He's been charged with assault. He's yet to be arraigned. He won't be in court until morning."

"Well, can I at least see him?"

"I'm afraid not until after he's been arraigned."

Mama's shoulders slumped and I put my arm around her. "Come on, Mama, let's go home. I promise I'll bring you back first thing in the morning."

Once we were out in the parking lot and the night air hit her, Mama perked up considerably.

"It's all just a big mistake, Kendra. Once that poor woman comes to her senses, she'll realize her mistake."

"And what if she doesn't?"

"We'll cross that bridge when we come to it. And who told you about Leonard's drinking? Have you been checking up on him? I thought we were past all that, Kendra?"

Her tone was more weary than accusatory and it was on the tip of my tongue to tell her about Leonard and Janette. But I didn't think she'd be able to handle one more negative thing about Leonard, let alone believe me.

"I wasn't checking up on him. I met a man who used to hang out with him years ago that's all."

"Janette Ramey? Why does that name sound so familiar?"

"She belongs to the same Ramey family that's been all over the news. She's the sister of that art dealer who got murdered last week."

"How the devil would Leonard know her?"

"I'm sure Leonard knows a lot of people you don't know."

"What's that supposed to mean?" she snapped.

"It doesn't mean anything," I said, getting annoyed. "Does Leonard know every single person you know?"

"I'm sorry, baby," she said, surprising me. Mama wasn't big on apologies and didn't say anything else the rest of the way home.

When I got home I sat down on the couch, and started to pull Carl's letter out of my purse, when there was a knock at my door. It was Rollins. He stood in my doorway looking contrite, and holding a Styrofoam carryout container from Frisch's.

"What's that?"

"A peace offering, and it's melting. Can I come in?"

I took the container and Rollins followed me into the kitchen. I pulled two spoons from the silverware drawer and we shared the large slab of hot fudge cake while I filled him in on what had happened with Janette Ramey and Leonard. Rollins let out a low whistle.

"So do you think he's guilty?" he asked.

"For Mama's sake I sure hope not."

"I didn't ask if you hoped he wasn't guilty," said Rollins, pushing the now empty container to the side. "I asked if you thought he could have done what he's been accused of."

I'd been so busy worrying about Mama and what could be in the letter Carl wrote me that I hadn't given Leonard's guilt or innocence much thought. But knowing what I knew about his probable involvement in his wife's death, I didn't have to think too hard about my answer.

"Yes," I said without hesitation. Rollins's eyebrows shot up in surprise.

"Really? You think he's capable of that kind of violence?"

"What I think doesn't matter. What I want to know is what made him take a drink after nearly two decades of sobriety? Why now?"

"Maybe he got bad news at the doctor's office. Didn't you say he told your grandmother he had appointments today?"

"If he even went to the doctor. That was probably a

lie," I countered. "And I want to know if he was drunk when Janette Ramey says he attacked her or did he get drunk *because* he attacked her and knew he was in trouble?"

"Too bad you can't ask him."

It was too bad I couldn't ask Leonard. And I doubted he'd tell me even if I could. But there was someone I could ask, Janette. She wasn't under arrest. Was she still in the hospital? The thought made me sit up a little straighter in my chair.

"Don't even think about it," said Rollins, chuckling softly.

"What?" I exclaimed in mock innocence.

"I know you well enough to know that look in your eyes, Kendra. You're just dying to talk to Janette Ramey."

"Oh, come on. I'm not that insensitive. The poor woman's been beaten up. No telling what kind of shape she's in. They probably even have her sedated."

Rollins eyed me skeptically before looking at his watch and standing up to toss the Styrofoam container into my trashcan. "Unfortunately, I can't babysit you to make sure you stay out of this mess."

"Hot date with Trish?" I asked casually, itching for him to leave.

"Nope, Bible Study at the church. And we'll be saying special prayers for Leonard and Janette."

Good, I thought as I walked him to the door, because they both needed it.

"We're okay, right?" He asked, pausing in the doorway. "You know I was just looking out for you when I wouldn't let you search Janette Ramey's apartment, don't you?"

"Yeah, I know," I replied grudgingly and gave him a smile. I had a sudden urge to hug him but thought better of it.

"Good," he said, returning my smile. "I know you probably don't believe this but you're important to me, Kendra, and I don't want to see you hurt or in trouble." He reached out and stroked my cheek leaving behind the warm imprint of his fingers on my face. Then he was gone.

I called the hospital and asked to be connected to Janette Ramey's room only to be told that she was no longer in the hospital, which really shouldn't have surprised me. If I were faking having cancer, the hospital was the last place I'd want to be. I bet Janette checked herself out against doctor's orders. To be on the safe side, I waited a good twenty minutes after Rollins left to make sure he wasn't lurking around outside waiting to follow me, before heading to Janette's apartment. I had no idea what I was going to say to her if she was at home. But I'd worry about that when I got there. As it turned out, I needn't have worried.

I could see there were no lights on in her apartment before I even parked. Either she wasn't home or she was already in bed. And as nosy as I was, even I didn't have the nerve to rouse an injured person from their bed. I parked in front of the building anyway trying to figure out what to do, when I spotted someone familiar coming out of Janette's building. It was Link Ramey. What in the world would he be doing here when according to Ingrid, he wanted nothing to do with Janette unless she had money to give him? Link was carrying a large duffel bag and slung it into the front seat of his Range Rover before getting behind the wheel and driving off. I quickly ducked down as he sped past me. I could have just accepted defeat and gone home. But since the only thing waiting for me at my apartment was a letter from my ex, I tore out of the lot after Link so I wouldn't lose him.

I followed Link back to his father's house in the country and was surprised Pia still hadn't kicked him out yet. I pulled up to the wrought iron gate and turned off the ignition. The gate had swung shut after Link had driven through. I was locked out. But I was able to see through the gate and saw Link getting out of his car with the duffel bag and heading up the steps to the front door. The door opened and Janette greeted him. I had to strain to get a get a good look. Was she so afraid of Leonard she was hiding out at her late brother's house or was she just using any excuse to spend time with Link?

I was too far away to see the extent of her injuries but the bright white bandage on her forehead, just over her right eye, practically glowed in the dark. Link promptly dropped the duffel bag at her feet and walked right past her into the house without speaking. Janette stared after him for several long seconds before slowly bending down to pick up the bag. I could tell by the way she moved that she was in pain. Broken ribs perhaps? But I bet the cold shoulder she'd just gotten from her own son had probably hurt a lot more. There was a buzzer I could have buzzed to try and get in to see Janette tonight. But I didn't bother. I went home instead.

FIFTEEN

Mama called me at six thirty in the morning to make sure I was awake and would be on time picking her up because she didn't want to miss a second of Leonard's arraignment. I hadn't slept well and had already been up for half an hour. Carl's letter sat on my kitchen table, still unopened, and I stuck my tongue out at it on my way out the door to pick up my grandmother. Neither of us had much to say on the way to the courthouse. Mama looked tired, old, and a little sad. I knew she couldn't have gotten much sleep, either, and reached out to squeeze her hand.

"It's going to be okay, Mama. There has to be a good explanation for all of this," I told her. I tried really hard to sound upbeat. She gave me a big smile and squeezed my hand back.

"You got that right," she said vehemently. "I know Leonard's not perfect, Kendra, none of us is. But I refuse to believe he beat up some woman and put her in the hospital. That's just not the man I know."

"Does Leonard ever talk about his first wife?" I asked. I never had the nerve to ask her before but since we were on the subject of Leonard and his imperfections, I figured what the hell.

"Not really," she said, shrugging. "He told me once they got married for all the wrong reasons but she never really comes up in any of our conversations. Why?"

"No reason. I just heard she died tragically and wondered if he ever talked about it."

"You heard, huh?" she said, cutting me a look. "Did you hear this from the same person who told you he used to drink?"

"No. I heard it from a friend whose aunt used to live across the street from him and his wife," I replied and tried not to choked on the lie that Joy was any kind of friend of mine.

"And what else did this *friend* say?" she asked, trying to sound nonchalant. But I could tell she really wanted to know.

Just a week ago I was dying to give her all the grizzly details surrounding Lila Duncan's violent death and Leonard's weird behavior afterwards. But Mama's reaction to Leonard being arrested for assault made me realize that not only would she not believe me, she'd defend Leonard even harder, which would just piss me off and then we'd be on the outs again. Clearly, I was not the right person to tell her everything I'd found out from Joy. But that didn't mean I couldn't use a little of what's she'd told me to plant the seeds of suspicion in my grandmother's mind.

"Nothing much. Just about how much they used to argue," I said. Mama sighed and let out a mirthless chuckle.

"All couples argue, Kendra. Doesn't mean they didn't love each other."

"Oh, I know that. And I also know Leonard must have *really* loved his wife."

"Why is that?"

"Because my friend said he gave all her stuff to Goodwill the day after she was killed: every last stitch of her clothes, all her shoes, jewelry, perfume, purses, everything. Packed it all up and donated it."

I glanced over at Mama. She looked taken aback and swallowed hard. So, naturally, I went in for the kill.

"And the only reason why I can think that a man would give away all his wife's belongings before she was even buried was that it must have just been too painful for him to look at it and constantly be reminded of his loss." Or his guilt, I was dying to say but didn't.

Mama didn't say one word. But I could tell she was thinking really hard about what I'd just told her and trying to convince herself that giving away all Lila's stuff, when she'd barely been dead a day, wasn't completely coldblooded.

There were only six people in the courthouse that morning: me, Mama, Leonard, his attorney, the prosecutor, the bailiff and the judge. I half expected to see Janette there but wasn't really surprised when she didn't show up. Mama kept waving and trying to catch Leonard's eye when he was led into the courtroom but he wouldn't look at her and was hanging his head, though I couldn't tell if it was because he was ashamed to have her see him in handcuffs and jailhouse scrubs or was so hung over he couldn't lift his head. I could smell the alcohol fumes wafting off of him from where Mama and I were sitting in the row directly behind the defendant's table, and I know she could smell it, too, though she pretended not to.

Judge Jolene Willis was a thin, elegant woman of about sixty with a sleek, silver, asymmetrical bob and hard grey eyes that had probably seen it all. She asked Leonard if he understood the charges against him and he mumbled something unintelligible. Mama sighed and shook her head. Leonard's lawyer nudged him gently and whispered something in his ear. I couldn't hear what he'd said but it did the trick.

"Yes, ma'am," Leonard replied, finally lifting his head.

"And how do you plead, Mr. Duncan?" asked Judge Willis. Leonard was silent and just hung his head again. His shoulders started to shake and soon his muffled sobs filled the courtroom. Oh, boy.

"He's not guilty," Mama whispered to me. "Why doesn't he say so?"

"Because maybe he *is* guilty," I couldn't help but point out. Mama looked at me like I'd punched her.

"I'm waiting, Mr. Duncan," said Judge Willis, sounding beyond impatient and not at all affected by the elderly man's tears.

Leonard's lawyer handed him a tissue and said, "My client pleads not guilty, Your Honor."

"That's all well and good, counselor, but I need to hear that from your client."

"Not guilty, Your Honor," said Leonard loud and clear, finally speaking up and sounding more like herself.

Mama reached forward and gave Leonard's shoulder a quick squeeze of approval and shot me a smug *I-told-you-so* look. And for her sake, I really hoped he was truly not guilty.

"As to the matter of bail?" Judge Willis tossed the question in the air and the prosecutor caught it.

I was expecting the prosecutor to be the same woman who'd prosecuted my sister, Allegra, when she had been arrested for murder. Instead, it was a man who'd been acting bored and doodling on a legal pad the entire time we'd been in court and only came alive when the word *bail* had been spoken.

"Your Honor, due to the violent nature of the crime, we ask that the defendant be held without bail pending the outcome of the trial," he replied, like he was reading from a script. But I got the impression that he could have cared less one way or the other whether Leonard got bail or not.

"My client is elderly and in poor health, Your Honor," said Jeff Parson, gesturing towards Leonard. "He was born and raised here in Willow and has ties to the community. He also has no criminal record. He is not a flight risk."

We all looked at the prosecutor expecting some kind of rebuttal but he just shook his head like he had nothing more to say. Obviously, he didn't consider Leonard to be a danger to society.

"And what is the nature of Mr. Duncan's health issues?" asked the judge.

"I have a bad heart," said Leonard before his lawyer could. Mama nodded her head in agreement as if to confirm Leonard's bad ticker.

"My client takes a variety of medications on a daily basis that would make fleeing all but impossible as filling his prescriptions would entail leaving a trail, you honor."

"Then I guess it's not such a good idea for you to be drinking then, is it Mr. Duncan?" asked the judge sarcastically like she was talking to a child. "Bail is set at twenty-five thousand dollars." She banged her gavel and we were free to go.

"I just don't remember what happened, Stella. I swear to God I don't remember!" exclaimed Leonard.

Once his bail was arranged, Leonard was released and we all went back to Mama's. And as much as she wanted to believe in his innocence, I was happy that she didn't hesitate to demand an explanation from her man. After she'd cooked us a big breakfast of eggs, bacon, hash browns, and cinnamon toast, which Leonard devoured like he hadn't eaten in a week, Mama cleared the table and it was truth time.

"You mean you're too hung over to remember?" asked Mama, pulling no punches.

"No. I mean I went to the doctor yesterday like I was supposed to and everything after that is a blank until I woke up in jail." Leonard sat back wearily in his chair. His eyes were bloodshot and he was still wearing the clothes he'd had on yesterday, which were wrinkled and reeked of sweat and cigarette smoke. He stunk and I hoped after his grilling Mama would toss him in the shower.

"So you don't know if you're guilty or innocent," I asked, ignoring Mama's indignant look, "And that's why you got so upset when the judge asked you about your plea."

"Kendra!" exclaimed Mama, startling me.

"No, Stella, Ken's right, much as I hate to admit it.

I've been sober for fifteen years and I have no idea what I was doing at the Spot yesterday," said Leonard.

"Getting drunk isn't the issue, Leonard," said Mama, getting up from the table and leaning over him. "You're accused of assaulting a woman and beating her up so bad she ended up in the hospital. And just who is this Janette Ramey to you?" There were tears in Mama's voice.

Leonard and I looked at each other, stunned, and then I finally got it. Mama wasn't just upset about the drinking and the alleged assault, which were bad enough. She was also upset because she had no idea what kind of relationship Leonard and Janette had. In other words, Mama thought Leonard was stepping out on her. If I had a hard time coping with Mama having a boyfriend, I was having an even harder time seeing her as a jealous lover. Where the hell was the woman who made me cheesecakes on my birthday, and made my prom dress, and sent me care packages when I was away at college? I wanted that woman back.

Leonard stood up and grabbed Mama's hands and brought them to his lips. He kissed them gently then said, "Janette Ramey is and old friend of mine, Stella, baby. We grew up together. She was never my woman. Not then and not now. I was never interested in her like that. Get me a stack of bibles and I'll swear to it!"

"Oh, Leonard!" Mama threw her arms around his neck. They embraced tightly and I felt as uncomfortable as I did when I'd walked in on them in their robes.

He may have Mama fooled, but as far as I was concerned, this man still had a lot of explaining to do. I wanted so badly to ask about why he'd been giving Janette money and liquor and why, if they'd never been involved, did he let her buy him a car, and why was another woman connected with him a victim of violence? I caught Leonard's eye over Mama's shoulder, glared at him, and mouthed the words, *"We need to talk."*

He shook his head no and looked away then blurted, "Queenie!"

In all the excitement, we'd all forgotten about Leonard's dog, Queenie, who hadn't been let out or fed since yesterday morning. It was as if fate had finally dropped the perfect opportunity in my lap and I jumped up from the table.

"You stay here with Mama, Leonard. I'm sure you two have a lot to talk about. Give me your keys and I'll run by and take care of Queenie.

Before Leonard could say no, Mama reached into his back pocket with one hand, pulled out his set of keys, and tossed them to me without breaking their embrace. Leonard looked momentarily panicked but knew better than to object. It was my cue to leave. And I was quite happy to get out of there before I saw something between the elderly lovers that would make my eyes bleed.

Queenie started barking up a storm as soon as she heard the key in the lock. But when she saw I wasn't her master, she cautiously sniffed my shoes then my fingers before letting me pet her. Leonard's house was immaculate, which didn't surprise me. What did surprise me was that it was decorated with modern, up-to-date furnishings. I was expecting old, flowered, or plaid stuff like Mama had not a tastefully decorated living room that could have been featured in House

Beautiful.

The kitchen was bright and cheerful and just as up-to-date and except for the pile of dog poop on the yellow linoleum floor, just as clean and tidy as the living room. Queenie didn't follow me into the kitchen. Instead, she paused in the doorway with her head hanging like she was awaiting punishment for her accident, the poor thing. I sidestepped the crap and opened the backdoor and the dog promptly flew out into the backyard to do her long overdue business.

I cleaned up the crap, as well as a puddle of pee near the stove, then found cleaning supplies and mopped the floor. I found dog food in the pantry and filled her dish with food and water then I got busy doing what I'd come to do. Snoop around to try to figure out what happened yesterday between Leonard and Janette and what if anything it had to do with the murder of Leonard's wife. If I was lucky, I might even find something that might tell me what happened to the Cadillac. The house had two bedrooms, one of which had been turned into a guestroom/office. I started there and searched the desk drawers and the closet. The only thing I found out was that Leonard was a meticulous record keeper and had boxes of neatly filed receipts and paperwork dating back a good ten years. I found cancelled checks for car repairs but they were for the car he currently drove, and not a blue Caddy.

I moved on to his bedroom closet and found it held only clothes, shoes, hats, belts and coats all neatly hanging on wooden hangers or in boxes and coordinated by color and season. I needed to have this man come organize my closet. His dresser was solely for socks, pajamas, underwear and sweaters. The top drawer was filled with prescription medicine bottles. There were at least a dozen of them for a variety of ailments including heart disease and high blood pressure. There was even a prescription for Viagra, which I pretended not to see. But I did have to wonder how Leonard could have dared mix all this medication with alcohol? According to each bottle, he was taking all of these pills on a daily basis and most of them warned against consuming alcohol. Could this be why he couldn't remember what happened yesterday? But I still needed to know why he took a drink in the first place. I had no idea when I'd get a chance to get him alone so I could ask. So I'd just have to ask Janette. I left the bedroom, and was heading back downstairs to let Queenie back in, when I noticed a door in the ceiling at the end of the hall that must have led to the attic.

Unable to resist the urge to snoop some more, I reached up and gave the handle a good tug and the door creaked open. There was a ladder attached to the door turning it into a makeshift staircase into the attic. I climbed up into the dark space and was hit by the strong scent of mothballs. There was a naked light bulb dangling from the ceiling at the top of the stairs and I pulled the chain to turn it on. It lit up the space but barely put a dent in the darkened corners of the attic where the shadowy shapes of sheet covered furniture and stacked boxes peeked out from all sides.

Leonard's housekeeping skills apparently stopped short of the attic. There was a thick coat of dust on everything and I could tell it had been a long time since he'd been up here. Once my eyes adjusted, I ventured further into the room where an old brass headboard for a king sized bed was propped up against a heavy oak chest of drawers. An old record player, with a 45 still on its turntable, sat on top of the dresser. I picked up the record, blew the dust off of it, and held it up to the weak light. It was The Isley Brothers' *"It's Your Thing"* circa 1969. Suddenly, the image of Janette Ramey in her glorious party girl days drinking and dancing up a storm at The Spotlight Bar and Grill popped into my head.

A quick perusal of the nearby boxes uncovered more old records and cassette tapes, old blankets and sheets. There was also folding chairs and card tables, an artificial Christmas tree, a broken vacuum cleaner, and a quilted sewing box with a faded floral print. I opened it and was immediately greeted by the scent of Chanel No. 5 perfume. This must have been Lila's sewing box. He'd obviously not given all of her stuff away. I wondered why he'd held on to it?

Inside was a clear plastic tray holding spools of colored thread, needles, and scraps of material. But something dark showed underneath. I pulled out the tray and found a bible. The bible was old and the gold lettering on the white cover was flaking off. When I started flipping through it, several loose pages fluttered to the floor and I bent to retrieve them. Most of them were long outdated store coupons and the others were bits and pieces of paper with recipes written on them. But there was one item that had fallen out that wasn't a coupon or a recipe. It was an old snapshot of two couples sitting at a table playing cards. Even though he had a lot more hair and looked about forty years younger, I recognized Leonard right away. He was clutching a beer bottle and I could tell by his squinty eyes and the goofy grin on his face that he was drunk.

The attractive woman sitting next to him wore a smug half smile and had her hand possessively over his. This must have been Lila.

The female half of the other couple looked much younger than her companions and was casting a sly flirty smile in Leonard's direction instead of looking at the camera. It was Janette. She barely looked out of her teens and was dressed in a very tight, black sweater that hugged her large breasts like a second skin. She was gorgeous. The muscular, clean cut man sitting next to her had a cigarette hanging from the corner of his mouth trying to look like a bad ass and not quite succeeding. His arm was draped around Janette's shoulders with his fingers dangling dangerously close to her breasts. Something about him seemed familiar but I couldn't place what it was.

On the back of the snapshot were the words: *Get thee behind me Satan.* I flipped it back over and got another, closer look and saw someone had drawn horns on Janette's head with an ink pen. It had to have been Lila. I knew from years of vacation bible school as a kid that the word *Satan* meant *adversary*. Lila had obviously known the beautiful young Janette was after her husband and had felt threatened enough by her adversary that she'd handed her burden over to a higher power by sticking this photo in the bible. And it had worked, to an extent. Leonard never left Lila for Janette, but in accepting her gifts and money, he'd still been unfaithful on an emotional level. Lila must have despised Janette. But Janette must have hated Lila even more because she had what Janette wanted, Leonard. And all of her beauty, money, and gifts couldn't lure the man she loved away from his wife. What would she have been willing to do to get rid of Lila forever? Maybe I should just ask her.

"Hey, girl, what are you doing here?" Janette looked taken aback by my appearance at the door. I walked forward practically forcing her to step aside so I could come in. Justin Ramey's house was just as impressive on the inside.

I stepped inside a large airy foyer with marble floors and a circular staircase. A large, crystal chandelier hung from a recessed ceiling. Light flooded in from a large round window above the front door.

"I heard what happened to you yesterday and stopped by to make sure you were okay. You weren't at your apartment so I took a chance that you'd be out here."

"How'd you hear about what happened to me? The report in the paper didn't have my name," Janette asked slowly, looking confused.

The bright light of the foyer made the bruising on her face even more vivid. Her bottom lip was puffy and in addition to the bandage over her eyebrow, there was also a knot on her forehead. But for all her injuries, I couldn't tell if she'd really been beaten up. She could have just taken a drunken tumble down a flight of stairs.

"I didn't say I read about it in the paper," I replied, my eyes never leaving her face.

"Then how did," she began before I cut her off.

"Because my grandmother dates Leonard Duncan, the man you accused of doing this to you." I gestured towards her face and her hand immediately touched her bottom lip self-consciously.

"Then you already know what happened." Her back straightened indignantly but her eyes wouldn't meet mine.

"No, I don't. Leonard claims he doesn't remember what happened and everything after he left the doctor's office yesterday is a blank. So, I thought you could fill in those blanks."

Janette snorted with laughter. "And just what the hell did you expect him to say? 'Yes, officer I beat the shit out of a sick old lady'."

It took everything in me not to roll my eyes at the sick part. I just let Janette vent.

"Leonard Duncan has been hiding behind that I'm too drunk to remember bullshit for as long as I've known him. Why would he change now?"

"But you drink, too? I bet you don't remember me giving you a ride home from The Spot on two different occasions and you driving off in my car, do you?" She gave me a startled look. "I can tell you don't remember so it is possible he doesn't remember what happened yesterday." Did I just defend Leonard?

Janette angrily turned on her heel and walked away leaving me with no choice but to follow her into a large living room with a set of French doors that led to a large patio. She threw open the doors like she was the lady of the manor, then stalked outside and then sank wearily down on a tan wicker patio chair like her little outburst had worn her out. The patio overlooked a large Olympic sized pool. Off in the distance there was a large building. I knew Justin Ramey had gone to art school and vaguely wondered if that was his studio.

"I really didn't come here to upset you," I said, sitting down in the chair opposite hers. "But accusing someone of assault is pretty serious business, Ms. Ramey. I just came by to get your side of the story."

"Fine," she said, finally looking at me. "I was at my apartment picking up a few things, minding my own damned business when Lenny showed up. We argued and the next thing I remember is waking up on my living room floor all bloody and bruised."

"You mean you don't actually remember him assaulting you?"

"Ain't that what I just said?" she snapped irritably.

"Were you drunk at the time of this argument?" She just glared at me and didn't answer, which I guessed meant yes.

"Is it possible you just blacked out and that's the real reason you don't remember being assaulted?" I asked.

"It don't take a genius to figure out what happened when I woke up all beat to hell! You think I did this to myself?" she said, putting a hand to the knot on her forehead.

"Well, what were you arguing about?"

"None of your damned business!"

"Was it because he wouldn't give you any more money?"

Janette's mouth fell open comically and she started to sputter. "How the hell did you—?"

"I know a lot of things, Janette." I pulled out the snapshot I found at Leonard's place and slid it across the table at her. She glanced down at it and then did a double take. She picked it up and let out a humorless chuckle. I looked really hard at her and tried to see the beautiful young girl in the picture but she was long gone.

"You found some old picture of me making eyes at Lenny and now you think you know something about me? Girl, you need to get outta my house with this mess and for your information, I don't need nobody's damned money. I got money of my own now."

"Your house? I thought your brother left everything to Pia."

"He did," she said smugly. "And being the loving and generous niece that she is, she turned right around and signed this house, and everything in it, over to me."

So that's why Link was still living here. His mother was hardly going to throw him out on the street. And not having any money or anyplace else to go, Link had no choice but to stay in this house with a woman he loathed. Janette finally had her son right where she wanted him, completely dependent on her.

"Does your loving and generous niece know that you don't really have cancer?"

"Of course she knows I don't have cancer," Janette replied, without missing a beat. If she wondered *how* I knew about her scam, she wasn't showing it.

"Pia knows you've been faking it and she still gave you this house?"

"As far as Pia's concerned, I'm in remission, and she wants her old aunty living the good life. Doesn't want me all stressed out cause the cancer might come back. Now ain't that sweet?" Janette sat back in her chair clearly satisfied with herself.

"I bet that must really have pissed off Ingrid, huh?"

"Like I care what that uppity heifer thinks! And it don't matter no more because I got what I wanted. See for years everybody's been talking about me behind my back and feeling sorry for me. Always talking about how I could have done something with my life if I had settled down with some old boring army dude and hadn't been so wild and always chasing a good time. And look at me know. I'm living in this sweet crib while all those folks who talked about me are barely hanging on."

"Was Leonard's wife, Lila, one of those people who talked about you?" I asked smoothly and was rewarded with a momentary look of panic on Janette's face. I'd found the chink in her armor.

Her eyes immediately fixated on something behind me and I turned around but couldn't see what she was looking at. The only thing behind me was a lush manicured lawn and the pool.

"Lila Duncan was never a fan of mine and the feeling was mutual. I couldn't stand her ass even before she married Lenny. She reminded me of that bitch, Ingrid. Always acting better than she was." Janette said, laughing.

"Maybe it was because you were after her husband and he didn't want to be bothered."

Janette laughed out loud. "I don't know where you got your information from, but my relationship with Lenny was a two way street."

"Really?" I couldn't tell if she was telling the truth or it was just wishful thinking.

"It's like I already told you, back in the day I was hot stuff and no man, including Lila Duncan's old man, could resist me." She grinned and then winced, touching her puffy lip again.

"Is Leonard Link's father? Is that why he was giving you money? Or were you blackmailing him for another, deadlier reason?"

Again Janette's eyes looked beyond me at something in the distance before she stood up abruptly and towered over me.

"Now, look, I've put up with these rude bullshit questions of yours but now you've gone too far. Like they say during last call at The Spot, you ain't got to go home but you got to get the hell outta here," she said through gritted teeth.

"You know what I think?" Janette just glared at me and I pressed on. "I think you've loved Leonard for so long that you're willing to do just about anything to keep him close, even blackmail him over something he didn't do just so he'd still have to come see you. His wife's been dead for fifteen years and he still doesn't want you because now you remind him of the worst night of his life. The night he ran over Lila, only he wasn't the one driving, was he? He was too drunk to drive. He must have passed out and you got behind the wheel and headed to Lila's job."

"Get out of my house!" she yelled. but I didn't move. I wasn't finished.

"What happened, Janette? Was it an accident or did all the anger and rage you felt for Lila Duncan all those years come bubbling to the surface and you mowed her down on purpose?"

"It's her own damned fault she's dead," she spat out at me. "Who the hell stands in the middle of a parking lot anyway? Her ass should have been waiting at the door." Her voice was so cold that I actually flinched.

"So . . . I'm right?" I said in a voice barely above a whisper. She laughed.

"What difference does it make when you've got no

proof?"

I pulled the title to the Cadillac that I'd found in her apartment from my purse and tossed across the table. Janette looked at it for a few seconds before picking it up, and tearing into tiny pieces.

"This doesn't mean a thing when there's no car to go with it," she said in amusement.

She turned on her heel and went back into the house, slamming the French doors behind her.

SIXTEEN

I headed through a side gate that led to the front of the house and spotted Link. He was in the driveway talking to a man in an old red pickup truck with the words Lehman Shaw's Antique Appraisals painted in yellow block lettering on the side.

"I told you on the phone the warehouse is out back, behind the house! You took the wrong road." Link shouted, motioning for the older man driving the truck to back up. But the man didn't budge. He just sat squinting at Link through the windshield like he was wondering what kind of a fool he was. And when he slowly got out of the truck instead of backing up, Link slapped his forehead and stomped his foot like a five year-old throwing a tantrum.

I could see the problem all the way from where I was standing at the top of the driveway. The man, who I assumed was Lehman Shaw, was quite elderly and was wearing a hearing aid in each ear. He was thin and stooped with wisps of white hair sticking up in tufts all over his liver spotted head. He slowly took a step towards Link and held out a trembling hand for him to shake. Link sighed and gave the man's hand a quick pump, then took a look behind him at the house. I jumped behind a tall bush before he could see me then ducked down behind the row of high hedges that lined the driveway and crept closer so I could listen.

"I got a call for an appraisal?" said the elderly man in a booming voice.

"I'm the one who called you but the building is separate from the house at the back of the property. I left very specific instructions on what road to take to get there when I made this appointment."

"No need to get testy, young man. I may be old but I'm not stupid. I like to know who I'm doing business with before I go gallivanting down back roads on someone else's property. Back in my day that was a good way to get yourself shot."

"I also made it very clear that this appointment was to be discreet." Link had lowered his voice and took another quick peak at the house. I looked as well and saw no one.

What in the world was Link's shady behind up to this time? Knowing him it was certain to be about money and even more certain to be about money that didn't belong to him. And since Pia would sooner French Kiss a rattle snake than give her estranged brother any money, Link was most likely plotting a way to get his hot little hands on a piece of his father's estate before she gave any more of it to Janette. Jeesh! Why was it so hard to get a job like a normal person? Surely, punching a clock would be a lot easier than this nonsense.

"Well, now that you've met me," said Link,

irritably. "Can we please go to where we were supposed to meet in the first place?"

"Go eat?" replied Mr. Lehman cupping both his ears in confusion. "I thought you wanted me to appraise some antiques?"

Link threw up his hands in exasperation and practically shoved the elderly man towards his truck and into the driver's side. Link quickly jumped into the passenger side and seconds later Lehman Shaw was slowly backing out of the driveway. Once they'd taken off down the road, I rushed to the end of the drive to see the truck a quarter mile away turning down a narrow dirt road that I hadn't noticed the other two times I'd been out here.

My car was still parked in the circular drive in front of the house so I jumped in and headed down the dirt road after them. The road was bumpy and uneven with large rocks so I had to slow down to a crawl for fear of puncturing a tire. Soon a large, squat, rectangular, white building came into view. Lehman Shaw's truck was parked in front but I saw no trace of him or Link. They must have already gone inside. I parked behind the building, closing my car door as softly as I could so Link wouldn't come outside.

A white sign posted on the side of the building declared that trespassers would be prosecuted but I ignored it, of course. Pausing near the entrance of the cavernous building, the faint voices of the two men inside told me they must have been at the very back. So I ducked inside and had to wait a few seconds for my eyes to adjust to the gloom. The building was a long one-story affair with a loft overhead and empty stalls along either side. It obviously used to be a horse barn and though the horses were long gone, the slight tang of hay and manure remained.

The building appeared to be mostly empty with the exception of a couple of old saddles hanging from rusty nails on the walls. A center path led to a large open area filled with boxes where Lehman Shaw was examining a tiny blue and white vase with a long thin neck resting in Link's outstretched hand. Neither man had noticed me, yet. I took the opportunity to quickly and quietly duck inside the closest stall and peered through a slat in the wood.

"Hmm," said Shaw, rubbing his chin as he examined the vase. "I believe what you've got here is a very well done fake."

"A fake! Are you serious?" growled Link indignantly. "My old man bought this from a well-respected collector. This is a genuine Ming vase!"

Lehman Shaw burst into wheezy laughter that made him double over. Link gripped the neck of the vase tightly like he was about the break it over the elderly man's head.

"Oh, don't get me wrong, young fella," Lehman Shaw said, straightening up. "It's a pretty good fake. One of the better ones I've seen. If we were back at my shop and I had my black light I could show you better. But look at the porcelain." Shaw took the vase out of Link's hands and held it up to the light.

"What about it?" snapped Link, straining to see what Shaw was referring to.

"It's opaque, that's what. If it was genuine Asian porcelain, made in China prior to the eighteenth century, It'd be translucent. Plus, this color blue is all wrong. It's too light. Should be cobalt."

"You're telling me this vase is worthless?" said Link, incredulous.

"I wouldn't say worthless. It was made in China sometime in the eighteenth century and is probably worth about a thousand bucks or so."

"A thousand bucks?" Link looked deflated. He apparently thought he was going to get enough money by secretly selling off his father's antique collection to stick it to Pia and get out from under Janette's thumb. And since Pia owned the property and Janette owned the house, would Link now be considered a trespasser?

"No need to get all distraught," said Shaw, patting Link on the shoulder. "What else have you got?"

Lehman followed Link through another door and I lost sight of them. I strained to hear but could only catch snatches of their conversation. I stood up, and had crept closer to try and hear what they were saying, when they started coming back out of the room. I froze in my tracks. Link was in the doorway with his back to me. All he had to do was turn around.

"Take your time, Mr. Lehman. I'll be back in a about an hour. I have some business to take care of.

Mr. Lehman grunted and I backed up, stepping on my own untied shoelaces and fell on my ass with a thud that seemed to vibrate off the walls. I barely had time to crawl behind a large box when Link turned. Why the hell had I followed them back here? Link being sneaky and trying to make a buck by selling Justin's stuff wasn't my problem. As usual my nosiness had gotten the better of me and if I got caught, I knew Link wouldn't hesitate to have me arrested for trespassing.

"Did you hear that?" Link asked aloud. And getting no response from the other room, added under his breath, "Of course you didn't hear anything you deaf mother—"

"Now this might be worth a pretty penny," interrupted Lehman.

Link rushed back into the room to see what of his father's antique collection was about to net him a small fortune. And as curious as I was to know what the old antique dealer was talking about, it was time I got the hell out of Dodge. I quickly tied my shoelaces and was about to leave when what Link said next stopped me.

"Are you kidding me? You mean this piece of crap Caddy is worth something?"

Did he just say Caddy as in *Cadillac*? I slunk over to the doorway and peeked in. The room was the size of one of the storage units at Storage Solutions Self Storage Units. It was crammed with boxes on the left side of the room. But a dark colored car, partially covered with a white sheet, occupied the other side of the room. The back end of the car was facing the back of the room, which I could now see was actually a barn door.

"I know a collector that restores and sells old Cadillacs. Bet he'd love to get his hands on this beauty," said Shaw, as he yanked the rest of the sheet off the car. It was definitely an old Cadillac but in the poor lighting I couldn't tell if it was dark blue or black. Could this be the same car that killed Leonard's wife? My stomach fluttered with excitement.

"What's so special about this old car?" asked Link skeptically. "Your friend could probably find one in just about every junkyard or used car dealership from here to California."

"It all about the paint job, son," replied Shaw. "But

I need to get a better look to be sure. Help me with this door so we can get some light in here." The old man pulled feebly at the wooden slat holding the barn door shut.

Link nudged him aside with a sigh and pulled with all his might before the slat came up with a loud scraping sound that set my teeth on edge. Each man pushed a side of the door open, flooding the darkened room with much needed sunlight and fresh air and revealing the car in question to be dark blue that was almost black, the same color Cadillac as Leonard's Cadillac or rather the Cadillac that Janette bought him.

"So what about the color?" Link impatiently trailed Lehman Shaw as he inspected every inch of the car.

"Well," said Shaw straightening. "It's kind of like that fake Ming vase of yours. This color blue was a mistake. Fifty cars were made with this midnight blue color before they caught it and now these cars are collectors items."

"How much are we talking?" asked Link.

"I'd say upwards of a hundred grand or more." Link let out a low whistle.

"You've got to be shitting me," he said.

"Scouts honor," said Mr. Shaw.

"And you're sure this friend of yours would be interested?"

"It's like I already told you. He's a collector and this car is worth a pretty penny.

"Well I'll be damned," said Link.

I could practically hear him grinning. "I never thought this car was anything but a piece of junk. My old man's had this car since I was eleven. He told me he was saving it for when I turned 16. I couldn't wait to drive this thing. But by the time I actually turned sixteen, driving this hooptie was the last thing on my mind. I didn't have the heart to tell him I didn't want the car anymore. But it turned out that I didn't have to."

"Why's that?" asked Mr. Shaw.

"It was really weird. For years he'd been talking about getting this thing fixed up for me to drive but instead he gave me a BMW convertible for my sixteenth birthday and never mentioned this car to me again. I forgot this old thing was still out here."

If Justin gave Link this car when he was eleven that would put the timeframe at around the time of Lila Duncan's hit and run. This had to be the same car. And there was only one reason why Justin would have hidden this car away in an old barn at the back of his property. He was protecting his little sister, Janette. Her killing Lila must have been the straw that broke the camel's back and caused her estrangement from Justin. I had to go tell Harmon before this car was sold off. Before I turned to go I glanced through the open barn doors and noticed something. Off in the distance, across the open field, was a very clear view of Justin Ramey's back yard and the stone patio where I'd sat talking to Janette barely 20 minutes ago. Now I knew what she'd been looking at so nervously.

Ten minutes later I was cruising through downtown Willow on my way to the police station. I had tried to call Detective Harmon but she wasn't answering her phone. I left an urgent message for her to call me but knew she probably wouldn't. I had a pretty good idea who she was with and resisted the urge to head out to Rollins' house. The last time I'd been to his house I'd watched the two of them slow dancing through the patio window. I winced at the memory. But if I didn't hear from her soon, I may have to take a trip out there whether I wanted to or not. I also called the hospital to check on Mason but all the nurse was able to tell me was that he was still in the hospital but with strict instructions from his doctor that he rests and not to be disturbed.

I was stopped on Main Street at a red light when someone I knew crossed the street in front of me. It was Ray Wallace the bartender at the Spot. I blew my horn and waved but he was so lost in thought he didn't even look up.

Once across the street, he headed into the Super X pharmacy. I don't know why but I've pulled over and parked in front of the pharmacy. I started to get out and go inside when Ray came out. He had a pack of cigarettes in his hands. If his hands hadn't been shaking so badly, I probably wouldn't have noticed how bruised his knuckles were. He finally freed a cigarette from the pack and shoved it in his mouth. He pulled out a cheap red lighter from his pocket and shakily lit the cigarette. Then he took a long drag and slowly blew out a cloud of smoke. And then he finally noticed me standing there staring at him.

"Hey there, Mr. Wallace. Remember me?" I asked. For a second his eyes were blank then he finally let out a chuckle.

"It's Kim, right?" He ventured. "You were in the Spot the other day, weren't you?"

"Actually, it's Kendra. But that's okay. We only met one time. I hardly expect you to remember my name."

"Pepsi with a cherry," he said with a smile. "I may not remember names but I always remember what people had to drink." He blew out another stream of smoke and settled the cigarette into the corner of his mouth where it dangled limply.

That's when it hit me. This was the same man that had been with Janette in the picture I'd found at Leonard's place. I remembered when I've been at the spot and he told me a little bit about himself and about how he been in the military and how Janette could've had a nice man and a family of her own. He'd been talking about himself.

"What happened to your hand Mr. Wallace?"

"Oh, this?" He flexed his fingers and pain flash across his face. "The wind blew the door shut on it. It hurt like the devil."

"Really?" I said. "Remember what we talked about when I was at the Spot?"

"I'm sure we talked about a lot of things, young lady. I can't be bothered to remember every conversation I ever had with someone I was serving drinks to.

"You don't remember telling me about how sad Janette Remy's life was and how it could've been different if she gone with the right man?"

He didn't say a word just looked off into space for a few seconds before dropping his cigarette on the ground and mashing it with his foot.

"I've got to go, sweetheart. But it's been real nice talking to you." He took off walking down the street the way he'd come. I called out after him.

"You were talking about yourself, weren't you?" I ran to catch up with him but he kept on walking. "You were the nice guy she could have had a family with. You were the one she dumped because she thought you were boring." He stopped so abruptly I almost ran into him. His back stiffened.

"Netty never had eyes for anyone but Lenny Duncan," he said, with a low simmering anger that practically made him vibrate. "She only went out with me to make him jealous. Didn't matter that he had a wife. Didn't matter how much I loved her. She didn't have to give me a dime to be with her. I would have given her the world. But she didn't want me." His voice caught but he didn't cry.

"You're still in love with her, aren't you?"

"With that drunk old hag? No," he said, wearily. "But with the beautiful young woman she used to be, yeah. I still love that Netty. Just being around her made me feel alive. She was fearless. She could have been so much more. Instead, she wasted her life chasing after a man who could never love her."

"Is that why you beat her up? You were mad because of how she wasted her life." He gave me another blank look.

"I don't know what you're talking about. I never laid a hand on Netty in anger."

"Maybe not the beautiful young Netty you loved years ago but what about the woman she is now?"

He fumbled for another cigarette. Inhaling another lungful of smoke seemed to calm him.

"How would you feel if you'd paid child support for a son you thought was yours for eighteen years? A son you never got a chance to know because his mother wouldn't marry you and you were in the military and always traveling. You sent letters and gifts and the mother of your son swore she gave him those letters and gifts. But he never wrote back. You thought he just didn't want to know you and you stopped writing. In reality, not only did he never get what you sent; he wasn't even your son. You find out you were lied to all along and the son you thought was yours could have been fathered by one of at least a dozen men? How would that make you feel?"

"Janette lied and made you think Link was your son? No wonder you snapped. So what happened? Did you go to her apartment and overhear her asking Leonard for money and you wondered why? So you waited for him to leave before confronting her. She was drunk and told you the truth about Link and you went off on her?"

"I never touched her."

"Did you know she thinks Leonard assaulted her? He got arrested yesterday and spent the night in jail. He's being held responsible for what you did."

"I said I didn't do anything to Netty!" he shouted, causing some passersby to look at us. "And besides," he said, lowering his voice, "Lenny Duncan was in the Spot most of yesterday drinking. And I can vouch for him because I was the one serving him."

"Really? And why did Leonard start drinking again after fifteen years of being sober?"

"Because his lady, your grandma, was about to get some bad news about him by way of Netty. He wouldn't say what it was but it must have been pretty bad for him to fall back into the bottle again after all these years. And whatever he did, Netty knew and he'd been paying her to keep her mouth shut about it for years. But he'd stopped paying and Netty was about to spill the beans. And you're right. I did wonder what she had on him and if it had anything to do with Link. "

"I went to her place to ask her and as usual she was drunk as a skunk. We argued. After she dropped that bombshell on me about not knowing who the hell that boy's father was, and laughing about how she spent up the money I'd sent her every month partying, I punched the wall and called her a whore. She swung at me, missed, lost her balance and fell flat on her face. She busted her lip and knocked herself out cold and I left her lying right there on the carpet just like a stain. And I'd have told the police that, too! But they never asked." He glared at me indignantly.

"Are you still willing to tell the police what happened?"

"Of course. I can't have Lenny getting locked up over Rats' lies and foolishness!"

"Rats?" I said in confusion.

"That's Lenny's nickname for Netty. When we were kids, Netty loved Minnie and Mickey Mouse. Still does. Lenny always used to tease her and say any mice big enough to sing and dance and wear clothes weren't mice. They were rats. She always hated that nickname."

Rats? Suddenly something else made sense. Now I had to see if I was right.

"Thank you, Mr. Wallace!" I flung my arms around his neck and kissed him on the cheek.

"Where you off to in such a hurry, sweetheart?" He called out after me.

"I've got to see a man about some rats!"

The little park near the Ramey Gallery was empty of people. But the trace of breadcrumbs on the ground near the bench indicated that Handy Randy had recently been here and I really needed to talk to him. It had occurred to me that when I'd asked him about what he'd seen the night of Justin's murder, he'd mentioned seeing rats. I thought he'd meant real rats. But thinking back on the way he'd said it, I now wondered if he'd been talking about someone *named* Rats.

"Hey there. You got some more work for me?" Randy said, startling me. I hadn't heard him sit down next to me. His clothes looked slept in, his eyes were glassy, and his hair was coming loose from its ponytail. Someone apparently had a good time last night.

"Hi Randy." He also reeked of weed and I scooted a little further down the bench.

"That cop boyfriend of yours isn't with you, is he?" he asked suspiciously, making me feel guilty that I hadn't been to the hospital to see Mason today.

"Of course not," I sighed "And I already told you he's not my boyfriend."

"Good. So what brings you to the park this time?"

"Actually, I'm looking for your friend, Rats."

"Rats?" he said, looking confused.

"You know, Rats. You said you saw Rats the night that art gallery owner got killed, remember?" Could I have been wrong about what he'd said that day?

"Oh, that Rats." He shook his head as if to clear it. "What about her?"

"Her name wouldn't happen to be Janette Ramey, would it?"

"No clue. I never asked her her real name. She's just Rats and I'm just Randy."

"Well, have you seen her lately?" I asked, trying not to sound as impatient as I was feeling.

"I only see Rats when I've got a new batch of dandelion wine to sell. I sell it for two bucks a bottle. It's cheap but it's strong. Really packs a punch. Rats is my best customer, especially when she's low on cash and can't afford to go to the bars to drink. Hell, most of the time I give it to her for free."

So I was right. Rats was Janette and she was in the vicinity of the gallery the night of Justin's murder when she was supposed to be at home. And after finding out everything I had about Janette, I had a bad feeling I knew why. And it was connected to Lila Duncan's death.

"Do you remember if you saw her before or after you saw the pretty black girl crying and talking on the phone?"

"Hmm," Randy said, as he started to nod off. I gave his knee a hard nudge.

"Randy! Wake up! This is really important."

"Okay. Okay," he said, jerking awake. "Calm down. You know you could really use some of my special herbal blend. Would do wonders for your—"

"Randy!"

"Sorry. What was the question, again?"

"Did you see Rats here in the park before or after you saw the pretty black girl?"

"After. . .I think, though it could have been before. Sorry. I'm a little fuzzy on the exact details. So why are you looking for her anyway? I didn't think Rats had any friends except me."

It was on the tip of my tongue to tell him but since his dislike of the police would probably make him sympathetic to her, I kept it to myself.

"Um. . .I owe her some money."

"Oh. Well, I'll make sure and tell her you're looking for her next time I see her."

"And when will that be?"

"Next time she needs some. . .hey, wait a minute!" He started laughing hysterically.

"What is it?"

"What the hell was I thinking? I never saw Rats here in the park that night. I saw her at my place. That's right! She showed up at my place late that night. We smoked a little herb and got shitfaced drunk."

"Oh," I replied. Just great. I was wrong and this had been a huge waste of my time when I should have been tracking down Harmon. For all I knew, Lehman Shaw had called his collector friend and the caddy that killed Leonard's wife could be halfway to God only knew where by now.

"Thanks, Randy. I'll see you around." I got up to go.

"Hey, Kendra?"

"Yeah?"

"Could you give me a ride home? My bike's got a flat tire. And I'm not feeling too good. Partied a little too hard last night," he said, chuckling. "You know how it is."

"Sure, Randy."

I kept all the windows of my car rolled down all the way to Randy's place so he wouldn't leave his pungent herbal odor in my car. He lived out by the fairgrounds in a rusted out old trailer in the woods. I parked by the side of the road and followed Randy to his door to make sure he didn't pass out in the woods.

"Can you come in for a minute?" he asked.

"There's a bottle of my homemade peach wine with your name on it. It's the least I can do to pay you for the ride."

"That's okay, Randy. I really need to get back to town."

"It'll only take a minute. Loosen up will ya?" Randy pulled out his key to unlock the trailer door but when he placed his hand on the door, it swung open. "What the hell? I don't remember leaving my door unlocked." He pushed the door all the way open and stumbled inside with me on his heels. The inside of the trailer was a mess.

"Oh cool," he said, letting out a sigh of relief. "For a minute there I thought I'd been robbed."

"You mean it looks this way all the time?" I mumbled.

"Have a seat while I get the wine. But not on the recliner it's broken. Ain't worked right since Rats was last here. I haven't had the time to fix it."

I stepped gingerly around a pile of dirty clothes on the floor. One end of the trailer was a kitchenette with a sink full of dirty dishes and a round kitchen table scarred with cigarette burns and sticky rings left behind by coffee mugs along with a partially disassembled radio. In fact, small appliances, that I assumed Randy was repairing for people, were all over the counter tops and even on the floor. The trashcan was over flowing, as were the ashtrays. The blinds were greasy and pulled shut making it dim inside. A lopsided brown couch and a leather recliner filled the opposite side of the trailer.

The couch had a large old TV lying screen side down on it with the back panel removed. A pair of pliers, a screwdriver, and a multitude of screws and small wires covered the coffee table. I absently sat down on the recliner and immediately the footrest sprang out. Not wanting Randy to see I'd messed up the recliner even more, I tried in vain to push the footrest down. But every time I pushed it down it sprang back out. Frustrated, I looked underneath and could see something was caught in the hinges preventing it from staying down. I tugged at it and pulled it free. It was a black, plastic bag with something heavy inside.

It was a roundish chunk of light colored wood with a deep crosshatched diamond pattern all over it and a carved stem on top. One whole side of it was stained dark red with dried blood and when I looked closely could see silver strands of hair stuck in the blood as well as bloody bits of dried pinkish tissue. Brain matter. I almost dropped it. This was the missing pineapple sculpture used to kill Justin Ramey. And when Janette had gotten drunk, she must have forgotten and not remembered where she'd left it. Janette was the one who'd killed Justin aka the only other person who knew she'd killed Lila Duncan fifteen years ago. Did he threaten to turn the car over to the police if she didn't stay out of Pia's pockets?

"Randy!" I called out as I got unsteadily to my feet. "Randy!" I headed back through the kitchen towards the room he'd disappeared into and was greeted by soft rhythmic snoring. Randy was face down on a mattress on the floor fast asleep. And shaking him only made him snore even louder. Great.

I paced nervously for a few minutes wondering if should stay put and call Harmon or take what I'd found to the police station. In the end, a sense of urgency drove me out of the trailer. But I was no sooner out the door, than I was struck hard on the back and sent flying off Randy's stoop and flat on my face. The black bag with the pineapple sculpture went flying across the yard. I rolled over to see Link Ramey framed in the doorway with a lead pipe in his hands.

SEVENTEEN

Now I knew what Link had been talking about when he'd told Lehman Shaw he had something to take care of. We both eyed the black bag.

"Don't even try it," he said in a low growl as he walked down the steps of the trailer towards me. He was slapping his palm with the pipe like he wished it were my head.

"Help! Randy! Help! Somebody!" I screamed to no avail.

"Randy's in dreamland and he'd better not wake up or he'll get what I was planning to give him if he'd come home alone."

"Why kill Randy?"

"Because I was afraid he'd found that bag my aunt Janette left here by accident. By the way, thanks for finding it for me. I'd have gone crazy if I had to spend another minute searching this shit hole."

"But he wouldn't have even known what it was!"

"I couldn't take that chance." Link was now less then twenty feet away. I started inching away from him.

"You killed Justin? But. . .but. . . he was your father!"

"But Pia was his little princess. I hardly existed once she came along. Then came Lauren. It was bad enough she used me to get to him. But what was I supposed to do when she kept crawling into bed with me even after she married him? She came after me! But *I* was the one he was so angry with!" he shouted.

"She didn't force you! You could have said no! What did you expect Justin to do, give you a medal?"

"Women like Lauren are a dime a dozen. He could have gone out and bought another one. But I was his son, the only son he had, and he wanted nothing to do with me! It was like I no longer existed. We were living in the same house. But I may as well have been invisible! It was all Lauren's fault!"

"So, instead of apologizing to your father for sleeping with his wife, you killed him?"

"I didn't go there to kill him!" To my surprise a fat tear slid down his cheek. "He called me and told me to meet him at the gallery that night to talk about my future. I just knew he was going to forgive me and things would go back to normal. Instead, he told me he wanted me out of the house by the end of the week. I begged him to change his mind. I even cried. But he told me to get out. Then I saw it, an anniversary card on his desk. It was for Lauren. He had forgiven her. But he wouldn't give me, his own son, another chance. I just lost it. I grabbed the first thing I could get my hands on and swung it at him and I hit him over and over and over again. Then he was dead and there was blood everywhere. I heard a noise behind me. It was Aunt Janette just standing in the doorway."

"What was she doing there?"

"Pia called her in tears about dad cutting the funding for her stupid art program. She said she came by to reason with him. But when she saw me covered in his blood she never even blinked. Didn't even ask me what happened. She just took the sculpture out of my hands and told me to go home and get myself cleaned up and she'd take care of everything. I was in shock. I just took off. Later, I kept asking her what she'd done with the damned pineapple but she wouldn't say. She said it was best I didn't know then she finally admitted she'd gotten pissy drunk that night with some old hippy named Randy and forgot it at his place. I never should have trusted her. She must be the stupidest woman on the planet!"

"Well, the apple doesn't fall far from the tree," I blurted, without thinking. But to my surprise Link laughed.

"You sure are mouthy for someone about to die."

"Aren't you going to ask me what I'm talking about?" I added quickly.

"I don't care." He raised the pipe and took a step towards me. I quickly scooted backwards ending up next to the black bag.

"Aren't you the slightest bit curious about why Janette helped you that night? And why she always wants to spend time with you, even if she has to pay you? I know you've been getting money from her."

Link stopped mid-step. "What are you talking about?"

"She's your mother, Link. Janette is your mother!"

"You lying bitch!"

"It's true, I swear!" I said, scooting back further.

"Justin and Ingrid adopted you when you were two because Janette was unfit and when Justin turned his back on you, Janette started scamming Pia. She's been pretending to have cancer and using the money Pia gave her for treatments to give to you! She loves you so much she'd do anything for you! And I have to admit; you're just like her. Did you know she killed someone, too? She ran over a woman with that old Cadillac in your father's horse barn. Didn't you ever wonder why a man with so much money, who could afford any car he wanted, had an old car like that hidden away in that barn? He was protecting your mother, his sister, just like Janette protected you!"

"Liar!"

He swung the pipe at me and I managed to roll away before I got my head bashed in. I grabbed the black bag, swung it at him, and knocked the pipe out of his hands. But my palms were sweaty and the slick plastic bag slipped out of my hands. Link and I both lunged for the bag at once. I reached it first and managed to get to my feet. But before I could get away, he tackled me to the ground then flipped me over.

"You nosy bitch! I should have done this when I caught you snooping around Venus Studio. Lauren told me to meet her there, but when I got there, she was gone, Paul was dead, and the wall safe was empty. She killed him and tried to frame me!"

So Link was the one who used the stun gun on me and stole the computer, files, and the investors list from my pocket. Too bad I'd never get a chance to tell anyone. Link put his hands around my throat, and squeezed. I frantically writhed and clawed at his fingers to no avail, causing him to squeeze tighter.

I was starting to lose consciousness. Then there was a thud. Link grunted and let go of my throat. His body went limp and he collapsed on top of me. I was gasping to catch my breath when none other than Margery Warfield rolled Link's limp, unconscious body off of me.

"What a nasty man! Kendra, are you okay?" She dropped the lead pipe she'd clobbered Link with, knelt down, and put her arms around me, hugging me close in a warm cinnamon scented embrace.

"Margery. . .thank. . .God!" I gasped, tears streamed from my eyes. "You. . .saved my life! Where in the world did you come from?"

"I live in the trailer park across the road. I was taking my trash out when I heard someone scream. I ran over here and saw that man choking you. What happened, Kendra? Who is this person?" she asked, helping me to my feet.

"It's a long story, Margery, but first we need to tie him up and call the police."

Since Randy had no phone, Margery offered to make the call from her trailer. I managed to wake up Randy, hoping he'd babysit Link and make sure he didn't wake up and break free of the duct tape we'd bound his wrists and ankles with. But once he heard the police were on their way, he packed a duffle bag and took off for parts unknown, vowing not to come back until the dust had settled. Link lay so still on the ground I had to check his pulse every few minutes to make sure he was still alive. Margery had whacked him pretty hard. After ten minutes, and still no police, I made my way through the woods and crossed the road to the trailer park in search of Margery.

Woodside Trailer Park had been cut out of a three-acre section of the woods with trailers lined up neatly in rows of six or eight in each block. The yards were an eclectic mix of well-tended manicured lawns with flowerpots and above ground pools in the backyards and dirt lots with trash and debris strewn about. Almost all the trailers, including the most run down ones, had satellite dishes. It didn't look much different from a lot of the neighborhoods in town. I remembered Rhonda describing it as 'dicey' and wondered how long it had been since she'd been out here.

Aside from a few kids riding their bikes, there weren't any other people outside. It was getting dark and several dogs barked, a couple of them straining at the ends of their chains, to try and get at me, as I wandered around looking for Margery's trailer. Realizing that unless her trailer sat under a large blinking neon sign that read Margery's that I was never going to find it, I waved one of the kids on their bikes over and asked if they knew where Mrs. Warfield lived.

"You mean the cookie lady?" asked the kid, a boy of about seven who dug in his nose the entire time I was talking to him.

"Yeah, that's her," I replied. My mouth watered involuntarily at the thought of her chocolate chunk cookies.

The boy turned and pointed, "She lives in that one with the white fence."

There were three trailers with white fences where the kid had pointed but he'd pedaled off before I could ask him which one. But as I approached, I guessed the one with the large terra cotta pot of pink impatiens on the steps must be the one, that and the initials MW stenciled on the lid of the mailbox. My fist was poised to knock when the door flew open. A scented wave of baking cookies wafted out into the night air.

"Kendra?" Margery seemed confused to see me at her door.

"I'm sorry to bother you, Margery, but the police still haven't shown up. Can I come in and call again?" She rolled her eyes and sighed in exasperation as she held the door open for me to come in.

"I'm so sorry, Kendra. I should have warned you that it might take a long time for them to respond. I'm afraid this area has a bit of a reputation for crime and they'll probably take their sweet time getting here. But come on in and I'll call again."

I waited inside the doorway while Margery made another call to the police. While she was on the phone, I looked around. The inside of her trailer was the exact opposite of Randy's, meaning it was so clean there probably wasn't a surface anywhere that I couldn't have eaten off of. Aside from being clean it was pretty sparse on furniture with just two floral recliners and a TV stand in the living room and a dinette set in the kitchen.

"I had to sell almost everything to pay the bills when my husband left," said Margery, gesturing for me to sit down at the kitchen table when she got off the phone. There was flour, sugar and eggs sitting on the kitchen table along with a rack with cookies cooling on it.

I didn't know what to say and just gave her a smile. It was also freezing in the trailer and goose bumps popped up on my arms. I didn't want to be rude but it was taking everything in me to keep my teeth from chattering. If it were just a few degrees colder, I could probably see my breath.

"Sorry about the air conditioning. I'm going through menopause and it's like summer all year long. It's especially bad when the oven's on."

"No problem, Margery. Did they say how long it might be?"

"They said they'd send someone right out. You shouldn't have much longer to wait."

"Well, you should probably come back with me. The police will need to talk to you, too"

"Why?" she said with alarm.

"Because you're a witness. You saw Link Ramey try to kill me."

Margery slapped her forehead. "Of course I am! I'm sorry, Kendra, I don't know what in the world I was thinking."

"I know you've got a lot on your mind," I said, referring to her mother's death. "When is the funeral?"

"The what?" She looked confused again.

"Your mother's funeral? I'd like to pay my respects and I know Rhonda would, too."

"My mother was cremated yesterday. I couldn't afford a funeral."

"Oh," I said, for lack of anything better to say. "Um. . .we should probably get back to Randy's trailer before the police get there."

"Sure. Just let me put this batch of cookies away first."

"Is there anything I can do to help?" I asked, anxious to get back before Link regained consciousness.

"Can you grab me a container from the cabinet over the sink, please?"

Margery pulled plastic wrap from a nearby drawer as I reached up and pulled open the cabinet above the sink. Plastic bowels and Tupperware containers were stacked neatly on the bottom shelf, while round cookie tins filled the upper shelf. The tins were all the same. They were all red with white horses galloping around the sides. All the cookies she'd given away at work had been in the same kind of tin. I quickly grabbed a Tupperware container, and was about to hand it to her, when I froze.

I had the same cookie tin with horses on it at home. Tin. Horses. That's what Mason had said when I'd visited him in the hospital. He'd said ten horses. I'd thought he'd meant the number ten. But he'd meant tin, as in cookie tin. I already knew from the cobbler he'd eaten at Mama's that he had a massive sweet tooth. He must have found the tin of cookies at my place and eaten them and that's what had made him sick. That was also what had been making me sick. It was the cookies. By why hadn't I gotten as sick as Mason? Why would Margery do this? Had her husband leaving her pushed her over the edge? Then another thought hit me hard. Were poisoned cookies what had killed Margery's mother?"

"Kendra?" Margery was holding her hand out for the container. But I just stared at her. I took a step back and dropped the container. "What's wrong?" she asked, looking concerned.

"Nothing. Just feeling a little lightheaded."

"It's no wonder. You were almost choked to death. Sit down and I'll get you some water."

I didn't want any water. I wanted to get out of there. But I sat down at the kitchen table anyway. Margery poured me a glass of water from a pitcher in the refrigerator, sat it down in front on me and waited for me to take a sip. If the cookies were poisoned, then I wasn't about to take a chance on what could be in the water. The sound of police sirens in the distance made me stand up and head for the door. Margery stood up, too, and blocked my way.

"You're in no shape to go anywhere, Kendra. Now sit down and finish your water." She commanded. The smile was still on her face but her words were as hard as her eyes.

"They must be at Randy's. I need to get back there!" I tried to push past her but she shoved me hard making me stumble backwards.

"No, they're not." She replied calmly.

"Yes, they are! What's wrong with you? Don't you hear the sirens?"

"That's just my next door neighbor's TV. He's watching Cops and he's deaf as a doornail and jacks the volume up sky high."

"But that doesn't mean the police haven't already gotten to Randy's," I insisted.

"Yes, it does." Her eyes narrowed. "Because I never called them," she said in an odd, low voice that wasn't at all like her usual voice.

She took a step towards me. I grabbed the glass of water from the table and hurled it at her. The shock of the ice-cold water made her gasp and curse. As her hands flew to her face to wipe the water away, I tried to get past her to the door. Again she blocked my path. I ran around to the other side of the kitchen so the table was between us.

"Why are you doing this? What did I ever do to you?"

"It's all your fault! Everything is your fault!" Margery shrieked and lunged at me.

"What the hell are you talking about?" I didn't wait for her answer. Instead, I shoved the table, pinning her against the door, before tipping it up on its side and taking off down the hall.

I didn't turn around but could hear Margery cussing up a storm as she struggled to free herself. There was a room at the end of the hall and I ran inside and locked myself in. I pressed my ear against the door and the sound of the doorknob rattling from the other side made me jump back. I was breathing heavily and my breath came out in frosty puffs. That's when I finally noticed how cold it was. It was much colder in this room then in the rest of the trailer. As Margery started savagely kicking at the door, I rubbed my arms and looked around wildly for a phone or anything I could use as a weapon. There was only one piece of furniture in the room. It was a bed. And someone was lying on it.

A woman wrapped in a white sheet was lying on the bed. Only her head and wrinkled face were exposed. Was this Margery's mother? Why lie about having her cremated? I took a step closer. The bedroom door behind me shook in its frame as the crazy woman on the other side continued to kick it. I got to the edge of the bed and forced myself to look down. What I'd first thought to be the wrinkled face of an elderly woman was actually sagging, heavily scarred and patchy red and white from numerous skin grafts. Her head was mostly bald with patches of white blonde hair. I gasped and I sank to the floor beside the bed. This wasn't Margery's mother. It was Stephanie Preston. And she was very dead. All this time I'd thought Stephanie was out there somewhere waiting to pounce. But the woman lying on the bed would have been in no shape to come after me, at least not without help. How long had she been dead? And where was the prison doctor who had helped her escape?

Suddenly, there was silence from the other side of the door for several long seconds then a low moan. I crept over and pressed my ear to the door. I heard the moaning again but realized it wasn't coming from the hallway. It was coming from inside the room, the closet to be exact. Someone was in there and it sounded like they were in pain. With trembling fingers I slid one side of the mirrored closet door open half expecting to see a wounded man.

Instead, curled on her side with her hands tied behind her back, ankles bound, and a gag in her mouth was a petite blonde woman in a soiled pink sweat suit. Her eyes were closed. My eyes watered as the strong smell of urine hit my nostrils. From the state of her clothes, I could tell she had to have been in there a long time. I quickly untied her and pulled the gag from her mouth.

"Ma'am," I said, rolling her over and shaking her gently. "Are you okay?"

Her eyes flew open and she clutched my shirt. "Help me, please?" she said in a horse whisper. Her eyes were sunken and she could barely hold her head up.

"It's okay. I'm going to get us both out of here. I

promise," I said, trying to reassure her. "My name is Kendra. What's yours?"

"Margery," she croaked. "Margery Warfield."

I don't know what I'd been expecting her to say and was so stunned I just gaped at her in shock. "You're. . .Margery Warfield?" I whispered. "But. . .but. . .then who the hell is that out there?"

"My ex husband, Walter. He kidnapped me a month ago."

"Dr. Walter Dillon?"

The sound of a splitting wood cut off her response as the tip of an ax sliced its way through the bedroom door taking out a chunk big enough for fake Margery to stick her head through. The blonde wig sat askew on his head revealing short, dark hair matted under a stocking cap. The water I'd thrown in her—I mean his—face had caused his makeup to run, making him look like a waterlogged clown and exposing a five o'clock shadow. How I'd not been able to tell that Margery was a dude all this time, I'll never know. I guess I could blame it on being heartbroken and distracted. More than likely it was because when I looked at her all I saw was tasty baked goods. And had the situation not been so dire, I'd have had time to ponder just how truly messed up it was that for the past month I'd had a lunatic doctor in drag not only working along side me at my job, but trying to kill me with poisoned cookies. Rollins was right. This crap only happened to me.

"Go," said the real Margery.

"But I can't leave you!"

"I'm too weak. I won't make it," she insisted. "Out the window. Go get help."

She passed out and I had no choice but to close the

closet door and sprint for the window on the far wall of the room. I managed to get it open just as Walter Dillon chopped a hole in the door big enough for him to get through, though he could have just reached a hand in and unlocked the door. Go figure. The window was narrow but I was able to swing a leg over the sill and get my head and right shoulder out before Walter let out a battle cry and—looking like he was reenacting a scene from the movie Psycho—came charging across the room at me with his ax held high.

I screamed and jerked the rest of my torso through the narrow opening and fell out onto the ground below mere seconds before Walter embedded his ax in the windowsill so deep that he couldn't pull it free. He struggled with the ax and I took off running in a blind panic into the dense woods behind the trailer. Idiot. I was probably fifty feet into the woods before I realized I was going the wrong way. But turning back would lead me straight into Walter.

I paused to catch my breath and get my bearings when the sound of running feet made me jump behind the nearest tree. It was Walter. I was still breathing hard and clamped both hands over my mouth so he wouldn't hear me. He was looking around wildly for me in every direction and growing angrier by the minute. By now he was wigless and I was happy to see he was also axless.

I had planned on staying right where I was until he gave up and left. Then I'd double back to the trailer park and get help. But that plan was soon squashed when I felt something run up my arm. That something turned out to be a spider the size of Toledo. If rats were at the top of my phobia list, then spiders were a close second. I let out an involuntary shriek and did a spider jig, twirling and spinning to get the damned thing off of me. Bad move. I spun myself right out from behind my hiding place right into Walter's line of sight.

"You murdering bitch! My Stephanie's dead because of you! She was everything to me: my mother, my lover, and my best friend!" He buried his face in his hands and started to cry. What a whack job.

"Me? You're the one who broke her out of prison where she was getting medical help. If anyone killed her, it's you!"

"She was never going to get any better! She didn't want to die in prison. I was just fulfilling her dying wish."

"Then why kidnap your ex wife and impersonate her? Why poison me if you were just fulfilling Stephanie's dying wish?"

"Because that was *her* wish," he spat out at me. "*My* wish was to see the woman who helped put her behind bars die a slow, painful death like she did." He started crying again.

"I'm really sorry about Stephanie, Walter," I ventured. His head jerked up.

"How dare you!"

"No, really. I am sorry she died," I said as the thought of all the people she killed and everything she'd put my family and me through filled me with anger. "I would have rather she'd spent the rest of her miserable life rotting in prison!"

I took off running. Branches tore at my hair and scratched my face and arms. I ignored the stinging pain as well as the stitch in my side. I could see what looked like the road up ahead through an opening in the trees. I didn't look back but could hear panting and wheezing and knew Walter was gaining on me. I emerged from the woods next to the road just as a semi went flying past. I yelled and waved my arms but it kept on trucking. A hard shove from behind sent me sprawling into the dirt. I rolled over to see Walter looming over me. Somewhere along the way he'd managed to pick up a large, thick, tree branch and was about to bash my head in with it. Here we go again!

My hands scrabbled around frantically for a weapon of my own but the only thing besides pebbles, twigs, and pine needles that I could get my hands on was a big dead possum. Walter started to swing the branch down on me like a giant fly swatter. And you know what they say about desperate times and how they call for desperate measures, right?

I grabbed hold of the possum's thick tail with both hands and—praying it was truly dead and not playing possum—swung it. I was hoping to fend off Walter until a car came along and saw me being attacked by a man in a denim skirt and peep toe espadrilles, and would stop to help me. But the possum's bloated body broke free of its tail and sailed through the air, hitting Walter in the face, and exploding like a road kill bomb.

The stench was unbelievable. Putrefied entrails, fur, blood, body fluids, and a goodly amount of maggots were in Walter's eyes, nose and mouth. He couldn't even scream. All he could do was stagger around blindly gagging and franticly clawing at his face. I watched in horror as he staggered out into the road. I didn't see the truck until it whooshed past me, filling the night air with a loud blast of its horn.

"Look out!" I screamed.

But it was too late. The eighteen-wheeler hit

Walter head on. He was briefly pinned to the front of the truck like an insect before falling underneath and being crushed by the heavy wheels.

EPILOGUE
Three days later.

Link Ramey was arrested for the second-degree murder of his adoptive father and uncle, Justin Ramey, and attempted murder for almost killing me. Lauren Ramey pled not guilty to killing Elton Paul. Lauren claims she was acting in self-defense when she shot Paul, who she said tried to rape her. Janette Ramey was also arrested for the hit and run murder of Lila Duncan, as well as being an accessory after the fact for her brother Justin's murder.

Janette was willing to help cover up her son's crime, but Link was more than willing to feed Janette to the wolves. He was the one who told the police where to find the car that killed Lila Duncan in an attempt to make some kind of deal with the prosecutor in exchange for helping them solve a cold case. And in light of her son's betrayal, and the evidence against her, Janette finally confessed that she was the one driving the car that killed Leonard's wife. But she'll probably never serve one day in prison. Ironically, routine tests done at the hospital after her alleged assault revealed that she had liver cancer and had about three months left to live.

Mama and Leonard are still going strong. The charges against Leonard for Janette's assault were dropped based on Ray Wallace's statement. It turned out that the money I'd seen Mama giving him was actually money she owed him that she borrowed when she came up short at the grocery store. I apologized to both of them, again. And since he was off the hook for his wife's murder, I guess Leonard wasn't so bad after all. But I still hated being called Ken.

Pia plans to move to Paris with her mother and open an art gallery. That's what they'd been celebrating that night at Estelle's and why Joy was so upset. But she promised Pia she'd take over the running of her art program, Graffiti, in her absence. Those poor kids.

Handy Randy was still in the wind. But I'm sure I haven't seen the last of him. At least I hoped not. He still owed me a bottle of peach wine.

Detective Blake Mason was sitting up in bed when I arrived in his hospital room after visiting the real Margery Warfield. She was still in bad shape but was expected to make a full recovery. Mason was naked from the waist up and shaving. A tub of soapy water sat on a hospital tray in front of him. I tried hard not to stare at his rock hard chest and muscular arms. A semper fi Marine Corps tattoo arched across his torso, right above his six-pack. Damn. Why did this aggravating man have to be so fine?

"Are you going to say something or are you just

going to stand there staring at me," he asked without even looking at me.

"You're looking a lot better," I commented as I walked over to the side of the bed.

"And you're looking a little rough." He gently touched one of the thin scratches on my cheek that I'd gotten while running through the woods. His touch was like fire wrapped in silk.

"It's a long story," I replied and quickly turned so he wouldn't see how flustered I was.

"I get the feeling it always is with you, Kendra," he said, chuckling.

"So have they figured out what you were poisoned with yet?"

"Whatever it was, Dillon took it to his grave. But what I want to know is why you never got as sick as me?"

"Well, according to the doctor, it may have been because I always ate the cookies with milk or ice cream or chips or pizza and that must have coated my stomach, lessening the effects of the poison. Your no fat and no dairy diet made you more susceptible."

"Meaning?"

"Isn't it obvious? Being a gluttonous pig saved my life," I concluded with deadpan seriousness. Mason threw his head back and laughed long and hard, and I laughed with him.

"Hey, you missed a spot." I grabbed the washcloth from the tub of water and absently wiped a spot of shaving cream that he'd missed on his neck. He caught my hand and pulled me down next to him on the bed.

"Thanks for getting me to the hospital so quickly that night, Kendra. You probably saved my life," he said softly and without warning kissed me on the cheek just as Harmon and Rollins walked through the door.

Harmon was on her cell and had missed the whole thing, but Rollins hadn't. The anger that instantly flashed across his face at seeing Mason and me in such close proximity said a lot, though I couldn't figure out what. Maybe having Blake Mason around might be fun after all.

When I got home, I grabbed Carl's letter and settled down on the couch with a glass of red wine. Although my stomach was in knots from wondering what the letter might say, I knew whatever was in it wouldn't change anything. Despite our misunderstanding, there were good reasons why we were no longer together. It wasn't anyone's fault. It just hadn't been meant to be. And I was mostly okay with that. I took a deep breath, opened the letter, and began to read.

ABOUT THE AUTHOR

Angela Henry was once told that her past life careers included spy, researcher, and investigator. She stuck with what she knew because today she's a mystery writing library reference specialist, who loves to people watch, and eavesdrop on conversations. She's the author of five mysteries featuring equally nosy amateur sleuth Kendra Clayton, as well as the thriller, *The Paris Secret*. She's also the founder of the award-winning MystNoir website, which promotes African-American mystery writers, and was named a "Hot Site" by USA Today.com. When she's not working, writing, or practicing her stealth, she loves to travel, is connoisseur of B horror movies, and an admitted anime addict. She lives in Ohio and is currently hard at work trying to meet her next deadline.

Also by Angela Henry

The Company You Keep
Tangled Roots
Diva's Last Curtain Call
Schooled In Lies

The Paris Secret

Made in the USA
Lexington, KY
27 January 2013